LOOSE WIRES

Meet the dead, the doomed and the dangerous.

BARRY JOHN WATSON

SPINETINGLERS
PUBLISHING

Loose Wires
By Barry John Watson

ISBN - 978-1-906755-90-4

Spinetinglers Publishing
22 Vestry Road
Co. Down
BT23 6HJ
UK
www.spinetinglerspublishing.com

In Barry John Watson's second collection of short stories, visit places where the line between reality and the unknown becomes blurred; places where something dark twists tales of love, loss and loneliness into nightmare scenarios.

A son uncovers unwanted truths regarding his late father. A polar expedition ends in horror that leads to unexpected consequences. What strange secret do four paintings hold? How can a salesman of the year repeat past glories and why does an astronaut become obsessed with his craft's ejector bay?

Discover what happens when a childless couple move into an old house and find a dummy's head hidden in the attic. Learn of Jack the Ripper's true identity, how a hangman regrets his moment of cowardice, and of the terrible game a small boy is forced to play in a Second World War concentration camp.

These and a host of other tales make 'Loose Wires,' a read guaranteed to raise hackles and chill the blood.

Reality and the unknown; don't get lost between the two.

For Beej, Sam and Jake.

Three of the four best things that have ever happened to me.

Also by B.J. Watson: 'LIGHTS OUT!' *A Collection of Chillers Killers and Thrillers.*

Contents

A LOOSE WIRE

The father I never knew died a guilty man. Whatever drove him to take his own life after he'd stolen others could be traced back to an imbalance of the mind. At least that's what the doctors claimed; a faulty connection that pushed him over an invisible edge. As I grew older I gradually discovered the circumstances surrounding that terrible time; what the man had done and why he claimed he'd done it.

His killing spree had only begun after he'd married my mother, as if the union had somehow triggered in him something unstoppable. The press had feasted on the story, glorying in details I reluctantly memorised each time I went back to the events of that long ago winter. Below the lurid headlines and a copy of his scrawled suicide note were images of him staring into the camera, a man I didn't recognise but whose eyes mirrored mine. It was like looking into the face of a ghost. I was glad I'd never known him.

That was when I realised all it takes is a loose wire to rob a man of his sanity; a poor contact carrying the wrong signals into the over-loaded nerve-endings of somebody's brain. The frightening thing is no-one knows when that wire may work loose or what it might lead to. And it could happen to anybody.

My father's passing dragged my mother into a future she couldn't possibly have foreseen. Who knows what it must have felt like to be branded a murderer's widow, to have to bear the daily routine of malicious gossip and whispered blame? I can only imagine what she went through.

The few memories I possess of her are vague; half-formed images of a woman whose smile and good humour had been robbed from her by the death and deeds of her husband.

One clear recollection clings to my mind: a pushchair ride along the banks of the Mill River, the two of us below a vast stormy sky, her soft flat voice attempting to explain things an infant couldn't possibly hope to understand. Across the water the skeleton of Burley Mill rose into the clouds. I remember the sound of reeds bending in the river as the breeze brushed faint eddies across its surface. I didn't realise it then, but her words filled me with a fear of the future. It's a fear that's stayed with me ever since.

She left my life on a winter's morning when I was three years old. The front door closed, leaving behind it the faint scent of a perfume I've never discovered the name to. I didn't see her again. A neighbour found me late that evening, crying in the dark on the hallway floor as I waited in vain for her return.

Where she went nobody knew, but the Mill River flows fast and runs deep. Its black surface holds secrets. I suspect a body could enter that cold embrace and disappear forever.

It seemed my young life wasn't enough for my mother, she felt a compulsion to go seeking the one that had caused her so much heartache. Either that or she couldn't bear living under the stain her husband's name had marked her with.

It was a long time ago.

Since then I've always found winter a time of unbearable loneliness; a season where the short dark days are overshadowed by a desperate need to go in search of something that resembles love. The brief impressionable period of childhood stretches a long way: an orphan's memories last a lifetime.

I met my wife on a December morning, on a day when the past had made its seasonal return in an effort to threaten and torment. I was lucky, I could have walked passed the store and never known she was there. But a picture in the window caught my eye, a framed watercolour print of a man carrying a small child on his shoulders. They were both laughing. The father was barefoot, the beach they walked along shimmered in the sun. It stirred in me a longing for something I'd never known.

As I entered the shop the woman who would become my wife looked up and smiled. For a strange moment I imagined us in the painting, her walking beside me as I carried our little boy along the shore.

"Can I help you?" she asked, and I instinctively knew she could. Whether or not she would be able to help me enough, I didn't know; that was something only time would tell. But when I looked into her face I had the feeling my lonely searches were over.

Ours was a summer wedding, a day full of light and warmth and laughter. I wish it could have lasted forever. For a while my happiness made me realise there was more to life than looking back. For once where I came from didn't seem as important as where I was going.

But that year, as the first frost layered the ground, something happened that jolted in me memories of the father I'd never known.

A young girl's frozen body was discovered dumped on wasteland. The news she'd been strangled filled my mind with unwanted knowledge and the image of a ghost face. But there was worse to come. February snow hadn't fallen hard or long enough to blanket the corpse a passer-by almost stumbled over in an alleyway. It was a copy of the first murder; the woman's life had been squeezed from her.

The winter weather hampered a search that went on for weeks and revealed nothing. It was as if the killer had vanished along with the melting snow. As days slowly lengthened the police investigation hit a wall: leads tailed off, questions remained unanswered, and all the while a frightened public waited for news of the murderer's next victim.

There wasn't one. The killing stopped. March came and went. April left behind it only heartbreak and an unsolved mystery. By the time spring ran into summer, people had hesitantly settled into the belief that perhaps the madness was over.

It was, but only for a while.

Later that year, as an unseasonably chill autumn breeze stripped bare the trees and blew colour from the sky, the killer struck again. He left his victim's body lying on the towpath at the side of the Mill River; another young girl whose last moments had been spent fighting for breath.

Once again the police were left chasing shadows as they floundered in the wake of a man who seemed able to kill and then disappear without trace.

The 'Winter Killer,' the press have named him, with the strange habit they have of romanticising violent death.

I loathe him. His actions have brought back unwanted childhood recollections. I've longed to find him and make him suffer, to do to him what he did to those girls. I can imagine him as my father reincarnated, picking up from where he'd left off, stalking me through time, showing me what a parent could do when wires worked loose and connections failed.

My wife knows of my past, it was something I shared with her soon after we met. She realises how these killings have affected me, haven't I told her of my father's distant sins? It's the memory of those misdeeds that sometimes drive me from the house, to force me to flee the warm shelter of love she's built around us. Words go unsaid, but she understands; there's some pain a man has to bear alone. My absences are a thing of habit.

"Where were you?" she asked, the first time I went missing. What could I say? How could I tell her that I'd been kneeling at my father's grave, asking a dead man questions he could never answer? I shivered and when she folded her arms around me, I cried into her shoulder like a baby.

Now I read of how the Winter Killer has taken another life. My heart beat so hard I could feel it in my throat. It brought back the past and all the baggage I've never been able to unload.

I pictured the abduction, how he lured his victim into his car with soft words and friendly smiles, and then drove her to a remote woodland setting that became a murder scene. I heard her futile cries for help, and as he placed his hands around her throat, I could imagine him smelling a scent he'd never been able to name.

My tears stained the paper.

"Are you all right?" my wife asked.

I saw the worry on her face, the way it had formed lines across her pale skin. It was a question I couldn't answer, but she needed reassurance.

"Of course I am," I said. She smiled and clouds left her eyes.

Love can lead you down a pathway of lies; you just have to be careful where you tread. Once upon a time I thought it was possible for a man to change, to discard those lies and shed the past the way you'd throw away an old coat.

But now I'm not so sure.

I keep thinking of loose wires and what they can lead a man to do; of winter streets and longings impossible to satisfy.

How a father's genes can be handed down to his son.

Sometimes when night closes in and sleep won't come the urge to leave my bed becomes almost unbearable. I listen to my wife's soft rhythmic breathing and feel those unnatural connections sparking in my brain. Then I wonder how it would sound if she stopped breathing.

The police say they believe the killer will strike again.

I think maybe they're right.

THE THAXTON QUARTET

"Are you sure it's genuine?"

Cowdrey appeared offended by the question. He raised his hand and swept it in a graceful arc through the air, as if he were a member of royalty acknowledging his subjects. "Sir, these are *all* genuine."

Powell ran his eyes over the oils and watercolours adorning the walls. It was a fabulous collection; paintings worth millions, but there was only one masterpiece that interested him; the Thaxton: Portrait Number Four.

"So, Mr Ivanovich is willing to do business with me?"

The custodian of the gallery looked at him, his expression unreadable. If the eyes were the window to the soul Powell suspected Cowdrey didn't have one.

"It's most unusual sir, but yes. Mr Ivanovich isn't in the habit of selling, only buying, but when he heard you owned the other three Thaxton's he was intrigued. One, by how you managed to acquire them, and two, to discover if the rumour concerning the paintings was true. So, in your case he's made an exception." The custodian chuckled. "A very expensive exception."

Powell's heart beat faster; the final canvas was just a banker's draft away.

"And does he believe the rumour?"

Again Cowdrey stared at him, his face a blank. "Do you?"

The two men stood facing each other in the deserted gallery; the faint sound of evening traffic drifted in from the street.

"If I did I'd be foolish to want Portrait Number Four."

Cowdrey raised an eyebrow, whether in disbelief or agreement it was impossible to tell. He turned and wandered along the gallery, then stopped with his back to Powell, his interest seemingly taken by the Van Gogh he was examining.

"So, how *did* you manage to acquire three of the most sought after works of art in the world?"

Powell grinned; it was a smile that held dark secrets. There was no way he could tell Cowdrey the truth, there was no way he could tell *anybody* the truth, but that didn't concern him, he'd mastered the art of lying a long time ago.

"I inherited Portrait Number One from my mother. She had a passion for collecting art and although her portfolio wasn't anywhere near as extensive or valuable as Mr Ivanovich's it was still impressive. After she died a number of works came into my possession, one of them being the Thaxton. I had it valued, and that's when I first discovered how much his quartet of portraits was worth, and also the rumour surrounding them."

That much of his tale was true, it was the background concerning the other two he would have to change. Cheating and murder wasn't something he wanted to share with the minion of the man he was purchasing the final Thaxton from. The custodian had turned his attention to a Monet, but Powell had an uneasy feeling he was dissecting every word.

"Go on," Cowdrey said. It sounded more like an order than an invitation.

"Portrait Number Two." He shook his head and laughed, as if he couldn't believe how easily the painting had fallen into his hands. The custodian turned and frowned, seemingly puzzled by his jocularity. Powell swallowed and decorated the story until it bore no resemblance to the truth.

"So you won it in a card game?" Cowdrey's incredulous stare forced him to look away; he sought sanctuary in a Picasso. "My, my, how careless of Leonard Harper, I presume he doesn't play poker anymore?"

"He can't," Powell said, "he's dead."

"Ah yes, that's right." The custodian scratched his chin, as if recalling something inconsequential that had slipped his mind. "Didn't the police find his body floating in the Thames?"

"Evidently." Powell knew exactly where the police had found the late art dealer's body. After Harper had refused to sell him the painting Powell had offered to prove there were no hard feelings by treating him to dinner. He'd plied the man with drink and then convinced him that a walk along the embankment might help clear his head. It had been a dark night. There'd been no witnesses. He could still hear Harper's cries for help as the current dragged him under.

It had been perfect. There was no proof Powell hadn't won the Thaxton at cards and it was assumed Harper had been so distraught at the loss he'd flung himself off Blackfriars Bridge. Obtaining Portrait Number Three hadn't been as bloodless.

Cowdrey was looking at him intently, as if he could read every thought running through his mind. "And how did you obtain Thaxton's third painting?"

Powell remembered a summer spent tracking down the owner of that particular canvas and being shocked when he found it belonged to one of London's most brutal crime lords, Eddie Shaver.

It had taken him months to infiltrate his organisation and then work his way into a position of trust; soon after that Eddie was dead, the victim of a revenge killing by the McNaughton gang.

Powell had been behind the scheming and double-dealing that led Eddie to believe the McNaughton's had stolen his masterpiece. Feelings became even more inflamed when Powell got word to Gerry McNaughton that Shaver was in league with the police and in the process of attempting to stitch up his biggest rival. When the two gangs met there'd been a bloodbath. No-one knew who fired the bullet that killed Gerry but Powell had come out of it suspicion-free and in possession of the third Thaxton.

He looked at Cowdrey, hesitated for a moment and then explained he'd bought it from an anonymous seller.

"That's strange," the custodian said, "I was under the impression it had belonged to some underworld figure." He smiled disbelievingly. "I must have been mistaken." He reached up and lifted Portrait Number Four from the wall. "Now, let's get down to business."

They walked towards the front desk, the thick-pile carpeting silencing their footsteps. Above them painted faces watched from the walls. Cowdrey carefully stood the Thaxton in a corner and offered his buyer a seat. As Powell took the banker's draft from his jacket pocket Cowdrey sat opposite him and leant his elbows on the desk.

"Refresh my memory," he said, "what exactly is the rumour surrounding the Thaxton Quartet?"

Powell laughed; the sound drifted along the gallery like the last words of a condemned man.

"It's a ridiculous story," he said, and he truly believed that. His sole reason for wanting the final portrait was money. Together, the four canvases would be priceless. Cowdrey leant back in his chair, linked his hands behind his head and closed his eyes.

"Tell me anyway," he whispered.

The gallery was silent now, the shadows broken only by the soft glow of strip lights illuminating the hanging canvases. It seemed to Powell as if a thousand eyes were watching from those walls. He cleared his throat.

"As you probably know Edwin Thaxton only completed four paintings in his entire life; The Thaxton Quartet. When the last one was finished, he killed himself."

The custodian nodded slightly, as if affirming the story.

"Each portrait was of the same girl, but painted from a different position. Her identity remains a mystery, but what is known is that Thaxton became besotted with her. Unfortunately, he was unaware she regarded their relationship as nothing more than an amusing fling, an opportunity to earn money and flaunt herself in front of someone who could never have her.

"When the final painting was complete he couldn't bear the thought of losing her and begged her to marry him. She laughed at his proposal and ridiculed him. He was a penniless artist; why would she choose him when she could have any man she wanted? She was still laughing when he pulled a pistol from his belt and shot her. Then he cursed the paintings and blew his brains out.

"Death tainted his legacy. After that the portraits were regarded as unlucky and sold separately at auction. Since then it's been rumoured if ever the four works of art were assembled again they would bring whoever owned them bad luck."

Cowdrey opened his eyes and Powell grinned. "I told you it was a ridiculous story."

The custodian stared at him and for a moment, just before he smiled, Powell thought he saw contempt in the other man's eyes.

"A strange tale indeed." Cowdrey stood up and flicked on the main light switch. "Now, I believe you owe Mr Ivanovich a lot of money."

Powell did, but it was only a fraction of what the Thaxton's were worth.

***

Cowdrey hadn't shaken hands once the transaction had been completed. He'd folded his arms and watched Powell climb into a taxi clutching his precious painting. The man had been so obsessed with his purchase he'd been willing to risk carrying a masterpiece around London in the back of a cab. He shook his head; it was strange how greed could get the better of a man's judgement and also make him careless.

Back inside the gallery he locked the door, pulled out his mobile and called a number. Somewhere on the other side of the world, it was answered.

"Mr Ivanovich, Cowdrey here. Just to let you know, the Thaxton is sold." He listened for a few moments, smiled, and ended the call. His employer was happy; Cowdrey's promised bonus would be in his account by the end of the week.

The gallery manager had worked for Mr Ivanovich for over thirty years. The Russian was a wealthy man, and one of the reasons why was because he was careful.

He was also superstitious; a childhood spent in isolated rural towns had shaped him that way. Aware of the story behind Portrait Number Four he'd asked his assistant to look into the background of the myth surrounding the Thaxton Quartet.

Cowdrey grinned, Powell had only uncovered half the tale, and even if he'd known the rest the custodian doubted he would have believed it. His obsession had blinded him to any other reality.

When Ivanovich heard the full story he'd instructed his employee to sell the portrait to the highest bidder. No-one had come close to Powell's offer. The sale had eased a bad feeling the businessman harboured concerning the painting; letting it go hadn't been a hardship, there were plenty more masterpieces he could afford.

The end of the tale had been an interesting one, the bad luck Powell referred to made clear in the version Cowdrey had unearthed.

Rumour had it that if ever the four paintings were again hung together the first person to view them would fall hopelessly in love with the mystery girl. Captivated by her beauty, her admirer would be unable to look away. The legend said the girl's face would then slowly fade from each canvas, leaving the onlooker so distraught they'd end their life the same way the artist had ended his own.

Cowdrey stared at the space where the portrait had hung. He hadn't liked Powell; the man was a liar and probably a thief and murderer as well. As he switched off the lights and set the alarm he found himself wondering if the story was true.

He thought he'd leave it until the morning and then give Powell a call, just to see if he was satisfied with his purchase.

Maybe the man would answer his phone.

Maybe he wouldn't.

Barry John Watson

A DARKER SECRET

'ANTARCTIC EXPEDITION ENDS IN HORROR AS SURVIVORS RESORT TO CANNIBALISM.'

It's a headline that holds a darker secret, although that may seem hard to believe. I was one of the two men who returned from that fateful Polar mission. Before our rescue, when all hope seemed lost, three of us made a choice. Frozen and starving to death, it was a decision that separated us from humanity. We ate the living.

***

'SIX YOUNG MEN WITH DREAMS OF GLORY.'

Today the Hughes' expedition sets off on its historic attempt to reach the Pole. Their aim is to follow the route taken by Dutch explorer, Peter Heckman. In 1911 he endeavoured to reach the Polar cap via the Western Approach, and so beat the expeditions led by Amundsen and Scott.

His decision to take the shorter course was a dangerous gamble and proved fatal. The unstable terrain, notorious for shifting ice, blinding spindrift and avalanche, was believed to be impassable. It's a belief that's held to this day. A fortnight after entering that frozen wilderness the Dutchman and his team disappeared. They were never seen again.

Since then the Pole may have been conquered on numerous occasions but never via the legendary Western Approach. These brave young men have a chance to make history!

***

It was a patriotic article that camouflaged the problems we were already experiencing. The press were unaware we'd been advised to hold fire. A cyclone was building, pushing the worst weather it could gather towards the Polar cap. The forecast meant we either left hurriedly or took the safer option and waited until the following spring.

The decision to continue was one based on finance, too much time and money invested in the project had made our backers impatient. To delay would have meant losing public interest and the financial support on which we so desperately relied.

In my opinion, it was a foolhardy choice. Our mission was dangerous enough, why increase that risk for the sake of a timetable? But I wasn't the one leading the expedition, the final say came down to Hughes. He'd been waiting a long time to show the world how he could accomplish something no man had ever before achieved. His vanity meant he would wait no longer.

We set off with words of praise and visions of glory. How soon those words were silenced and how rapidly the visions faded.

***

We were cursed from the start. Forty-eight hours into our trek a problem with one of the sledges meant valuable time was lost as we carried out repairs. Hughes was full of fake bonhomie, offering encouragement and making jokes in an effort to disguise his impatience. It was all a show. Now and again I caught him furtively checking his watch, frowning into the distance as he mentally calculated the arrival of a distant storm.

That day we tried to make up for lost time, pushing ourselves too hard as a gale sharpened itself against us. The weather worsened before we had a chance to properly set up camp. By the time the blizzard blew in we realised how inadequate our preparations had been. In our rush to beat the storm Morton was careless securing the huskies. When we emerged from our tents the following morning the dogs had broken free. Their tracks were lost in the snow. Precious hours were spent in a fruitless search that sapped energy and shortened tempers.

After that we had no choice but to pack fewer supplies and manhandle the sledges. It was a decision we'd later come to regret.

Progress was slow; gradually we fell behind schedule. The weather constantly played on my mind. It was bad enough now, what would happen if we were still out here when it turned? We struggled on through terrible conditions. I'm sure I wasn't the only one whose thoughts strayed to Peter Heckman and his vanished expedition. Staring into a whiteout can expose fears a man never knew he possessed.

Late one afternoon we watched an avalanche cascade down a distant mountain slope. Tons of ice and snow thundered into the ground and then rose into the air like smoke. It was as if we were listening to the end of the world.

Halfway into our journey we lost Wallace.

The weather had cleared and we woke to a morning where the sky had tented itself in a perfect blue above the landscape. After a scratch breakfast we loaded the sledges. For once the going was smooth. Spirits had begun to lift. Jokes were shared as we penetrated a world wiped clean by freshly fallen snow.

Wallace was leading the way. I think out of all of us he was the one most determined to make our mission a success. Hughes might have craved the fame he believed his ambition deserved, but Adam Wallace had a point to prove. As an only child whose father had constantly assured him he would never amount to much he was a man carrying the past on his shoulders; this expedition was giving him the chance to walk off those assurances and prove the past a lie.

I was following in his tracks, placing my boots where his had been moments earlier. When I looked up, he was gone. The snow beneath me suddenly gave way and as I fell someone grabbed my arm. O'Brien dragged me back from the edge of a crevice that looked as if it went on forever.

"Are you all right, Sandy?" he asked.

I couldn't answer. Perhaps I'd gone into shock. A body that had marched miles suddenly wouldn't function. My gaze was drawn to the dark crease that had spread itself like a stain across the snow.

Daniels crawled to the edge of the drop. When he called out, the sound of Wallace's name echoed into the abyss, spiralling through blackness until falling silent. There was no answer.

Morton looked at each of us. "What shall we do?"

"We'll have to leave him there," Hughes said. "We've come too far to turn back,"

He'd pulled off his goggles and was staring into the ravine. Nobody spoke. "Wallace would have wanted us to carry on."

It was a statement full of ego and ambition, the same self-centred attitude that had led us out here against good advice. I thought we should turn back and voiced my opinion.

"Let's take a vote on it," I said.

When Hughes glanced at me and scowled, I knew we would never be friends again.

Daniels was my only ally, Morton and O'Brien sided with our leader. We formed a single file and trekked further into that murderous landscape.

***

The driving snow disfigured any landmarks we might have recognised. Walking blind, placing our faith in charts and compasses, we spent the next forty-eight hours with our bodies bent into the storm.

Provisions were becoming dangerously low, in our effort to lighten the load we'd underestimated how much we'd need. Falling behind schedule had meant we'd stretched ourselves. It was another worry to mentally stack up with the others. We began to ration food and listened as our stomachs complained.

When the weather briefly cleared I took in our surroundings and suspected we were off course. Maps I'd studied of the Approach had given no indication of the immense glaciers we were attempting to traverse. When I raised my concerns to Hughes, he took it personally, as if I were questioning his judgement. The stand-up row that followed almost developed into a fist-fight. We had to be pulled apart.

The rest of the day was spent in silent procession; a line of men silhouetted against a backdrop of glistening ice. We must have looked like winter nomads in search of the sun.

That night we camped in the shadow of a frozen overhang. As I watched the moon trace a slow path across the stars I thought of Wallace and wondered if any of us would live to tell his father how wrong he'd been about his son.

***

We were taking unnecessary risks. I think even Hughes had come to believe something he previously couldn't face: we were lost. His eagerness to extract us from that situation cost him his life.

It was an afternoon of bitter wind and blinding sunlight, a time when the landscape revealed what cruelty it possessed. We were perched high above the world, inching our way across the ice as we tried to short-cut our journey. Hughes was lead man, cajoling us to hurry, still determined to prove he could tame the Western Approach. Two days had passed since our disagreement and relations between us still hadn't improved.

I remember watching his shadow mirror his actions against the cliff face, a busy silhouette that suddenly wasn't there anymore. He slid thirty feet, his arms pin wheeling in a desperate effort to find purchase. His body disappeared beyond the cliff edge and then he was hanging in space, clinging to the handrail of a ledge as he made a futile effort to haul himself to safety.

For one tantalising moment it looked as if he might succeed. I crawled towards him trying to ignore the drop that invited death. As I reached out the ledge gave way. His scream followed him two-hundred feet down into a snow-packed canyon.

By the time we recovered his body, it was almost dark. We buried him as best we could and then came to a decision: it was time to go home.

I think it was that night, camped beside his grave, when our morale and purpose began to falter. Turning back was a decision easier made than done. Provisions were low and the knowledge of what lay ahead sapped our energy and drained our will. We fell asleep listening to the wind whine its way across the tundra.

The food ran out before we were even halfway into our homeward journey. After that it was a case of bowing our heads and placing one foot in front of the other.

The days drew themselves in my mind, images of relentless repetition as our fight for survival became more hopeless. We hardly noticed Morton falling behind. It was only when he collapsed that O'Brien made me aware he was no longer with us. We reluctantly went back for him. Unnoticed by us he'd flung off his goggles and gloves. Snow blind and frostbitten his exhausted body had reached the end of its journey. We struggled to lift him and when he fell again we knew it was a choice of either leaving him there or making camp.

An endless snow-scape stretched ahead of us. There was a blizzard on the horizon. It seemed easier to pitch the tent and wait for whatever another day would bring. We crawled into our shelter, dragging an almost dead man with us. As we huddled below a growing storm the need for survival planted a dark seed in our minds.

***

Morton was unconscious, trapped in a coma we were sure he'd never wake from. Outside, the wind tore at our flimsy shelter, causing the storm lantern to swing drunkenly from the ridge pole.

Our hunger had taken us to a place we'd never before visited. The thought of the provisions we'd abandoned roused in me a hate for Hughes I couldn't quell. The gale blew and the snow fell and our despair grew deeper. There are things a man can lose and still be able to carry on, but hope isn't one of them. I think we believed then it didn't matter what we did, that soon the frozen wilderness would claim us the way it had claimed Wallace and Hughes.

Our discussions had been conducted in whispers, as if we were afraid our dying friend might overhear the terrible plan we were concocting.

"No-one need ever know." O'Brien coughed into his sleeve and left a mouth-shaped blood stain on his cuff. I was trembling, but for once it had nothing to do with the cold.

Daniels hugged his shoulders in a futile attempt to rub warmth back into frozen bones. "It's the only way," he said.

We listened to the gale beat snow against the tent. It was like being cocooned, separated from the world and a code of values that no longer mattered. Suddenly we were outlaws.

"Who's going to do it?" My question was a tipping point, after that there was no turning back.

O'Brien opened his journal, tore off three strips of paper and then slung the diary back onto his sleeping bag; there would be no record of what we were about to do. He placed the fragments between his thumb and palm and held them up. "Choose," he said.

Daniels went first. His fingers were shaking as he reluctantly pulled a sliver free. O'Brien looked at me. I raised my hand and hesitated. *How could two slips of paper appear so frightening?* I closed my eyes and fumbled at his fingers. Then we laid out our choices.

Mine was the short straw.

I turned and gazed at the shape huddled beneath the blankets. Morton didn't appear to be breathing. I said a silent prayer and pulled out my knife. Shadows see-sawed around the tent and then for a moment the gale died. When I dragged back the covers and thrust the blade into Morton's belly, he didn't make a sound. Daniels and O'Brien were staring, their eyes saucer-wide and as blank as the snow-shrouded landscape. I could hear their teeth chattering as they fought the cold and waited for a meal they dreaded tasting.

I sliced the skin from Morton's forearm and watched the blood run to his wrist. God forgive me, my mouth began to water. And then he moaned; a half-dead sound that chilled me more than the sub-zero temperatures we'd been forced to endure. I looked at the other two.

"Don't stop," O'Brien whispered. Daniels closed his eyes and nodded silent agreement.

The knife blade shone in the lamplight.

I don't think our companion felt a thing.

Two hours later the storm died.

Trapped in that tent, without the strength to dig our way free, we survived on melted snow and human flesh. It was a time of fevered dreams and strained conversation; of half-remembered actions and sullen silence. I think each of us was trying to come to terms with what we'd done and how to live with it.

Although we were still alive, none of us could face the fact that Morton had also been until hunger drove us to perform an unforgivable deed. The hours passed slowly. We rationed out his body and wondered at what we'd become.

On the third morning I was roused from a sleep in which I kept hearing a dying man's final moan. It took a moment to get my bearings. Daniels was crouched over me. For a second I thought he was Morton and stifled a scream.

"What's wrong?" I asked. I could smell the sourness on his breath; there was panic in his eyes.

He pointed to the open tent flap. Beyond it a triangle of white dazzled in the sun. "O'Brien's gone," he whispered, as if he were afraid to be overheard.

I propped myself up and squinted into the glare. The triangle looked inviting. I longed to crawl through it and feel the frozen air against my face; to lose myself amongst the drifts as I left a decaying body and Daniels far behind.

I didn't even have the strength to rise from my sleeping bag. How O'Brien had managed to do so I could only guess at. Guilt's a powerful motivator. At some point during the previous seventy-two hours I suspected he'd come to a decision and realised he couldn't live with what we'd done. Walking out into the ice and snow had been the only way to silence his conscience.

That was when I knew all was lost. I lay back down and waited for the end.

"What shall we do?" Daniels asked.

When I didn't answer, he pulled the flap back into place and rolled onto his bed. Before I fell asleep, I thought I heard him crying.

We were getting weaker. The cold was extreme. Eventually our bodies could fight no longer.

Daniels passed into unconsciousness before me. I remember listening to his breathing gradually slow and then staring at Morton's remains. Killing our friend hadn't saved us after all. As I drifted into darkness I could taste human blood on my tongue.

***

Neither of us was aware of our rescue. Who knows what thoughts ran through the minds of the search party that discovered our camp? I doubt if they expected to find two unconscious men and a decomposing corpse.

The sleep before death meant that Daniels and I were spared the gruesome headlines later paraded before a shocked world. When we did eventually surface from that slumber we were famous.

It was a long recovery, overshadowed by a baying press demanding answers to questions we were in no fit state to answer. Accusations of an inhuman act were balanced against public opinion, there were a lot of people who'd placed themselves in our position and seen what they could become. Our survival had depended on consuming human flesh; we could be forgiven for eating the dead. For us it was a smokescreen, our sympathisers still had no idea of how inhuman our final act had been. It was a truth that could never be told. Our secret was safe with me, but I was worried about Daniels, concerned his conscience might lead him down the same path O'Brien had taken.

The unexpected silver lining our survival gifted us meant that for a while we were too busy making money to reflect on past actions. A greedy media courted us. The bidding war that took place for the publishing rights to our story made headlines itself. Chat show appearances and lecture tours were hastily arranged. Hughes would have loved every moment.

But I was becoming more and more uneasy. Due to the nature of our fame Daniels and I were forced into spending large amounts of time together. I was witnessing his gradual decline as he tried and failed to come to terms with notoriety. His excessive drinking had become a danger, one slip of his tongue and both our reputations would be shredded. I lost count of the evenings I spent with him where he talked late into the night, rehashing previous conversations in an attempt to exorcise memories.

"We have to tell people the truth."

It was a rare night off. We were staying in the Chamberlain Hotel as guests of yet another TV company. I'd gone to Daniels' room, more out of an instinct for self-preservation than concern for his well-being. His drunken statement left me in no doubt that sooner or later our money-making merry-go-round would stop abruptly. I dreaded to think of the legal recriminations and public backlash that lay in wait should he confess. I fed him more champagne and watched his eyes grow heavy. Then I suggested we both write confession notes.

A look of grateful relief flickered across eyes that struggled to focus. "It's the right thing to do," he slurred. I smiled. He had no idea how true that was.

I fetched pen and paper from the bureau and dictated our confession. "You go first," I said. His untidy handwriting looked like that of a man on the edge of a breakdown.

'I can't take any more. The memory of what happened in that tent has scarred me and I can't live with the burden any longer.' His eyes were closing.

"Sign it there," I whispered. "We can finish it in the morning." He did as he was told and then struggled to swallow the drink I handed him. Five minutes later he passed out.

I dragged him into the bathroom, dumped him fully clothed into the tub and turned on the taps. Then I went to the cabinet and took out a new razor blade. When I held it up to the light I could see myself reflected in miniature. It was the face of a man who knew how to keep a secret.

I turned around. For the first time since our return Daniels looked at peace. I slid the blade across an exposed wrist and watched blood dribble from his veins. It stained the water red and reminded me of a Polar sunset. As my mouth began to water I asked God to forgive me again.

VACANT POSSESSION

It was the third time she'd seen the little girl. The sighting finally made clear what she'd already suspected but found almost impossible to accept: her new home harboured a ghost and George Pallister, the previous owner, was the one person who might be able to explain why.

***

Railway Cottage wasn't the house of Maria Robinson's dreams, but she'd never expected it to be, a limited budget had lowered any previous hopes. How many depressing two-up two-down's had she viewed accompanied by an estate agent attempting sincerity? The list seemed endless, as did the hollow words used in an attempt to convince her that all damp walls and crumbling brickwork needed was a little TLC. Railway Cottage would require attention, but at least the dry walls and sound brickwork made it a more attractive proposition. The agent seemed to sense her mood.

"It used to be the station-master's house," he said, as if that information somehow elevated it above the others. Maria gazed at a kitchen that would have been basic when the cottage had last been renovated thirty years earlier. That was another detail her guide had offered in an attempt to show he was a salesman with nothing to hide.

His mobile rang. "I'll leave you to explore," he said, as if the cottage were a mansion, and made his way back out into the lane.

Maria wandered through the house and tried to picture what she might do with the empty rooms and featureless walls. When nothing came to mind, she gave up and went out into the back garden.

Years of neglect had left another project to be tackled. An old stepping-stone path by-passed a dilapidated garden shed and lost its way in the long grass. At the end of the property a row of stunted conifers fought for space amongst a mass of shrub and hawthorn.

She picked her way along the trail until she reached the boundary. Beyond the bushy screen a wooden gate was set into a six-foot-high timber fence. *'I'll leave you to explore,'* the agent had said; it seemed like a good idea. She squeezed between the twisted limbs and edged along a natural passageway branches had formed over the fence line.

There was a bolt rusted into place at the top of the gate. Maria loosened it with an old house brick she found lying in the leaves and dragged it open. In front of her a grassy slope ran down to a disused railway line. Beyond the far embankment a stagnant pond lay motionless beneath colourless willows. The grimy surface of the water showed no reflection.

She stumbled down the slope and climbed onto the tracks. Clumps of chickweed and tangled dog-rose grew tall between weather-blistered sleepers. In front of her the rusted rails narrowed until they were lost from view. It was so quiet she could hear the breeze ruffling the branches of the willows.

She turned around and took a step backwards. Thirty yards away the mouth of a tunnel yawned from the base of an overgrown bank. It seemed to fill the space where the tracks ran into darkness, as if the opening were too wide and too tall.

As she approached, she could hear water dripping from the arched brickwork. She rested her fingers against the wall and stared into darkness. There was no sight of the tunnel's end; it could have gone on forever.

"Mrs Robinson!"

The call startled her. From the top of the bank the agent was waving. His smile looked strained, as if he were trying to disguise an impatience only a sale might calm.

Maria felt an irrational surge of anger. She was tempted to march back and explain to the salesman that she wasn't a *'Mrs,'* any longer; that the debt her unfaithful husband had burdened her with was the reason she was viewing properties such as Railway Cottage. The thought of fake concern and professional sympathy prevented her from doing so. Instead, she took one more look around. There was a desolate feel to the scene, a loneliness that conjured up images of a past where the discarded rails and empty tunnel had still been vital links.

She clambered back up the slope and slipped into the garden. As she closed the gate, she caught a glimpse of the upper half of Railway Cottage perfectly framed between a gap in the branches. Something moved from shadow and passed across a bedroom window. Maria shaded her eyes and squinted into the sun. Surely the agent hadn't returned to the house that quickly? *But it wasn't a man, Maria, was it? It was a little girl.* The thought came and went before she had time to even consider it. She gazed at the window and watched reflected clouds move slowly across the glass. "A girl, indeed," she said to herself, and laughed, but when she pulled the bolt back into place frozen pinpricks had risen across her arms.

The salesman was waiting for her in the kitchen. "Well, Mrs Robinson, what do you think?"

Maria recalled damp walls and crumbling brickwork: an endless line of houses that made this one seem like a bargain. "It's *Ms* Robinson," she corrected, and made an offer just below the asking price.

It was accepted the next day.

***

The first weeks in her new house were a time spent making the strange familiar. Freshly decorated and newly furnished Railway Cottage began to feel like home. That changed on a day when early morning sunlight flooded the rooms with warmth and a false promise of summer.

She'd been balanced on a stepladder, attempting to hang a print in the hallway, when a reminder of death wandered across the landing at the top of the stairs. Maria sensed movement and glanced upwards. The little girl she saw trailing a teddy-bear behind her passed soundlessly from view. For a moment the newly familiar became strange again.

"Hello?" Her voice broke the stillness like a stone shattering glass. She climbed from the ladder and listened for sounds of an intruder's movements. Railway Cottage slumbered above her.

The stairway treads creaked as she slowly made her way up onto the landing. Had she closed the bedroom door? She couldn't be sure; it wasn't something she normally thought about. She pushed against it and stepped into the unknown.

The room showed no trace a child had ever entered. She gazed at the wardrobe and was transfixed by the slit of shadow that formed a perfect rectangle between the doors. Maria could imagine a phantom infant crouched in the darkness, a tiny spirit waiting for night to come and a chance to jump out and demand she join in games only the dead can play. It was a ridiculous notion. She strode across the room and pulled open the doors. The sight of hanging dresses and shelved shoes only reinforced the feeling she was overworking her imagination.

She leant her forehead against the window and stared outside. Below her the overgrown garden begged for attention. Beyond the disused railway line willow branches hung limply into the grey pond. A question she couldn't answer filled her mind: had she seen a ghost? It was a thought that only minutes earlier would have seemed absurd, yet something had been in her house; it had crossed the landing and then disappeared.

Through habit she bent down to smooth the bed sheets. As her fingers brushed away a faint indentation she was shocked to realise it resembled the shape of a teddy bear.

***

"I hear you've moved into Railway Cottage."

Audrey Newton ran the tiny post office serving Manor village, an old lady whose main job seemed to be the receiving and passing on of gossip. It was the first time Maria had visited. "I have," she said, and smiled.

The shopkeeper's beady eyes examined the newcomer. "I bet George Pallister left it in a mess." It was a statement made with the certainty of someone who knew they were almost always right.

"Who?" The property had been listed as vacant possession, other than that Maria knew nothing of its history.

"The station master," Mrs Newton said. As Maria recalled the agent's words Audrey rested her elbows on the counter and gave a detailed account of Railway Cottage's former owner.

Apparently Pallister had spent most of his retirement years there. The end of his working life had coincided with the closure of the line. The house was surplus to the railway company's needs, the station master had been a loyal servant; he purchased it for a price well below its market value.

"Kept himself to himself, did George Pallister," Audrey said, as if a need for privacy were a crime. "Only ever wandered into the village when he had to. Even had his groceries delivered, probably thought he was too grand to mix with the likes of us."

"Why would he think that?" Maria suspected Mrs Newton's opinions were formed on the basis of one unshakeable rule; never have a good word to say about anybody.

"His job," she said, as if that explained everything. "He was Mr High and Mighty while he ran that station. I think poor old Derek Hill must have gone through hell trying to keep his boss happy."

Audrey Newton folded her arms and waited for Maria to ask who Derek Hill might be. When she didn't the old lady willingly told her.

"Derek did most of the donkey work at Manor Halt station," she said. "Now and again a couple of part-timers would help out if needed, but it was only a branch line so that didn't happen often. I think Pallister liked the fact he could lord it up over Derek. When you get down to brass tacks George was nothing more than a small-town bully."

"Where is he now?" Maria asked.

"Being looked after in a care home," Audrey said. "I heard that's why the cottage had to be sold. The money from the sale is going towards the cost of his care."

"What about his wife?"

The old lady snorted. "George never married," she said. "His mother made sure of that. He might have bossed his way around that station but when he went home, mummy ruled the roost."

Audrey Newton narrowed her eyes in thought. "I think she died just before Pallister bought the cottage. Her death almost broke him, I can tell you. For a while the locals were sympathetic, bully or not no-one likes to witness another man's grief. But then the little girl went missing and opinion changed." Mrs Newton saw the colour drain from her customer's face. "Are you feeling all right, love?"

Maria nodded unconvincingly. The memory of a child trailing a teddy bear across her landing passed like a shadow through her mind. "What girl was that?" she asked.

A grim look of satisfaction settled on Audrey's face, gossip was gossip no matter how ancient or tragic. "Emily Reagan," she said.

Maria's frown was the only introduction Audrey needed.

"It was probably before your time, dear," she said. "But there are still a lot of people around here who believe George Pallister had something to do with her disappearance."

"I don't understand." Maria was trying to connect the image of a dead child with that of an of an aging station master. The shopkeeper continued with her revelations.

"The little girl, Emily, was being cared for at a kiddies club while her mother worked mornings as a receptionist at the local clinic."

Maria listened to a story every parent dreads.

Somehow Emily Reagan had wandered unnoticed from the crèche. The panic following that discovery continued when her favourite toy, a dog-eared teddy bear, was found discarded on a seat in the empty waiting room at Manor Halt. It was presumed the little girl had managed to slip into the station and climb aboard a train. How no-one saw her was a question that couldn't be answered, but Everfern was the next stop on the line, all that was needed was a telephone call to the station master there. He could search the train, an inspection which hopefully would lead to a happy reunion between parents and daughter.

That happy reunion never took place.

Somewhere between Manor Halt and Everfern the little girl went missing, never to be seen again. No body was ever found: no footprints ever traced: no last sighting that might have led to the location of an infant corpse. The only reminder that Emily Reagan had ever walked this earth was the ragged teddy bear left on a waiting room seat. Thirty years of heartache baptised with a stuffed toy.

"In a place like this it takes no time at all for rumours to do their rounds." Audrey Newton shook her head as if she were disgusted at the thought. Maria could imagine the old lady embellishing those rumours and then helping them on their way.

The shopkeeper continued. "Like I said, they never found the girl." She shrugged her shoulders. "You'd have thought Pallister might have seen something."

"What about Derek Hill?" Maria asked. "Didn't he notice anything strange either?"

"Derek was off sick that day," Audrey said. "Something Pallister never stopped harping on about. He reckoned if Hill had been at work then the police wouldn't have given him such a hard time. But that was typical of George, half of the village had volunteered to search for the missing child and all he was worried about was himself."

The shopkeeper puffed out her cheeks as if the relaying of gossip was something she wasn't used to. She smiled her beady-eyed smile and gazed at Maria. "What can I get you?" she asked.

***

Three days after a child wandered across Maria Robinson's landing, the weather worsened. As the temperature fell so Railway Cottage mirrored the change. The chilly rooms and icy hallway remained that way despite a log fire and heating turned to full.

That night, as Maria lay huddled beneath blankets attempting to shiver her way into sleep, she wondered if perhaps there was something structurally wrong with the house, something a surveyor might have missed. Worries strayed through her mind until eventually her eyes closed and she drifted into uncomfortable slumber.

When she woke the next morning Maria wasn't sure if she'd dreamt she'd heard a child crying in the night or if it had actually happened. As she lay in bed she recalled a face at a window and the shape of a stuffed toy moulded into bedclothes. Traces of Emily Reagan clung to Railway Cottage and Maria needed to know why. George Pallister was in care; perhaps Derek Hill could help. Audrey Newton was sure to know his address.

Later that day the sun reappeared, forcing its way through the windows of a house that seemed reluctant to thaw its way back to normal.

***

Derek Hill's retirement flat bore tribute to the fact he'd spent his life working on the railway. Mementos of the past hung from walls and cluttered the front room, giving it the appearance of a miniature railway museum. Maria's surprise visit had been welcomed. Once she'd explained she'd moved into George Pallister's old house Hill hadn't hesitated in inviting her in.

As Pamela, his wife, served tea, her husband proudly guided Maria through his memories. A procession of knick-knacks and photographs were followed by stories of days Derek Hill clearly still missed. Pamela had retired to another room, her resigned smile signalling her husband's recollections were well told tales.

"So what do you think of the cottage?" Derek was pouring them more tea.

"Actually," Maria said, "that was one of the reasons I came here. I wanted to ask you if George ever mentioned anything strange happening there?"

For the first time since meeting him she noticed Hill's good humour fade. He handed her a cup and sat back down.

"Mr Pallister was a hard man to know," he said. "If I'm honest with you I never particularly liked him." He sipped at his tea as if confession made him thirsty. "But I loved my job," he continued. "I wasn't going to let someone like George Pallister spoil it. As for talking about Railway Cottage, Pallister believed work was work and social was social, we only ever shared the former."

"Do you mean to say he didn't ever chat about his home life?" Maria wondered how two men could spend their working lives together and never reveal anything personal.

Hill was silent for a moment, as if now he couldn't believe it either. He shrugged his shoulders. "The one occasion I ever remember him opening up a bit was when the little girl went missing. That was about the only time he ever confided in me."

Maria leant forward. "What did he say?"

The old man's face coloured; it was the one part of his past he seemed reluctant to share, as if he felt he was trespassing on another man's trust.

"Only that he missed his mother," he said, "and he swore to me that he'd never laid eyes on the child that morning."

"Did you believe him?"

Maria's question brought more colour to Hill's face. This time his silence lasted longer. He placed his cup back on its saucer and sighed. "I don't know," he said. "I honestly don't know." He stood up. Maria sensed the tea party was over.

"Has he got any family?" she asked, as her host escorted her into the hallway.

Derek Hill shook his head. "Nobody," he said. "Once his mother died George became a recluse. Now he's alone in that care home and I think that's the way he likes it."

"Do you ever visit him?" she asked.

Hill looked at her in surprise. "No," he said. "Why on earth would I want to do that?"

As she left the house a sly question entered her mind: *could Derek Hill have been responsible for Emily Reagan's disappearance?*

Maria felt a sorrow for George Pallister that went beyond sympathy. He seemed to have been a man wrongly suspected of a crime on the basis he was a loner, a social misfit who rubbed people up the wrong way. Pamela Hill had confirmed her suspicions when the old lady had said her goodbyes. They'd been standing on the doorstep, her husband had gone back inside to tidy away his past. "Derek's a good man," she whispered. "I'm afraid I can't say the same about Pallister."

***

She was lying in bed hoping that sleep would erase the image of a lonely old man who seemed to cherish his isolation, when she heard the voice. *'Maria.'* The sound was like a feather against her skin. As her eyes grew heavy the voice spoke again. *'Maria.'*

She opened her eyes and listened. From somewhere far away her name drifted across the night. She climbed from her bed and went to the window.

Outside the moon was like a splinter caught in the clouds. Beyond her garden the railway cutting sank into a shadow-filled hollow. She wondered at how dark it must be in the tunnel; if the old bricks were still dripping water onto forgotten rails. For a brief moment the sky cleared and as Maria peered into the night she saw movement.

A little girl she recognised was standing at the top of the far embankment clutching a teddy bear. Behind her the dark surface of the pond lay like a motionless shadow. Maria felt a cold fingertip trace its way down her backbone. The child raised her arm, whether in greeting or farewell Maria couldn't tell, and then she turned around and stepped into the stagnant shallows.

Maria called out and reached for the window but the more she pulled on the handle the less it gave. When it refused to open she beat her fists against the frame and screamed a warning. Rain suddenly speckled the glass. Maria watched in horror as the little girl brushed aside trailing willow branches and waded deeper. By the time clouds snuffed out the moon she'd disappeared beneath the surface.

Floating weed crept over the watery trail the child had left, as if an invisible current was knitting it back together. Moments later it looked as if she'd never been there at all. A thought entered Maria's head: *'Perhaps she hadn't.'*

She threw on clothes and hurried down the stairs. There was a torch in a kitchen drawer. She pulled it out and ran into the garden. Silvery flecks of rain fell through the beam as she stumbled down the path. By the time she reached the fence she was soaked. The gate swung open easily. Maria scrambled down the bank and across the tracks. An old plank lying beside the rails gave her the bridge she needed to span an overflowing drainage ditch.

Trying to climb the far embankment proved more difficult. The grass was wet and slippery underfoot. Water appeared to be seeping through the earth, as if the saturated ground was gradually losing its fight to contain the pond. She dragged herself up the incline and shone the torch across the surface. There was nothing. No footprints on the bank: no slight disturbance that might have given a clue that a little girl had entered the water minutes earlier.

As she lay on the grass attempting to make sense of what she'd seen she heard movement behind her. She swung the torch around and shone it into the mouth of the tunnel. Shadows danced around the soot-stained walls.

"Who's there?"

A sound that might have been the slow tread of footsteps on rails suddenly stopped. All Maria could hear was rain beating through the trees.

She slid down the bank, crossed the makeshift bridge and climbed onto the tracks.

"Who's there?" she called again.

The beam of light ran into darkness. Just before the battery died and the night folded itself around her she thought she heard someone laugh. For a second she was unable to move. Then she was running, tripping over sleepers and clawing at the bank as her headlong flight took her closer to safety and the sanctuary of Railway Cottage.

The torch shone itself back into life the moment she stepped into the kitchen.

Later, as she lay in bed unable to sleep, images of a little girl walking to her death ran themselves through her mind. Each time the child disappeared beneath the water Maria heard again the laugh that had drifted from a darkened tunnel.

She woke to daylight and the thought that Emily Reagan had appeared to her three times. Why would the child do that unless she was trying to tell Maria something? As she puzzled over what it might be George Pallister's name slipped into her mind. Maybe he could help.

***

The ex-station master was spending his twilight days cocooned in the comfort of the Shady Vale Nursing Home. Maria had been given his new address from the font of local knowledge that was Audrey Newton.

A crisp white uniform did nothing to enhance the stern features of a receptionist who seemed reluctant to lay down the paperback she was engrossed in. She stared disbelievingly when Maria gave her name and informed the woman she was a friend of Pallister's.

"That's strange, he's never mentioned you," she said, and glanced at her watch. "He's not well but it might do him good to get a visitor. You can have ten minutes, he's in room twenty-three." She ignored Maria's thanks and returned to her book.

The old man was on the first floor, positioned where all those at the top of their final downward slope were placed. When Maria entered, the curtains were drawn. Pallister was nothing more than a thin shadow propped against pillows. His breathing was shallow and slow, as if each intake of air might be his last and needed to be savoured before he let it go.

"Mr Pallister?" she whispered.

He sighed in his sleep and brushed a feathery hand over the bedclothes.

"George?" Maria placed her fingers over his and was surprised at how cold he felt.

"George?" she repeated

The old man stirred. It was like watching a corpse slowly come back to life; the thought ashamed her. He opened his eyes and squinted into hers.

"Who are you?" The voice was cracked and tired but still carried a trace of arrogance, as if Pallister had never got used to the fact his days of ordering others around were over.

"I'm sorry to disturb you, Mr Pallister," she said. "My name's Maria Robinson, I bought your old house."

He stared at her blankly. Maria wondered if he understood.

"Railway Cottage," she prompted. "I've moved into it."

Something flickered beneath Pallister's sick eyes. He studied her warily and managed to withdraw his hand from beneath hers. "What do you want?" he said.

She looked at him and realised he was a man who'd never mastered the art of friendship; a man who'd probably never felt the need to.

"I wanted to ask you about where you used to live."

Pallister coughed and winced. He pointed at a jug of water placed next to a glass on the bedside table. "Get me a drink," he said, and added "please," as an afterthought. When Maria handed it to him she noticed how badly his hand shook. He caught her staring.

"I wasn't always like this," he said, and sucked at the edge of the glass. "What do you want to know?"

She suddenly felt foolish. What was she doing questioning an old man about something she wasn't even sure was real?

"Well?" he said. His impatience tripped her tongue.

"Do you remember anything strange ever happening in Railway Cottage?"

Pallister's cautious stare remained in place. He sipped at his water again as if he were giving himself time to think.

"What do you mean, strange?"

Maria had the feeling the old man knew exactly what she meant. His narrowed eyes and guarded answers betrayed him.

"The little girl; did you ever see her?"

"Get out!" Pallister's anger was sudden and unexpected. "I suppose you're another interfering busybody who thinks her disappearance had something to do with me!" Saliva had formed at the corners of his mouth. "Well lassie," he spat, "I'll tell you exactly what I told the police all those years ago. I never saw the girl and I had nothing to do with whatever happened to her! Do you hear me?"

He began coughing, reaching for breaths that took an age to come. As the glass slipped from his fingers she backed out of the room and ran down the stairs. "It's Mr Pallister," she told the receptionist. "He's having trouble breathing."

The girl folded her book and placed it on the counter. "He was fine earlier," she said, "I think you'd better go." She hurried past, leaving Maria to wrestle with her conscience and wonder if visiting Shady Vale had been the right thing to do.

***

George Pallister had been hiding something. She realised that later when she recalled his sly expression and the sudden anger an innocent question had unleashed. She also realised she'd been wrong in her earlier judgement;

the people she'd spoken to had known him far better than her, now their criticisms seemed justified.

What had upset him so? She guessed she'd have to discover the answer to that question alone, the same way she needed to find out why the spirit of a little girl lingered in Railway Cottage. Derek Hill had been unable to help, Pallister had refused; Audrey Newton's observations were those of an old lady whose memories were tailored to suit her tongue.

Emily Reagan had disappeared almost thirty years ago.

There was a trail somewhere.

Maria's journey to the truth began with an anonymous phone call and ended in a ramshackle garden shed on a day when she feared George Pallister had returned to Railway Cottage.

***

After an internet search had led her in circles Maria had gone against her better judgement and sought out Audrey Newton. Hinting at the strange happenings she'd experienced in Railway Cottage piqued the shopkeeper's interest. *'Was Mrs Newton aware of any rumours concerning the missing girl?'* The old lady was. Maria's heart sank as Audrey's greedy tongue ran its way over a number of stories that became more implausible as one ended and another began. She was glad to leave the shop.

The phone rang five minutes after she'd arrived home. A weary voice answered her greeting with a question.

"Are you the lady who's moved into George Pallister's old house?"

"I am," she said. "Who is this?"

There was a pause; the caller ignored her question.

"The little girl never got on that train."

Maria heard another voice; it was the same one that had told her she'd seen a child passing across a bedroom window. This time it was telling her to listen.

"How do you know?" she asked.

"Check the old timetables," the stranger said. "If she'd boarded that train, she'd have still been on it when it pulled into Everfern. It left Manor Halt on time and arrived on schedule, that meant it couldn't have stopped anywhere. The carriages were searched thoroughly and there was no trace of her."

Her caller hesitated as if he feared he might have said too much. "Take my advice," he continued, "go back and ask George Pallister about that day. He's the only one who knows what really happened."

Maria recalled an angry old man whose eyes held secrets. "I don't think he'll tell me anything," she said.

The silence that followed seemed to suggest the stranger already knew that.

"Who are you?" she asked.

"Someone who doesn't want to get involved again," the caller said. "But I'm telling you what the police chose to ignore; Emily Reagan never got on that train."

The line went dead.

Maria stared at the receiver and then placed it back on the handset. She suspected Audrey Newton had been busy, why else would a complete stranger have rung her so soon after her visit? She wondered who else the old lady was spreading news to, if she was telling anyone prepared to listen that the woman who'd moved into Railway Cottage was seeing ghosts.

It was too late to worry about that now, she was more concerned with who her mystery caller might have been. *'But you already know, Maria, don't you?'* The voice was right again; the internet might have led her in circles but in the reports she'd scanned three names had cropped up continually. She'd spoken to George Pallister and Derek Hill, two of the three who'd been rigorously questioned by the police. The other man, John Underwood, had been station master of Everfern at the time of Emily Reagan's disappearance.

If Mrs Newton had given him her number she was sure the old lady would have no hesitation in passing on Underwood's address.

***

"Mr Underwood, my name's Maria Robinson."

The old station master's house was located on the edge of Manor village. Maria had been right; Audrey Newton's loose tongue was already primed, a simple question and the floodgates opened.

John Underwood was a man who looked as if he'd grown comfortably into old age and was glad he still had tomorrows to look forward to. He stared at Maria; there was no invitation to enter.

"I know who you are. Why are you here?"

"I think we both know the reason for my visit," she said.

She held his gaze. For a moment Maria thought he might order her to leave, then he shook his head and reluctantly made way for her. "I suppose you'd better come in."

He led her into a comfortably furnished lounge that lacked a woman's touch. She took the seat he offered.

"Why didn't you want to give me your name when you called?" she asked.

John Underwood rubbed at the tired lines age had formed across his face, as if doing so might smooth them away.

"Do you have any idea what I went through when that little girl disappeared?" The old man's eyes looked haunted, full of a past he'd tried to forget.

Maria could guess, she'd read the newspaper reports. Underwood had been the main suspect until suspicion fell on Pallister. The station master continued.

"The police were convinced she was still on the train when it stopped at Everfern." He looked at her. "I'm certain that was due to what George Pallister told them. After all, he found the teddy bear and swore there was no sign of her at Manor Halt. His statement made my life a nightmare. I can't tell you how many times I was hauled into that police station and questioned. At one point they even threatened to charge me." He paused. "As I said on the phone, I believe George Pallister is the only one who knows what happened that day, and as you said to me, he'll never tell."

The old man picked up a photograph from a coffee table and handed it to Maria. A younger John Underwood smiled self-consciously into the camera. The lady who clung affectionately to his arm was laughing and pretending to straighten his tie.

"That was taken at my son's wedding," he said. "My wife, Marion, died ten years ago and I miss her as much now as I did then." He sighed. "I sometimes think the strain of what happened affected her more than it did me, and I don't think I'll ever stop blaming myself for that." He ran his fingers over the photograph.

"Time doesn't soften tragedy," he said. "It just allows you the space to get used to it. I've found that space and I'm not letting anything invade it again. That's why I don't want my name mentioned if you go talking to anybody else. I don't think I could bear it."

He placed the photograph back down and held out his hand, an old man who still believed someone's word was their bond. "What I've told you is between us and goes no further than this room. Agreed?"

Maria smiled and took his hand in hers. "Agreed," she said.

For the first time since she'd entered John Underwood's house he visibly relaxed.

"Would you like a cup of tea?" he asked. When he smiled the lines left his face.

***

The questions still needed answers.

George Pallister had lived up to his reputation but did that make him a murderer? If he had done something to the girl how had he got away with it? Maria had watched a dead child wade into stinking water, as if it were her final resting place, but that didn't make sense. She'd scoured reports, the pond had been dredged and no body had been found. Now she was scared, frightened of a disused tunnel and worried what other visions Railway Cottage might hold. She needed to do something; something physical to take her mind off a mystery that wouldn't be solved. Maria gazed through the window; the overgrown garden had been last on her to-do list. She slipped on a pair of boots and stepped outside.

Pallister had been a hoarder. The old shed Maria thought might house a mower was full of rubbish. Tins of out-of-date paint were stacked in neat rows along with buckets full of nails and rusted work tools that could never be used again. Stacks of rotting newspapers had been thrown in a corner. She was placing them in the garden ready to be dumped when she saw a face she recognised staring at her from beneath a faded headline.

Emily Reagan was smiling shyly into the camera, a little girl with no idea of what torment the future held. As Maria picked her way through the papers she realised they all featured reports on the missing girl. Endless details of a lack of progress were coupled with grainy photographs of Manor Halt and Everfern railway stations. There were pictures of the three men she'd spoken to as well as that of a policeman who she learned had been the inspector leading the investigation.

Detective Alistair Mackay looked and sounded like a decent man. He'd been quoted as saying he'd carry on searching for the missing child until his dying day. He'd been as good as his word. Even in retirement, after years on the case, Mackay had continued in his quest to find the answer to a mystery he was certain one day he'd solve. But that day never came.

His body was found sprawled on railway tracks half a mile from the tunnel that so frightened Maria. A heart attack had ended his obsession. Clasped in his dead fingers was a notebook. On an open page he'd scrawled five words. *'I will find the killer.'* Even then Mackay knew the little girl was dead. What he didn't know was that he'd been wrong: he ran out of time before he could fulfil his vow.

Maria stared at the face of a man intent on discovering the truth. Perhaps Mackay had been unlucky she thought, or maybe there were some questions that could never be answered. Either way, time had let justice take a back seat, and all those yesterdays had buried a trail the detective had spent his life trying to follow.

Pallister's name featured heavily in many of the reports, as did Derek Hill's and John Underwood's. Most of them hinted that either Pallister or Underwood might have been involved in the girl's abduction. One faded article even suggested they could have been in it together.

Maria couldn't help thinking that Pallister seemed to have collected the papers as trophies, the way a hunter might gloat over a kill. *'Kill,'* it was a word that seemed eerily appropriate.

As she bent to pick up another bundle her foot slipped through the rotting boards. If she hadn't lost her balance she would never have seen the tin concealed beneath the shed floor. The words, *'Cadbury's Finest,'* were stencilled across the lid. She pulled it out and shook it gently. There was something inside. When the rusted lid wouldn't open Maria took it back to the house. A kitchen knife did what her fingers had been unable to.

It was then she discovered vague answers to a mystery that had begun thirty years earlier.

The vandalised diary lying in the old biscuit tin was torn and weather damaged. Maria carefully opened it. On the few pages that were still intact neatly formed handwriting detailed the disappearance of Emily Reagan and the subsequent search. Pallister had taken a keen interest in the case. The rest of the log was smudged and faded, partial sentences ended suddenly by frayed edges and crumpled fragments. It was like trying to piece together the bones of a recently unearthed skeleton.

From the odd snippets Maria could read a picture slowly began to form of events that had taken place in and around Manor village on and after that long ago day.

Mother spoke to me today. I've done what…

The girl wouldn't…

Hill should have been there.

Underwood seems to be taking…

The pond; mother's right, no-one will…

I had to wait until after it had been dred…

Maria was confused. Hadn't Audrey Newton told her Pallister's mother had died before he bought the cottage? Yet in the words she could decipher it appeared he'd been talking to her.

Outside cloud and rain had cast a shroud over the fine spring day. Inside the kitchen Maria had grown cold. She began to shiver as a terrible truth formed in her mind.

The girl was in the pond and George Pallister had put her there.

It was all here, in the ripped pages and weather scored words. The station master's past had caught up with him.

Still, she was puzzled. Why keep a diary of your wrongdoings and live with the fear it might be found? The answers came as she recalled the comments levelled at Pallister. His arrogance: a need for control: the bully who cared nothing for other people's lives.

She realised the memoir was another trophy to go with the rotting newspapers. But something had panicked him, the remains of torn-out pages made that clear. Maria wondered if it had anything to do with Emily Reagan. Had she come back? Had his first sighting driven him to try and obliterate something that couldn't be changed?

As she read the final entry she thought she heard movement from upstairs. At first she wondered if the little girl was making another of her appearances. She laid the book on the table and listened. It was no child. The footsteps were slow and heavy. Whoever was above her sounded as if they were searching the house. She crept to the door and gently pulled it open.

'Look.' A child's voice drifted into her mind. Maria had no choice but to do as it said. She gazed up the stairs.

Somehow Emily Reagan had opened a window to the past.

Shadows formed above her. Maria watched in horror as George Pallister pulled a body across the landing. There was a grim determination on his face. He looked down and met her gaze. Then he shook his head and grinned. Maria knew what he was thinking. *'You should have kept your nose out of matters that didn't concern you, lassie.'* He let go of the corpse and placed a hand on the banister rail.

Maria slammed the kitchen door shut and pressed her body against it. There was no lock. Footsteps were making their way down the stairs. George Pallister, the frail old man conducting a hopeless fight against the inevitable, had somehow returned as his younger self with scores to settle. Maria could feel his presence. He was back in the place where he'd committed a deed so terrible the memory of it lingered inside the walls and stretched beyond the garden to where the railway cutting disappeared into darkness.

She listened and waited as a thought clouded her reasoning: how could a man be a ghost when he wasn't yet dead? A fist beat against the door. Maria watched it bow inwards and waited for the wood to split. It took a moment for her to realise the threat of violence was an outpouring of frustration. George Pallister could do nothing.

Somehow he'd come back, borne on the memory of a little girl who couldn't leave, and yet he'd arrived powerless, as helpless to change the future as he could the past.

When the house fell silent Maria listened to rain beat against the window and cried with relief.

The pond with no reflection had been dredged without success and now Maria could guess why. George Pallister hadn't dumped poor Emily Reagan's body in there until after that grim operation. She wondered how long he'd waited; if he'd sweated as the search continued, concerned the house to house inspections might be repeated. But that hadn't happened and now the little girl lay beneath cloudy green water, endlessly staring upwards at the willows shrouding her secret grave. Maria was sure; as certain of that as she was that Emily Reagan had been waiting years to be found. The girl wouldn't have to wait any longer. Maria knew what she had to do.

There was an old spade hanging on the shed wall. Maria took it down and tested her weight against the handle. When it held she closed the door and made her way down the garden.

'Wait.' It was the child's voice.

Maria frowned, surely Emily Reagan wanted to end this?

But the voice was persistent. Half-formed thoughts that weren't her own came and went.

'Leave your search until tonight.'

"Why?" she asked, and instinctively knew it had something to do with George Pallister.

The little girl's voice drifted across the garden as if it were a leaf caught on the breeze. *'Because then the time will be right.'*

Maria watched clouds blossom and felt the rain fall harder. She thought of a stagnant pond and a saturated bank ready to burst; of a torch dying on her in the darkness. Daylight would be better to do what was needed but if Emily Reagan wanted her to wait then she must. Tonight she was going to finish a search that had led to the death of Alistair Mackay. She prayed history would be kinder to her than it had been to him.

***

Railway Cottage seemed to have taken on a personality of its own. Dusk had settled early, bringing with it an unnatural silence that reminded Maria of the first time she'd climbed onto the tracks.

Now the ceiling lights shed a dusty glow, as if they were old and in need of change. Occasionally Maria thought she heard the muffled sound of heavy boots making their way through the house. She could imagine George Pallister stomping up and down the narrow staircase, impatiently waiting to get rid of a corpse as a search team dragged stagnant water.

She jumped as the front door knocker suddenly banged. The sound echoed through Railway Cottage. She crept from the kitchen and stared into the hallway. Beyond the opaque glass a shape that might have been George Pallister stood motionless. Silently she made her way along the length of the hall and rested her fingers on the handle. When she steeled herself to open the door there was nobody there. Anger took the edge from her fear.

"I know what you're trying to do!" she shouted, "but you're not going to stop me! Do you hear?"

It might have been her imagination but just before she closed the door she thought she heard the distant sound of a train whistle echo across the night air.

***

It was almost midnight. The cottage had grown cold. There'd been no more phantom footsteps or sightings of a dead child unable to rest. It was almost as if the house sensed someone else might soon be joining the departed and was preparing itself for that eventuality. It was time to go. She took out the torch, closed the back door and picked up the spade.

Below a moonless sky rain hissed through the trees. The torch beam picked out a broken pathway she reluctantly followed. When the gate wouldn't open she almost turned back, only the memory of a little girl clinging to a teddy bear gave her the strength to force it open and continue.

The abandoned railway line lay below her like twin snakes curving into the night. Maria slid down the bank and climbed over the tracks. Water was still seeping through the far embankment, saturating the mossy cover and filling the slow moving drainage ditch below.

The plank she'd left lying across the stream bowed alarmingly as she carefully made her way to the other side. Again the climb was a succession of slips and stumbles. Halfway up the bank the earth was springy underfoot. She picked a spot, laid the torch down and pressed the spade into the ground.

The dig was easier than she'd anticipated. Wet earth came away in chunks, and the deeper she went the softer it became. She could hear the water gurgling beneath the soil, forcing its way to the surface as the pressure lessened. Sweat and rain ran down her face, soaking her body as she bent to her task. Suddenly the blade sank further and as she slipped backwards the bank finally burst.

Water cascaded down the slope, sweeping Maria into the swollen drainage ditch and forcing her below the surface. As her feet found purchase something clawed at her face. For one terrible moment she imagined Emily Reagan in there with her. The waterlogged branch she pushed away spun crazily in the unnatural current. The force of it pushed her against the side of the tracks and as she feared going under again her hands found the rails. Straining to stay upright she pulled against them and dragged herself up onto the line.

Gasping for breath she lay on the tracks and as her breathing slowly returned to normal she heard the distant sound of impossibility. A train that couldn't be running was heading towards her. The rails hummed and rattled in anger, and as the sound grew louder she stared into the tunnel.

A small white circle of light began to blossom. When it pinned her in its beam she found it impossible to move. She clung to the vibrating rails and found the rhythm strangely soothing. The speeding train seemed to be delivering a message through its wheels. *'Relax, Maria, it's time to die. Relax, Maria, it's time to die.'* Over and over the words clattered through her mind, a mantra she couldn't fight. She laid her head against the rough surface of a sleeper and as the tarry scent filled her nostrils she closed her eyes.

'*Maria! Maria!*' It was a child's voice. Emily Reagan was calling to her, telling her to open her eyes, to get off the tracks before it was too late!

She shook her head and sat up. It was like waking from the grip of a sleep that wouldn't let go. All she could hear was the rumble of the rails and a child's voice screaming a warning. The mouth of the tunnel filled her vision and as the approaching light blinded her she pushed herself off the tracks.

The train thundered from the tunnel, its whistle screaming, the engine trailing a slipstream of thick black smoke. She barely had time to press herself against the embankment before it careered past. For a second she caught sight of something that looked like George Pallister leaning from the footplate, waving his fists and shouting obscenities as he rode a ghost train into hell.

And then just as suddenly as it had appeared the engine was gone, a silhouette melting into darkness. Silence descended over the cutting. Maria watched wisps of coal-coloured smoke fade into the night air and listened as the stagnant pond emptied itself onto the tracks.

The skeleton was lying half-submerged in the shallow basin of water that hadn't yet drained. Maria stepped into the mud and crouched beside the remains of a little girl who'd wandered onto a station platform and never came home. "You can rest now, Emily," she said. She stood up and wiped her eyes. "I give you my word I'll make sure the person responsible pays for this."

Rain was still sleeting through the night as she hurried back to Railway Cottage. The police asked for more details after she called and told them where a body was lying and what she believed had happened. She hung up without mentioning the ex-station master's name. It wouldn't take them long to link the discovery with him, but first she needed to speak to George Pallister alone; to tell him that she knew what he'd done and that a little girl had been unable to rest because of his actions.

***

Dim lights showed from behind closed curtains. The Shady Vale Nursing Home looked like a mausoleum. Maria pulled into the car park and ran through the rain. When she pushed through the entrance doors the young receptionist looked up in surprise.

"I need to see George Pallister," Maria said.

The girl took in her mud-stained clothes and dishevelled appearance. "I'm afraid that won't be possible."

Maria wasn't in the mood to argue. She pushed her way past and hurried towards the stairs.

"Come back!"

By the time the girl bustled from the reception area Maria had reached the first floor. The shadowy corridor was stuffy and overheated. A sickly scent of disinfectant and medicine clung to the air.

She barged her way into Pallister's room and stopped. A bedside lamp illuminated the death mask of a face. Blankets had been kicked off the bed. The old man's body was twisted rigid, as if his last moments had been spent in agony.

"What do you think you're doing?"

Maria spun around and thrust her face into the receptionist's. "When did he die?" she demanded. The girl stepped backwards. Whatever she saw in Maria's expression drew the sting from her anger.

"About forty-five minutes ago," she said, and pointed to an overturned medicine bottle lying by the lamp. Pills were scattered around it. "He took an overdose."

Forty-five minutes; the exact moment a ghost train lost itself to the night. So that was why Emily Reagan had wanted the search delayed! Somehow she'd known Pallister was preparing to kill himself. The timing had to be right or the little girl might have been trapped in Railway Cottage forever.

She glanced at the clock on the wall and could imagine Pallister lying in his bed, fearfully watching the last minutes of his life tick away. Before he died he'd realised the secret he'd nursed for thirty years had been uncovered. *Had he been riding that train?* Maria didn't know, but if he hadn't been aboard then she thought he probably was now. It was a one way trip and George Pallister had booked his ticket a long time ago.

She saw a sheet of paper lying beneath the bedside table. "What's that?"

The girl shook her head. "I don't know. I didn't notice it earlier."

The distant sound of a police siren grew louder. The receptionist looked at her questioningly. Maria nodded at Pallister's corpse.

"They've come to ask him some questions," she said. "You'd better go down and meet them."

The girl seemed glad to leave the room. Maria bent down and picked up the piece of paper. Spidery handwriting filled both sides of a begrudging confession note.

I know you'll find this, Maria Robinson, you're good at locating things, aren't you, lassie? As soon as you told me you'd moved into Railway Cottage I had a feeling you'd be trouble. It's a strange house, isn't it? Have you seen the little girl yet? Of course you have, that's why you're here now.

I suppose you wonder why I killed her. You may find this hard to believe but I didn't mean to. When I saw her alone on the platform all I intended to do was guide her to safety. But then the thought came to me that I might be able to take her home, to make her the daughter I'd never had. It was an idea I was certain would have pleased my dead mother. After all, hadn't she sometimes treated me the way a wife might treat a husband? The memory of her fingers stroking my hair as she slowly unbuttoned my shirt filled me with a belief the child could have been the fruit of one of those unions.

There was nobody around. It was a wonderful opportunity.

I tried to be nice, but the little bitch wouldn't stop crying, and the tighter I hugged her the more she screamed. It was only when she stopped that I realised what I'd done. I started to panic but then I heard my mother's voice telling me what I needed to do and how it should be done. After that it was easy.

Does that shock you? I don't really care; I'm too old and ill to let it bother me. If I'd been a younger man I think I might have done to you what I did to the child, just to shut your mouth up and allow me the satisfaction of taking my secret to the grave. But it's too late for that now; it's too late for a lot of things.

I left Emily Reagan's toy in the waiting room, hoping the police would think she'd forgotten it in her excitement to board a train. That almost worked. It was a shame John Underwood managed to talk his way out of a prison sentence that could have been mine.

No-one saw me carry the body back to the cottage because I cut through the tunnel. That was a long dark walk. I could hear myself crying. It seemed to take forever. You know all about that tunnel, don't you?

When the police carried out their door-to-door searches I took a risk and hid her back in there. They'd already checked it once, but I wasn't sure if they'd do it again. My luck held out. After that I brought her back to the house and waited for them to drag the pond. I knew once they'd done that everything would be fine. Mother promised me.

Of course, the divers never found a thing. I watched from my bedroom window and laughed at their efforts. Two nights later I carried the girl back across the tracks and slid her body into the water. That should have been the end of it, how was I to know Emily Reagan would come back?

Have you any idea how hard it is to live with the ghost of the child you murdered? You can't imagine how many nights I woke to hear her crying outside my bedroom door, listening as she begged me to confess. Once I thought that sound might drive me insane, but over the years I grew deaf to it.

My mother never came to me in those moments. I realised she'd abandoned the son she swore she loved and had left me to face my demons alone. But I won my battle of wills with Emily Reagan the same way I've won now. You see taking my own life wasn't that much of a sacrifice I didn't have a lot of time left anyway. Now no-one can convict me, I've escaped justice and there's nothing you or the little girl can do about it.

Sleep well in your new home, lassie, I never could.

George Pallister.

Maria re-read the note and then folded it in two. She could feel tears working their way from the corners of her eyes. Pallister was a man who'd been suffocated, corrupted by his mother's unnatural love, yet he was still a murderer who knew he'd done wrong. How many lives had he ruined by concealing that evil?

You've won nothing, she thought. *Soon everybody will know what you did and Emily Reagan can rest in peace.*

Below her she could hear the sound of police cars pulling up and the opening and slamming of doors. She placed the note on the bedside table and took another look at the twisted grimace that had been George Pallister's last expression

'*I've escaped justice,*' he'd bragged, but Maria wasn't so sure. A short while ago she'd seen a ghost train with a dead man standing on the footplate, screaming obscenities as his dying attempt to silence her failed. The station master might have believed he'd escaped justice in this life but she was certain he hadn't in the next.

An officer entered the room as she was leaving. "Are you Maria Robinson?" he asked.

"I am," she said. "And I'm tired and cold and that's the last question I'm answering tonight." She smiled; "Unless you're going to arrest me."

***

Maria was visited early the next morning by the same officer she'd met at Shady Vale. There was nothing she could have told him that would have made any sense so she settled for a simpler option: she lied.

Why were you out on the tracks at that time of night?

I thought I'd seen a prowler.

Why did you have a spade with you?

For protection, what else?

Why did you visit George Pallister so late at night?

Because when I discovered the body I had a feeling he was involved.

Why?

She shrugged her shoulders. *It was a feeling; that was all.*

The policeman's face showed he didn't believe a word, but what could he do? She'd done nothing wrong. He asked her to get in touch if she thought of any other details that might help and then he was gone.

John Underwood and Derek Hill rang; both men seemed relieved to discover their names were no longer linked to a murder. Audrey Newton welcomed her into the store as if she were a long lost relative. The following week two funerals took place at Manor church. Maria only attended one.

***

Three days after Emily Reagan's memorial service Maria was getting ready for bed when she heard a noise on the stairs. At first she wondered if perhaps the little girl had come back, that maybe she was making one more visit to say farewell. She opened the bedroom door. A scrap of paper that might have been a goodbye note lay on the landing. She picked it up and turned it over. Written neatly in handwriting she recognised from a murderer's diary was one word: *Lassie.*

The truth wound its way into her mind like slow poison.

Emily Reagan was gone, but George Pallister had taken her place.

ASLEEP ON DUTY

When the artillery barrage finally ended the men could still hear it, as if their heads were so full of sound the noise would never go away. Across no-man's land smoke drifted through the wire and hung in the breeze like an invitation to come and join the dead.

"Right you wasters, five minutes. If anyone hangs back, I'll shoot them myself."

Private Jack Ambrose realised that Sergeant Mullins, the man who'd bullied them halfway across France, was now prepared to bully them to their deaths. In front of Jack, Harry Wilson, his best friend, turned and shook his hand. Along the trench, whistles were being blown. The sound rose into the dawn air, piercing the dreadful silence with its promise of death. Ambrose felt Mullins push him in the back, and as the first rank disappeared into no-man's land he scrambled up the ladder and ran into a world that lost all meaning.

***

When he regained consciousness the sun was dipping below the battlefield. Harry Wilson's body lay at the bottom of the shell-hole. Jack remembered trying to shield his friend as the mortars exploded around them, desperately searching for cover where there was none.

He scrambled to the lip of the crater and peered across no-man's land: for as far as he could see the ground was littered with the dead. He eased his back down the slope and watched light fade from the day. High above him a flare burst, illuminating the landscape like an angel of death.

***

It was dawn by the time Jack managed to crawl his way back to allied lines. As he rolled into the trench he recognised the frightened voice that challenged him.

"Who goes there?" Mullins had his revolver drawn.

"It's me, Private Ambrose."

The sergeant relaxed. "Well done, boy, I've only just made it back myself."

He looked at Mullins; there wasn't a mark on him. Jack instantly knew the truth, the officer hadn't gone over. The knowledge passed unspoken between them.

"Guard the trench," the sergeant snapped. "I'll see if anyone else made it."

He marched off and Jack sat down with his back against a stack of sandbags. Something cold had lodged itself in his heart. He still couldn't believe Mullins hadn't joined the attack. No wonder he'd been so eager to bully everybody else out of the trench. As thoughts of cowardice and betrayal ran through his mind exhaustion dragged him into sleep.

***

Someone was kicking him awake.

"Asleep on duty, Ambrose? That's a court martial offence."

Mullins had been drinking; Jack could hear it in his speech and see it in his actions.

"I always knew you were a slacker. Get up and follow me. You're going on report and with my say-so you'll be facing a firing squad."

The sergeant grinned and Jack could see the hate stored in that smile; Mullins intended to make sure his secret went no further. A feeling of helplessness stole over him; he hadn't been able to save his best friend's life and now he was unable to save his own.

The trenches they passed through were crowded with reinforcements, young men with tired faces and frightened eyes. They boiled their billy-cans as they shared out rations and spoke in whispers of home.

"Hurry up, Ambrose!" Mullins was cocky now, marching upright as if he were a hero. Jack realised that by the time the sun rose again he'd be standing in front of a firing squad and no-one would ever know the truth. Ahead of them the officer's quarters came into view, a ramshackle construction that housed his judge and jury.

They were almost there when Mullins stumbled. As he fell Jack saw the small circular hole in the sergeant's forehead. He instinctively dropped to the ground and heard something thump into the sandbags overhead. When he looked up, Sergeant Mullins lay in the mud with his eyes closed and a sniper's bullet lodged in his brain. It looked as if he were asleep on duty.

Barry John Watson

SPACE FEVER

Yesterday I gazed in awe as a meteorite shower burnt its way high above the surface of Mars. Flecks of light drove intricate patterns across the barren landscape. It was like watching tiny mirrors splinter into a thousand formations. The sight was so beautiful that when they flickered and died I wept. I was still crying when I fell asleep. I miss Ashton.

Now I'm alone, I can take the ship wherever I like. As I sit here and stare into the stars I remember a blurb from an old science fiction movie: *in space no-one can hear you scream.* I wish that were true. Ever since I lured Ashton into the ejector bay and dumped him into the cosmos I've been listening to his final cry. It's a sound that wakes me from sleep and fills the silent hours with accusations.

I remember watching his body drift away from the craft; he looked like a swimmer floundering in an invisible ocean. I grinned and waved to him. Who knows what thoughts went through his mind as he waited for his oxygen tank to gradually empty? Was he surprised at my betrayal? Perhaps; I think he believed we might still be able to repair our relationship. What he didn't realise was that I'd gone past that point. By then I'd gone past a lot of points.

His weightless form turned slow cart-wheels against a starry backdrop; they winked and glowed as if to reassure me they knew what I'd done but that my secret was safe with them. By the time I lost sight of him I was laughing. It was the first time in almost three months that I'd felt truly happy. It didn't last long.

Before this voyage I used to think space fever was a figment of the imagination, something the old-timers who'd pioneered deep-space exploration liked to talk about in front of us cadets. It was as if they'd experienced a hardship we would never know. On how many occasions had I heard them lecture us about how time and isolation can change a man? They compared it to the cabin fever early settlers sometimes suffered from, when days and nights spent alone in the wilderness could sometimes drive a man into the arms of madness. I remember how we younger astronauts used to laugh at their claims; how we thought they were too old for space travel and should have hung up their suits a long time ago. It's only recently that I've come to realise how right they were and that sometimes a man longs to be held in that embrace; to feel the cold caress of insanity unburden him of responsibility

I blame the selection committee who carried out the personality profiling, they got it wrong. They know how long deep-space missions last and the complications that can occur. You need a partnership that gels. Two men crammed together for six months can cause untold problems; it was the committee's job to make sure those problems didn't happen. It seems Ashton slipped through their net and so did I, because of that we ended up hating each other, or at least I ended up hating him. You'd have thought the profiling board would have learnt from previous mistakes. Who can ever forget what happened aboard Space Probe IV?

***

Captain Bob Clements had flown countless missions, an astronaut with more space hours under his belt than most of us put together, but something happened on that voyage that turned him into a madman. His final broadcast will live forever in the memory of those who heard it. By the time Houston received his radio message he'd already slaughtered Jeff Baxter his co-pilot, and was about to commit suicide in spectacular fashion.

"Baxter got what he deserved," Clements said. "I couldn't stand him any longer." His voice sounded as if it were made of ice. "Now I've reversed the propulsion system." He laughed, and then began a countdown to his own death. "Ten."

Everyone in the control room knew what his message meant.

"Nine."

Instead of driving power from the ship the system was forcing it back in.

"Eight."

Nothing could withstand that pressure.

"Seven."

"BOB! DON'T DO IT!" The controller screamed a command Clements ignored.

"Six."

Through the wall-speakers the gentle hum of the craft's engines grew in volume.

"Five."

"Think of your wife and kids." The operator was pleading with him, he sounded close to tears.

"Four."

The crew and technicians had fallen silent, each of them mentally picturing the explosion that was about to happen.

"Three."

The engines had gone into deafening overdrive.

"Two."

"Bob!"

"One," Clements said, and laughed again.

Every man in the control centre flinched as Space Probe IV disintegrated. It sounded as if an atomic bomb had been detonated. Somewhere far out in space a white light briefly lit up that corner of the universe and then died. Captain Bob Clements had succumbed to something a lot of us hadn't believed existed.

Heads rolled after that fiasco. New profiling systems were put in place. Background checks became more strenuous. A psychiatric unit guided each astronaut through rigorous tests. Those in charge were determined the disaster that was Space Probe IV would never happen again. And it didn't. Following missions departed and returned safely. The journeys grew longer and timescales lengthened. Still, there was no sign of bad history repeating itself. The new set-up appeared to be a success. But then Mike Ashton and I were selected as crewmates.

We'd met in training, two of a batch of twelve, the elite; hand-picked for the deep space missions we all craved to experience. We got on so well it was easy to see how the selectors believed we'd make a good team, back then even we did. The animosity and resentment that eventually tore us apart didn't show itself until later, when time and space and the tight confines of a long distance craft brought to the surface things that couldn't be taken back.

We should have recognised the warning signs. The bickering started a week in, pointless arguments that went nowhere. A lot of the time we managed to laugh them off, to fool ourselves that they were only superficial disagreements. But as the weeks passed it seemed as if we couldn't agree on anything. The lighthearted banter we used to share dried up. That was when we should have turned back, while there was still time. The problem was we were both too proud and stubborn to admit it wasn't working. Besides, the colleagues who'd have given their eye teeth to pilot this mission would've regarded us as failures. Neither of us were prepared to face that. So the arguments became fiercer, the silences lasted longer, and I came to hate the man I once looked on as a friend.

Now and again Ashton would offer an olive branch of an apology, even though he'd done nothing wrong. I think he was worried for the future and genuinely wanted our relationship to return to the way it was. I wasn't and I didn't.

By the time we were eight weeks away from earth I realised everything about him grated on my nerves. The memory of face to face shouting matches and traded insults festered inside me like poison. I couldn't stand to be in his company but I had nowhere else to go; apart from separate sleeping quarters privacy on these ships is limited; they're built for distance, not comfort. All I could think of was the thousands of miles we still had to travel and the time it would take. That time and those miles built a barrier no olive branch could span.

As I lay in my bunk on a rare moment alone an idea slipped into my mind and nested itself there. *'You need to get rid of him,'* it said, and I liked the thought so much I couldn't let it go.

After that it was only a matter of time.

***

"There's an air-leak in the ejector bay! It's escaping from the outer-seal!"

I faked panic. It was the first time one of us had spoken to the other in almost two days.

"Are you sure?" Ashton leant across me and checked the readings, unaware I'd doctored the instrument panel.

"What are we going to do, Mike?" My rehearsed concern unsettled him. I could tell, even after everything that had happened, he still longed to be friends. I never wanted to see him again.

"How long before it affects the cabin pressure?" he asked.

I shook my head. "I'm not sure, it all depends if the seal remains in place. It needs repairing."

He saw my worried expression and placed a hand on my shoulder. "It's alright," he said. "I'll do it."

We looked at each other.

"Mike," I said. "I'm sorry about the way things have gone. Perhaps when this is fixed we can repair our friendship." When he grinned I felt like smashing my fist into his teeth.

"Don't worry, buddy," he said, and left the cockpit. Fifteen minutes later he'd donned his protective suit and was waiting to enter the bay. I saw him on the monitor link giving a thumbs up as he waited for me to open the connecting hatch.

I returned his signal and grinned. "I'm not your fucking buddy," I whispered.

Once he'd entered and I'd closed the door, I rested my fingers on the ejector button. It would only take him a moment to realise there was nothing wrong with the seal but a moment was all I needed. I pressed the button. The outer hatch opened and he was sucked into space. That was when I was sure I heard him scream.

***

You lose track of time up here.

Houston have sensed something is wrong. I laughed when they ordered me to turn around, to abort the mission and return home. I've come to realise orders are made by people who don't have to follow them. I laughed even more when they told me they wanted to speak to Ashton.

"That might be a problem," I said. "He went outside three days ago and I haven't seen him since." I couldn't understand why they didn't find that funny. When they brought a psychiatrist to the microphone I severed radio contact. They don't seem to realise, I'm the one in charge now. They can't order me around.

I sat back and thought I'd try and count how many stars I could see. I got to eight-hundred-and-seventy-nine and realised I might have counted some of them twice so I started again. It's a big universe.

Last night I dreamt Ashton had returned to the ship. He floated just beyond the ejector bay door with only his helmeted head visible through the viewing window. I could hear him pleading to be let in. "What did I do wrong?" he cried. "What did I do wrong?"

I stared at him and mouthed a single word: *Everything.*

That was when he screamed and pulled off his helmet. Inside was a bleached skull; only the eyes were still alive. They gazed into mine and were full of hate. "Look what's happened to me," he moaned. "This is your fault."

He punched his fists helplessly against the window. I knew he wanted to drag me from the ship and make me suffer what he'd had to endure. My scream drowned out his.

I woke up with tears in my eyes and the sour taste of guilt on my tongue.

The command centre continue to try and contact me. Now they know Ashton's dead I bet they're worried sick I'm going to destroy another expensive spacecraft the way Clements destroyed his. They've good right to be concerned. I've ignored their communications, what are they going to do, send another craft after me? I don't think so. Now I'm plotting another course, one that has no destination.

***

I did a stupid thing today. I sent all my rations into space. I placed them in the ejector bay and got rid of them the way I got rid of Ashton. I think part of me hoped that he was still alive and might find them. Who knows, perhaps in years to come someone might see a food cloud drifting past their ship. I wonder what they'll think when they see it floating by?

I've taken to spending hours in the ejector bay. It's a thrill to gently run my gloved fingers over the activate button. All it would take is the slightest of pressure and I'd be joining Ashton on his everlasting journey.

Perhaps I'm hallucinating but I'm beginning to suspect my crewmate has got back on board. I can smell him. He grinned at me from a mirror yesterday. Sometimes I hear him whistling through his teeth, another of his annoying habits I'd come to detest. I don't know where he's hiding but I've searched the craft countless times without being able to find him.

When I do, I'll make him pay.

***

I'm hungry. I'd forgotten I'd emptied the ship of food until I looked in the storage units and found them bare. There wasn't even a bottle of water left. I licked condensation from the ejector bay wall instead. It had a metallic taste but after a while I got used to it.

I've written a letter to Ashton. I know he can't read it, but I felt I needed to explain a few things.

Dear Mike
How are you?
It seems only a short while ago that we weren't speaking. (I don't like to point the finger but you were to blame. Ha-ha!)
I'm sorry about what happened, it was an accident. Did you manage to fix the seal?
Perhaps we can meet up sometime? I'd like to know what you think of the solar system.
P.S. I sent you a food parcel, have you received it yet?

I hope he appreciates my effort.

My tongue's too dry and swollen to lick the walls any more. I'm not sure what course the ship is headed on now, I lost track a long time ago. I can't even remember the reason for the voyage.

It's strange, I thought I wanted to be alone but now I am I long for company, although there are advantages to this solitude. It gives a man the opportunity to think. I've come to realise there's a fragile line between life and death, a thin membrane separating sanity from madness.

Crossing that line and rupturing the membrane grows ever more appealing.

I think I'll reverse the propulsion system.

A HELPING HAND

England 1957

The sound of dogs barking drifted across the night, the excitement of the chase turning domestic animals into something wild. A gunshot went off nearby and Owen Trent could imagine his pursuers barely able to contain their excitement. He lay shivering in the undergrowth, listening as their shouts grew louder, they had him cornered and they knew it. The botched post-office robbery had turned him into a killer and now they were going to make him pay.

"Over here boys, if you see him shoot to kill, after what that bastard did to Marjorie he deserves it."

Trent shut his eyes and waited. Somewhere in the darkness he heard footsteps moving closer.

***

It was a village store that should have been an easy target. The gun had only been for show, he hadn't meant to kill anybody, but then again he hadn't expected anyone to resist. The old woman who'd tried to pull the firearm away from him had only herself to blame. She'd ignored his threats and refused to hand over money. He remembered the look of shock on her face as the gun went off; the way the life left her eyes and the feel of her blood soaking through his shirt as she clung to him.

He'd pushed her away and fled the store.

Outside, an old man stood admiring Trent's motorbike, oblivious to what had just happened and probably too deaf to have heard a thing.

"Triumph, isn't it? I used to have one of these when I was younger." He looked fondly at the bike and then his expression changed as Trent pushed past him. "There's no need to be like that, I was only…" The words died on his tongue as he caught sight of the gun and saw the blood staining Trent's shirt.

Trent straddled the bike and revved it into life. "Piss off, granddad," he spat, an insult that angered the old man, who lunged at him. The blow took Trent by surprise. It knocked him off-balance and when the machine toppled over he found himself trapped beneath the weight of its body. The back wheel spun around inches from his face, and as the bike bucked dangerously he managed to kick it away and then heard the engine die.

The old man stood in front of the store shouting obscenities as Trent climbed to his feet.

"Think I didn't face worse than you in the trenches, you little bag of piss?"

Trent had an overwhelming urge to knock him unconscious, to beat him until he screamed. He took a step forward and stopped as a tractor appeared from behind a bend further along the road. The old man ran towards it waving his arms.

Trent cursed. When he picked up the bike and tried to rev it into life it refused to start.

"Shit!" He looked around. Woods bordered the far side of the lane. Behind him, he saw someone climbing from the tractor. The old man was pointing in Trent's direction. There was nowhere else for him to go, he ran across the road and as he pushed into the undergrowth he realised he'd dropped the gun. Before he could turn back he heard angry voices.

"HE WENT IN THERE!"

"GET HELP, HARRY, BUT DON'T CALL THE POLICE. WE'LL SORT HIM OUT OURSELVES!"

Trent suddenly realised he wasn't going to be brought to justice. He'd murdered an old lady, for that the locals were going to kill him. He turned and ran blindly into the forest.

***

His pursuers had tracked him all afternoon. There were a gang of them, a lynch-mob with dogs. He could hear the animals baying like wolves each time they picked up his scent. The faster he ran the more frenzied their sounds became. Shouted threats carried across the hot, still air; violent promises of what he'd be forced to suffer at the end of the chase.

Now it was growing dark. Twilight filled the wood with shadows; they hung between trees and camouflaged the leafy hollows. As he lost his footing and rolled helplessly into darkness he realised he'd gone as far as he could.

His body came to rest amongst earth and leaves. Somewhere nearby a twig snapped underfoot. As he rolled over and stared into a sky full of stars he wondered if the mob would encourage the dogs to savage him before he was shot to death. He heard the metallic snap of shotgun bolts being drawn back in anticipation and braced himself for the impact. That was when the voice spoke to him. It was soft and cold and barely audible.

"Do you need a helping hand?"

He struggled into a sitting position and stared into darkness, certain he was hearing things.

"Who's there?"

There was a moment's pause filled with the sound of whining dogs and impatient voices. He felt his nerves stretching. A whisper drifted from the shadows.

"If you need a helping hand, I can get you out of here."

Trent felt a thin needle of fear travel down his spine. "Who are you?"

As he spoke a beacon of light shone through the undergrowth and pinned him in its beam.

"Hey boys, the murdering little shit's here."

The hunters had found their prey.

The strange voice spoke again; this time it sounded urgent. "Do you need a helping hand?" It was a last demand and Trent knew it.

"Yes I do!" he cried. "Yes I do!"

He saw lamplight glint off a gun barrel aimed directly at him and then cold fingers wrapped themselves around his wrist and dragged him into blackness.

***

The rattle of a truncheon being drawn across iron bars woke him from a sleep filled with impossible nightmares. He opened his eyes and sat up. It took him a moment to realise he was in a prison cell. The bunk he was sitting on was the only piece of furniture in the dimly-lit six by eight space. There was a slopping out bowl at his feet. The guard who'd woken him was standing beyond a locked door; he was holding a plate and looked as if he'd like to kick Trent to death.

"Your last supper's here, I hope it chokes you." He laughed. "Although that's already taken care of."

Trent climbed from the bunk and rubbed his eyes. His head ached. "Last supper? What do you mean? Where am I?"

The guard pressed his face against the bars and scowled.

"I mean it's your final meal. The food you get before the executioner hangs you by your neck. It's what we do to murderers." He tapped the truncheon against the bars. "That's why you're in here. Is that so hard to understand?"

Trent thought it was. The smell of the food made his stomach turn. He looked at the plate. Meat leaked blood into watery mashed potatoes; gravy curdled its way around something green and unrecognisable.

"I don't want that," he said.

The guard grinned.

"That's fine by me." He stretched his arm through the serving hatch and tipped the contents onto the floor. "The rats can dine on it later." He hawked up a wad of phlegm and spat into the puddle of food. "Bon appetite," he said, and sauntered back down the corridor.

Trent gripped the bars and tried to make sense of what was happening. Across the walkway another prisoner mirrored his position. The two of them stared at each other. When the man smiled sanity left his eyes.

"They're going to hang you before they hang me, Mr Lady-killer." His sing-song voice echoed along the passageway. He giggled. "Try not to break the rope because I'm next."

He squeezed his throat with his fingers, then tilted his head to one side and let his tongue loll limply from the corner of his mouth. "You'll get the hang of it," he said. His laughter was high-pitched and hysterical and went the same way as his eyes.

The guard came striding back along the corridor, pulled the truncheon from his belt and beat it against the bars. The other prisoner screamed as the cosh came down on his knuckles.

"Now shut your noise up and go to sleep. There won't be another warning."

He turned and gazed at Trent.

"That means you as well. We don't want you over-sleeping on such an important day." He tapped his baton lightly against the palm of his hand. "See you at dawn."

His retreating footsteps sounded like a death march. Seconds later the lights went out.

Trent lay on his bunk, and as he listened to sounds only a condemned man can hear his tangled thoughts dragged him into sleep.

When he opened his eyes it was still dark. He had no idea what hour it was but he could feel daybreak creeping nearer, bringing with it the certainty of a terrible death.

He'd been dreaming, the kind of dream where nothing makes sense and everything seems out of time. One moment he'd been on his motorbike, the next he'd been fleeing through woods into a prison cell. Then he was lying on a forest floor as an old lady bled to death beside him. The only constant behind those images was the vision of a noose hanging from a scaffold.

He could hear the crazy man muttering in his sleep, begging for another chance as his body twitched beneath the blankets. Tears formed in Trent's eyes, another chance was something he'd never get. His weeping was silenced by the voice that drifted across his cell.

"Do you need a helping hand?" The question hung in the air like an invitation.

Trent's body tensed. He lay in the darkness, trying to remember where he'd heard the voice before. It spoke again.

"If you need a helping hand, I can get you out of here."

The prison had fallen silent, as if the guards and inmates had deserted the building and all that was left inside were him and the owner of the voice. Something in the shadows waited for an answer.

Trent could feel a hood placed over his head; could see his legs dropping through a trap door and just before his neck snapped the grip of a noose strangling the life from his body.

"Do you need a helping hand?"

He didn't need to be asked again.

"Yes, I do," he said.

Cold fingers closed over his own.

***

He woke to darkness and silence; warm air and the feeling he was the last person in the world. It was an effort to stay awake. When he yawned and attempted to roll over he found he couldn't move. His head struck something as he tried to rise. He reached up, ran his fingers along a smooth-grained surface and frowned. He was in a tunnel, a narrow one by the feel of the walls pressing against him. As he wriggled backwards and forwards he found his way barred. He lay there fighting to stay calm, trying to make sense of the situation.

Understanding came suddenly: there were no wild dogs or hangmen waiting for him here; he was in a coffin, buried alive.

Something deep inside him rushed its way to the surface and then he was kicking and screaming, splintering fingernails as he raked his hands along the wood above him. He smashed his face into the ceiling of his tomb, feeling nothing as he beat his features into a bloody pulp. Eventually exhaustion weakened him. He gulped in lungfuls of stale air. Sweat soaked his body.

When the voice spoke it was close to his left ear: horribly soothing.

"Do you need a helping hand?"

Trent screamed then, a long drawn out cry that carried on it both desperation and death. Again and again he beat his fists against the wood and kicked his feet into the bottom of the box.

Before his air ran out he'd screamed himself into insanity.

DESAMPARAR

We dropped anchor in Powder Bay on an evening when the breeze had died and the air was still thick with daytime heat. Above us stars had crammed the sky. As we clambered into the longboat the moon ghosted itself over the horizon and painted a yellow path across the ocean.

We were a reluctant crew. Early into the voyage we'd begun to suspect we'd sold our souls for a handful of gold and a drunken promise, but now we'd gone too far to turn back. William Ellis was searching for a brother he still believed alive, and the closer we came to Desamparar the stranger our captain's behaviour grew.

"What does the name mean?" Goodman had asked him before we left England

Ellis stared into the rain.

"It's Spanish," he said. "It means, forsaken," and without us knowing, from that moment on we were.

Of the eight men who went ashore in that longboat I was the youngest, and the only one to return.

I'm an old man now and my memories are like smoke. I reach for them, but they drift and fade and are something I can never quiet hold onto, but still I remember Desamparar and that starlit night as if it were yesterday.

* * *

We dipped our oars and the blades formed circles that spread like broken mirrors across the surface of the water.

"Go easy, lads," Goodman whispered. I saw the bos'n stare into the green depths and followed his gaze.

Jagged lines of coral grew over rocks close enough to touch.

He guided us slowly across the reef and as we entered the lagoon we could hear the distant rhythm of surf breaking against the shore.

Goodman held up his lantern and peered into the darkness, lamplight picked out the weathered lines scored across his face. "Pull away now, boys," he ordered, and as we bent our backs and worked our bodies the silver strip of sand that was Beggars Beach drew slowly closer. Our captain sat silently in the bows.

The tide ran us into the shallows. We dragged the boat up onto the sand and listened. Sounds we couldn't name came from the dark line of jungle that grew in a tangled mass twenty yards from the shoreline.

Ellis stared into the undergrowth and then turned to face us. His eyes had narrowed into pale flints.

"My brother's here somewhere, men," he said. "I've come to bring him home. We camp here until dawn and then we find him. After that we leave."

It sounded like a simple plan, but we never did bring the captain's brother home, and seven men never left Desamparar.

We collected driftwood and built a fire, none of us keen to stray too far from the boat, there was something about the island that bred fear into our veins. The Spanish had named it 'Forsaken,' and you could feel why. An air of abandonment clung like a shadow to its wild beauty. The palm fronds seemed to wave a warning as they stirred in the breeze; even the sea sounded as if it were sucking life from the sand.

The captain sat apart from us while we passed around a jug of rum. The flames threw flickering shadows across the beach, and as the hour grew late Goodman kept us entertained with tales of storms he'd sailed into that no man had the right to live through.

The sun rose early with a heat so fierce it bleached the sky and blinded our eyes. Daylight had softened the line of jungle that had appeared so threatening the night before. Now a thick green canopy stretched along the beach until disappearing from sight around the headland. Beyond it an outcrop of rock rose above the trees. Out in the bay our ship, the Winter Swan, lay moored in water so blue it dazzled the senses.

As we breakfasted Ellis told us a story I knew to be only half-true. While he spoke my mind went back to a Portsmouth ale house and a night spent in the company of Ben Goodman. That was where I'd learned of the true reason for our captain's quest.

***

The Compass was a dimly-lit shanty inn that stood in one of the narrow back lanes off the sea front. The saloon was crowded and smelt of stale beer and tobacco. It was a week before we were due to set sail and as we drank our discussion roamed over where we were bound and why.

"Ellis is going in search of his twin brother," Goodman said.

His words surprised me; all our new captain had told us was that we'd be well rewarded if our voyage was successful. We'd assumed he was seeking trade.

"His twin? I didn't know he had a brother. What happened to him?" I asked.

Ben gazed into his beer. "Nathaniel Ellis was captain of the London Queen," he said.

The London Queen. There was a name that had been talked about endlessly some months earlier. Rumours of what had happened aboard had travelled from ship to ship and bar to bar. Somewhere on that journey the truth had either been embroidered or discarded, but the fact was there'd been a mutiny and the captain had been cast adrift a mile off the island of Desamparar.

It hadn't occurred to me that Ellis was his brother, let alone his twin. I was new to seamanship and still a novice. Ben knew more than most, he'd spent his life at sea; if there was a ship he hadn't sailed on or a captain he hadn't served under then he knew someone who had. He told me the story.

"The only reason Nathaniel Ellis was captain of the London Queen was because his father, Charles, owns the shipping company."

He saw my look of surprise and grinned.

"Mind you, that didn't help him when his men mutinied and left him to his fate in the middle of the Indian Ocean."

"Why did they do that?" I asked. "Surely the owner's son deserved some respect; after all he was their captain."

Ben Goodman snorted into his beer and gave me a look that bordered on pity.

"Respect is something that has to be earned," he said, "and the way Captain Nathaniel Ellis treated his crew meant that was never going to happen."

"What did he do?" I asked.

Ben didn't answer my question. He sipped at his ale, staring into something only he could see.

"The London Queen was lost in a storm on her homeward journey."

His voice had become distant; I could imagine his mind going over similar circumstances, times when the same thing might have happened to him.

"She hadn't been heading for England though," he said, "her destination had been Amsterdam. The mutineers had known there'd be no welcome waiting for them here, not after what they'd done."

He downed the rest of his beer. "They didn't deserve that death," he said. "Not after what they'd been through."

He waited as the landlord placed two more tankards on our table and then continued.

"Nathaniel Ellis was crazy," he said. "Ask anybody who's ever set foot on a deck and they'll tell you the same. Word gets around, we may not be the ones wearing fancy uniforms but we know what we're doing and we know when someone else isn't up to the job. If you're sailing a ship into the teeth of a gale you want a captain who can keep his head and lead by example. Ellis could do neither, and because of that he'd punish others for his weaknesses." He shook his head and looked at me. "I've heard about those punishments; good men died for nothing more than getting on the wrong side of Ellis.

"Listen, Scully," he said. "There's crazy, and then there's cruel crazy. A man might be mad and only bring hurt on himself, but when cruelty twists its way into that insanity then you've got a whole different creature: someone like Nathaniel Ellis." He paused. "Don't you find it strange that all you know of the London Queen is second-hand rumours?" he asked.

It was something I hadn't thought about, but once Ben mentioned it I realised he was right. The version of events handed down to me had never been confirmed.

"I'll tell you why," he said. "His old man loves him more than a father should love a son. He'd do anything to protect his golden boy, unlike his twin, who he regards as the runt of the litter. Charles Ellis hushed up what happened as best he could and told those in the know that if they spoke about it there'd be fierce repercussions."

Ben was in full flow; I let him carry on.

"It broke his heart when he heard what had happened aboard the London Queen. He'd have seen every one of those mutineers hanged if he'd had the chance, and probably strung them up himself. But that never occurred and so now he's ordered his other boy to sail halfway across the world to find his brother."

He glanced around and lowered his voice. "And I'll tell you something else," he said. "It's a well known fact they hate each other." He laughed humourlessly. "But William's got no choice in the matter; if he goes against his father's wishes he loses his position in the company as well as his inheritance when the old man goes to meet his maker." He rested his pint on the table. "What do you think of that?"

I didn't know what to say.

Ben went on to tell me of some of the disturbing incidents that had taken place on board the London Queen. How Ellis had men flogged for the slightest reason. How he fed his crew starvation rations when he discovered a barrel of salted beef had spoiled. Worst of all, how he'd hanged a young lad he'd caught attempting to steal extra provisions.

102

"The boy was sick with fever," Goodman told me. "He didn't know what he was doing.

"The turning point came when he ordered an old hand who'd been with the shipping line thirty years to be keelhauled, all because he had the nerve to suggest the captain break out an extra rum ration to help lift the men's morale." He looked me in the eye. "I told you he was crazy, and if I'm not mistaken I'd say his brother's not far behind him. It runs in the family."

I was shocked. "How do you know all this, Ben?" I asked. "If the London Queen sank there can't have been any witnesses to what happened."

He gave a secretive smile and tapped the side of his nose.

"Aye, the London Queen went down, all right," he said, "and as far as the powers that be are concerned the whole crew went with her." Again he smiled. "But that might not have been the case. Maybe one or two survivors were picked up by a Dutch fishing boat. Perhaps they made their way back to England." He shrugged his shoulders. "Who knows?" he said, and pushed his tankard across the table. "I'll have a tot of rum with mine, Scully, I don't know about you but this damp gets right into my bones."

* * *

On the day we were due to sail the weather changed. Clear skies had given way to cloud and rain. A strengthening breeze whipped the waves white. Above us gulls screamed their defiance as they tried in vain to battle the wind.

Goodman shaded his eyes and stared into the horizon. "There's a storm out there," he said. "I hope it's not waiting for us."

But it was, only it didn't show itself until we reached Desamparar; then it finally broke.

Before that we experienced a taste of what the crew aboard the London Queen had endured.

***

It was a voyage our captain had no heart for; seeking a brother he hated on the orders of a father who favoured his twin. The days passed and as the weather grew warmer so his mood darkened. Goodman had been right when he told me insanity ran in Ellis's family. William might have been able to disguise his more easily, or perhaps it didn't run as deep, but it was there.

He kept to his cabin whenever possible. Who knows what thoughts ran through his mind in those isolated hours, but when he did appear on deck you could sense something missing in his eyes. It was a look that silenced the banter between the crew and made each of us uneasy; as if we knew that sooner or later William Ellis was going to reveal the madness he shared with his twin.

The Winter Swan was making steady progress, her sails were full and a cloudless sky looked down on us as we ran with the waves. It was a fine day but that was soon to change.

"What are you staring at, boy?"

The captain had come on deck shortly after noon. His vacant expression left no indication of what went on beneath. His question was aimed at me.

"Nothing, sir," I answered.

He beckoned me over and thrust his face into mine. Close up his eyes looked colourless, as if there wasn't a soul behind them.

"Scully, isn't it?" he sneered. I noticed a thin line of spittle form at the corner of his mouth.

"Yes sir."

The blow took me by surprise. His fist caught me across the face and sent me sprawling backwards. I landed on the deck and tasted blood in my mouth. He strode towards me, fists bunched.

"Get up!" He shouted. A knot of men had formed around us. Ellis didn't seem to notice, he had eyes only for me and I saw murder in them. As I backed away Ben Goodman suddenly came between us and dragged me to my feet.

"I'll sort this out, sir," he said. "These youngsters need to know what discipline is." He slapped me across the back of the head, a blow I hardly felt. "Come with me, Scully, you need to be taught a lesson."

As he led me away, I could feel Ellis's crazy eyes boring into the back of my skull, but he didn't try and stop us, Goodman had caught him by surprise.

Below decks Ben gave me a word of warning. "If you're going to stare at the captain, don't let him catch you doing it," he said, then he grinned. "You might not be as lucky next time,"

Two days later Ellis ordered a barrel of fresh drinking water to be poured over the side of the ship. Why? *'Because men work better with a thirst,'* he said, as if it made perfect sense.

A week away from Desamparar he fired his pistol into the rigging and laughed. "That'll keep the look-out on his toes," he shouted. His eyes had reclaimed the soulless look I'd seen just before he struck me. When he strode into the sanctuary of his cabin the crew exchanged worried glances. More than one of us were thinking of the London Queen and a madman set adrift.

A feeling of unspoken relief passed amongst us on the evening we sighted our destination. I think most of us believed Nathaniel Ellis was dead, and hoped once we found his body our captain's behaviour might improve. After all, he was searching for someone he could never live up to: at least not in his father's eyes. With his brother gone there'd be no more need for competition, his father would have to love him.

***

"The Spanish might have raised their flag on it," Goodman said, "but they've never been back since."

We were on deck, watching the shape of Desamparar grow larger. The light was fading. Below us waves lapped gently against the hull, as if the warm water was caressing the ship.

"Fantasma." Ben whispered the word to himself. I'd never heard it before. He looked at me.

"It's a ghost island," he said. "That's why the Spanish left it alone."

When I grinned he shook his head.

"Think what you like, young Scully, but I've been places and seen things beyond understanding. Believe me, there's more to this world than what you can see or touch."

He pulled a small flask from his belt and offered it to me. The rum burned my throat. I handed it back and he took a long swallow.

"North, south, east and west."

He made the four points of the compass sound like a poem.

"They all hold mysteries," he said. "But sometimes there are places that don't feel right, and no matter how much you try to convince yourself otherwise they never will." He nodded towards the island. "That's one of those places," he said.

I gazed from the deck. Desamparar was transformed into a beautiful shadow as the sun drifted into the horizon. It was hard to imagine something so lovely could be bad. But it was, and I was soon to find out what Ben meant.

We discovered Nathaniel Ellis was still alive on the morning of the first day. We also found out the months he'd been forced to endure alone had broken his twisted mind completely.

***

After breakfast was finished we doused the fire. Ellis had given us his version of events: how his brother had been cruelly abandoned and that he'd taken it upon himself to come to Desampara and save him. Ben glanced at me while he told us his lies; there was a faint smile in his eyes.

The captain split us into three search parties. Apart from Goodman we were all junior ratings, he'd left the senior crew members on board the Winter Swan. Ben had told me Ellis believed we were less likely to question any of his ill-judged orders.

He sent Skinner, Patterson and Wright along the beach, telling them to walk a mile and then fan out and make their way inland. Ben and myself were ordered to do the same in the opposite direction while he, Pugh and Matthews formed a line and entered the jungle from our landing point. If any of us sighted his brother we were to fire one pistol shot and wait for help.

"Otherwise, we meet back here before dark," he said.

We watched Pugh and Matthews follow him into the undergrowth. The other three men were already blurred figures.

"Come on, Scully," Goodman said.

We turned and made our way along the sand. Ahead of us the sun threw a glare against the distant rocks; behind us our footsteps left a trail the tide was destined to wash away.

By mid-morning we'd almost reached the cliff and seen nothing. We stopped to rest in the shaded boundary at the edge of the beach and drank greedily from our water bottles.

"Do you think he's still alive?" I asked.

Ben wiped sweat from his brow and stared out at the ocean. "If he is, he might be armed," he said.

I looked at him. "Armed? How?"

Although we were alone Goodman lowered his voice. "I couldn't tell Ellis," he said. "He'd wonder how I knew."

"Knew what, Ben?"

Goodman corked his water bottle. "When the crew of the London Queen cast Nathaniel Ellis adrift they threw a loaded pistol into the boat."

"Why would they do that?" I asked.

Ben put a finger to his temple and made a downward hammer motion with his thumb. "One shot," he said.

"An easy way out for when he couldn't bear the loneliness any longer."

I sat there and shivered as I imagined a crazy man pressing a pistol to his head and pulling the trigger. Where would he have committed that final act? High at the edge of the cliffs so his body tumbled into the ocean? Perhaps in the cool green shade of a jungle clearing where it might never be found?

Ben had been right, Desamparar felt like a bad place.

We discovered the burnt out remains of a camp fire at the same moment the sound of a gunshot echoed its way across the hot morning air. The ashes were scattered across the sand at the entrance to a cave. We'd been about to head inland when Ben suggested we take a look at the blind side of the headland.

I gazed upwards. "Which direction did that come from?" I asked.

Goodman was still kneeling where a fire had been. He picked up a handful of ash and let it slip between his fingers. "Look, Scully," he said, and pointed into the cave. Beyond the entrance was a pool. The water was as dark and still as oil. We clambered over fallen rocks and stared into the shadows.

"Nathaniel Ellis!" Ben's words bounced off the walls and repeated themselves. "We've come to take you home!"

There was no answer. The cave was damp and cold and so silent it felt like a tomb. He looked at me. "We'd better find out where the others are."

We made our way back into the sunlight and climbed a sandy ridge. Soon the sound of the surf was lost as the jungle closed around us.

We hacked our way into heavy undergrowth, sweating through the shadows as mosquitoes danced in front of our eyes. It was slow progress, now and then we'd halt and Ben would call out. Just when we thought we might be lost someone shouted an answer. The land rose and as we climbed higher the jungle thinned. We broke through knotted branches into a clearing.

"Mr Goodman, Scully, over here!" Matthews waved to us. He was behind Ellis; the captain was standing at the lip of a steep gulley, staring into the drop. We hurried across and followed his gaze.

Forty feet below us Pugh was lying motionless on his back with his eyes open. A pool of blood had formed like a crimson halo around his head.

"What happened?" Goodman asked.

Matthews nodded towards his boots. A length of vine had been strung across the track and secured to the trunk of a palm. Someone stepping out of the jungle into the sun would have been blinded and had no chance of seeing it. Pugh had been leading the way.

Ellis still hadn't said a word. His colourless eyes were fastened on the corpse.

"Shall we climb down and get him, sir?" Ben asked.

His question went unanswered. Before he could repeat it Ellis spoke. "My brother," he said. "My brother did this."

Something moved in the undergrowth behind us. As we spun around and drew our pistols a bird flew clumsily into the sky and sent a shadow racing across the ground. We strained our eyes searching the tangled gloom. There was nothing there.

The captain forbade us to collect Pugh's body.

"We'll retrieve it later," he said, "when we've found my brother."

I saw Goodman about to argue and then think better of it.

We made a silent procession as we headed in single file back to the beach. I couldn't get the sight of Pugh's death stare out of my mind. Those eyes would stay with me forever. Ben seemed to know my thoughts. He patted me on the shoulder and forced a grin. "Forget about it, Scully," he said.

It was good advice, but although I tried I couldn't.

It was a relief to hear the sea again. We emerged from the jungle sixty yards from where we'd beached the longboat and it was like walking out of a nightmare.

Matthews rekindled the fire. After I'd scavenged driftwood Goodman uncorked a bottle of rum and handed it around. This time Ellis joined us.

"Fire a shot into the air," he ordered. "It's time the others were back. We need to eat and then plan for tomorrow. Nathaniel's here and we're going to find him."

By the time the sun went down Skinner, Patterson and Wright still hadn't returned.

That night I dreamt I was back at the cave pool. I could hear the sound of water dripping on stone and smell the rich salty tang of seaweed. Behind me the ocean sang of shipwrecks and lonely shores.

The surface of the pool was as I remembered it, oil black and as smooth as glass. I didn't know why, but for some reason it was important I reach the other side. I lowered myself into water so cold it took my breath away. My feet searched for a hold but found nothing.

111

As I swam into the milky darkness I sensed eyes watching me. When I looked back a figure stood silhouetted against the cave entrance. Nathaniel Ellis grinned; it was like watching clouds uncover a sickle moon.

"You're out of your depth, boy," he said.

Next to me Henry Pugh's head suddenly popped like a cork from below the surface. There was a grin beneath his dead-eyed stare.

"Let me help you, Scully," he whispered.

My scream was choked off as his fingers found my throat. I floundered in the water and then Pugh reached out and dragged me below the surface.

"Scully, be quiet!"

Goodman was shaking me awake. He pressed a finger to his lips and pointed along the beach. Fifty yards away a figure scribbled something in the sand with a stick. When he was finished, he stood motionless for a moment, as if he knew he was being observed. Before he stepped into the jungle he gazed in our direction and grinned. His smile resembled a sickle moon.

We woke Matthews and the captain, lit torches from the fire and drew our pistols. As we made our way along the beach the jungle seemed to come alive. Whoever we'd seen was making their way inland. I think we all knew who it was.

The scrawled message revealed Nathaniel Ellis's state of mind.

GO BACK TO THE LONDON QUEEN AND LEAVE OR I'LL KILL YOU ALL.

He believed we were the crew from his old ship, returning to complete unfinished business. I doubt there was any way we could have convinced him otherwise.

His brother grunted when he read the message. He held up the torch up and stared at the words.

"He's coming home, dead or alive," Ellis said. When he looked at us and grinned I saw the same smile as his twin's.

We returned to camp and huddled silently around the fire. Even Ben seemed subdued. As the captain organised watch duty a log broke and sent a shower of sparks into the night air. None of us slept easily that night.

The first thing we saw as dawn broke was Skinner's body rolling in the surf. The waves pushed it onto the shore and left it stranded there like a trophy. There was no sign of Tom Patterson or Arthur Wright.

We dragged Skinner up the beach and turned him over. One of his arms had been hacked off. There was a slash mark across his throat. Both wounds had been washed clean by the sea. Ellis swore. As we stared at the mutilated body a scream pierced the morning air, quickly followed by another. Our heads went up. Somewhere in that crowded jungle a man was dying.

"I'll find the bastard," the captain said.

But Desamparar was a large island, and as we were soon to discover, if a man wished to remain hidden he could.

We searched all morning with no success. The heat drained the strength from our bodies and made us long for the cool feel of English rain.

By noon we'd climbed out of the jungle and reached a plateau at the top of the cliffs. Inland, Desampara's wild beauty lay spread out like a map. Directly below us the tide washed waves against the rocks. Somewhere down there was a cave with a dark pool that fed my nightmares.

Ben saw the smoke first; a lazy tail that drifted upwards, barely visible in the midday sun. He pointed into the distance. Ellis searched the landscape, peering through his spyglass like a hawk seeking prey.

"It's him," he said. His eyes were feverish. "He can't be more than half a mile away."

We scrambled down the rocks, struggling to keep up with the man whose brother's madness had led us to this place.

"Form a tight line when we reach the jungle, men." Our captain had already pulled the pistol from his belt. "Shoot him if you have to," he said.

It was an order he appeared to relish.

The undergrowth slowed our momentum; it was almost impossible to move stealthily through the maze of dense foliage and tangled vines. Matthews had fallen behind. I looked back once and saw him leaning against a rotten log as he tried to catch his breath. He waved me on. I never saw him alive again.

Ellis was slightly ahead of us. Through a gap in the trees we could see smoke rising. The captain raised his hand.

"You two spread out either side of me," he whispered. "Wait until I break cover and then do the same."

We were close. We could smell meat cooking. Ellis's brother was preparing a meal he'd never finish.

Goodman and I split up and five minutes later we were in position. Crouched out of sight I felt the mosquitoes feasting on my face and tried to wipe them away. In my other hand was a loaded pistol I'd never had reason to fire. I listened to my heartbeat and waited.

Ellis shouted and I charged into the clearing at the same time as Ben.

Clothing was scattered across the ground. A sharpened stake stood propped against a tree. The fire still burned but Ellis's twin was gone. At the last moment he must have heard our approach and disappeared into the jungle. I saw the livid expression form on our captain's face. He looked at us and raised his pistol. For one terrible moment I thought he was going to fire.

"Get the food, I'm hungry," he said, and lowered his gun.

It was only when I walked over to the fire that I saw what it was his brother had been cooking. He'd skewered a human arm and was roasting it over the flames. As I vomited into the bushes I pictured George Skinner and realised Nathaniel Ellis was crazier than we'd thought.

We discovered Jim Matthew's body on our journey back to the beach. Ellis had battered his skull to a pulp and then left the rock he'd used resting on his victim's chest. Our crewmate's pistol was gone.

Ellis's expression was featureless; it was like looking into the eyes of a ghost.

"Scully," he said. His voice was as cold as the pool water I'd dreamt about. "When we get back I want you to row to the ship and return with extra men. Make sure they're armed," he added, "this has gone on long enough."

Ben stayed silent, he was still gazing at the body of a man he'd sailed across oceans with; a man who'd matched him drink for drink in more portside bars than he could remember.

Ellis ordered us to leave the body where it was. Before we left, Goodman pulled off his waistcoat and covered his dead friend's eyes.

***

Nathaniel Ellis had returned our visit. The fire had been kicked out. Our provisions were gone. The longboat was drifting away from the shore. As we ran along the beach a shot rang out. I turned and saw Goodman clutching at his chest. Then he collapsed onto the sand.

"Ben!" I cried. As I went to help, Ellis levelled his pistol at me. This time I had no doubt he'd shoot, I could see it in his eyes.

"Get the boat, Scully," he ordered. "I'll sort this out." When I hesitated he cocked the hammer. "I won't tell you again. Get the boat."

I glanced at Ben and then waded into the surf.

"What about your brother?" I shouted.

Ellis smiled, the same vacant, dreamy smile I'd seen before: one that only belongs on the face of a madman. "I'll find him," he said, and walked calmly into the undergrowth.

I knew he planned to kill his twin; as far as I was concerned, I hoped they killed each other. I dived into the waves and prayed Ben would still be alive when I returned.

By the time I reached the boat and hauled myself over the side I was exhausted.

It took me precious minutes to catch my breath and fix the oars. The swell was heavy, the boat cumbersome for one man. Eventually I managed to line up the bows with the shore and began to row. The tide fought me all the way.

I was thirty yards from the beach when I saw Nathaniel Ellis emerge from the undergrowth and run towards the shoreline. He was half-naked and covered in blood. At first I thought he must be fleeing his brother until I saw what he held in his hand. The horror of what he'd done transfixed me. I wanted to look away but couldn't. He raised his twin's head above his own and shook it. Blood patterned the sand. Ellis shrieked with laughter and then sniffed at his brother's face. I could imagine him taking it to the mouth of the headland cave and slowly roasting it over a camp fire.

It was only when he lifted his other arm that I saw the pistol in his hand. In that instant I realised what he planned to do, and although he was crazy he knew I was powerless to stop him. A sly grin came over his face. He walked over to where Ben lay wounded on the sand and pressed the muzzle against the back of his head. As I cried out he looked at me and pulled the trigger.

It was only then that I turned away.

Ellis's wild laughter carried across the water, and as tears stung my eyes I remembered Ben's words. *He might be armed. One shot for when he couldn't bear the loneliness any longer.*

But Nathaniel Ellis had never made that shot and his loneliness wasn't a burden: madness had driven him beyond such things.

I manoeuvred the boat around and let the tide pull me out towards the bay.

My pleas for a landing party to return and collect Ben's body were ignored. William Ellis's last moments had been witnessed from the deck of the Winter Swan. Her officers weren't prepared to risk their lives attempting to ship a madman home to his father.

We sailed on the evening tide.

***

I've often wondered what happened to Tom Patterson and Arthur Wright, the two bodies we never found. No doubt they're still on Desamparar, lost souls keeping company with a man who probably never had one.

Sometimes when I sleep I hear the surf breaking on that distant shore. It's a sound that always brings to mind a dead man's stare.

I remember laughing when Ben told me there were some places that never felt right no matter how hard you tried to convince yourself otherwise. I wish I could have told him I was sorry; sorry for laughing and sorry for leaving him on Desamparar.

North, south, east and west.

They all hold mysteries.

GRIMBLE

He found the head in a box hidden away beneath the eaves. The carton had been tucked out of sight and surrounded by the leftovers of other people's lives. Holly Lodge may have been empty for years, but there still remained a trail of discarded memories that needed to be cleared.

The top of the house was hot and full of dusty shadows. Christopher Page could hear Melanie, his wife, moving about somewhere below, as keen as him to chase away the old and bring in the new. He knelt down and reached into the narrow roof space. The box slid easily from its hiding place, as if it had been waiting to be discovered. Above him the dim halo of a ceiling bulb picked out faded lettering scribbled across the cardboard. *'GRIMBLE. 1932.'* It was a name and year that meant nothing but stirred in him an irresistible interest.

He wiped away cobwebs and gently lifted the lid. A layer of straw concealed a relic from the past. When he pulled the packing aside nothing was ever the same again.

Jagged shadows and unnatural silhouettes seemed to invade the attic. Beyond the bulls-eye window the day slipped into darkness. He thought he could hear rain beating against the roof and then realised it was the sound of pulses drumming in his ears. Whatever secrets he'd imagined a box from 1932 might hold, a decapitated head hadn't been one of them. He stared mesmerised at a mass of black hair and through it glimpsed the misshapen features of a dead man.

He suddenly felt like a grave robber caught in the act, as if he were desecrating some last resting place and the high ceilings of Holly Lodge bore witness to his crime. When he could look no longer he squeezed his eyes shut and then opened them. The attic had returned to its former harmless mess. Sunlight filled the circular window. His heart beat in normal time.

The death box was still between his knees. Like a reluctant sightseer unable to ignore an accident he peered closer. It was then he realised the head wasn't human at all and he was staring at some kind of doll. When he lifted it out he found himself face to face with a ventriloquist's prop. The dummy's head leered at him with an expression that bordered on a caricature of insanity. Its eyes were too bright, its grin too wide, the face had been painted in clown colours. Below the neck, control levers hung from a support stick, giving it the appearance of a deformed spine.

Melanie would have laughed at his earlier fears but there was something unnerving about the doll. *'We can share secrets,'* that over-wide grin promised. He could imagine one of the eyes winking in silent conspiracy.

The sound of footsteps on the loft ladder startled him. Melanie peered over the hatch and placed a mug of tea on the boards. "Thought you might need this," his wife said, and then saw what he was holding. "What the hell is that?"

Christopher laughed and held up the doll for her to get a better view. "It's the lodger!" he joked.

Melanie climbed into the attic. The dummy's eyes seemed to follow her approach. "That is seriously creepy. Where did you find it?"

He pointed into the eaves. "It was hidden in there. Look at the date on the box."

His wife examined the inscription and then peered into the carton. "What's that?"

Partly concealed beneath the straw was a book. She pulled it out and wiped the cover. The initials *'A.K.'* were inscribed on the front. She made her way across the attic and stood beneath the bulb. Christopher rested the head on the floor and joined her.

"Wow, look at this," she said.

The opening page contained a grainy black and white image of a smiling middle-aged man. Dressed in evening wear and seated on a bench on what appeared to be an old music hall stage, he had a dummy balanced on his lap. The doll was dressed identically to its owner. It was staring into the camera, as if it wanted the photographer to know exactly who the star of the show was. The head lying on the attic floor matched the one in the picture. The clipping was dated 1931.

I SAY, I SAY, I SAY!

'Arthur King, globe-trotting ventriloquist, performing at the London Coliseum with his best friend, Grimble. (Arthur seems to be the only one in the theatre unaware he's not in charge!")

Melanie looked at her husband. "Grimble?"

He shrugged his shoulders. "I've never heard of him, or Arthur King."

The following page contained a photograph of a different theatre and another stage. This one had been made up to look like a room wrecked in the process of being decorated. A ladder lay on the floor next to an overturned table. Ripped sheets of paper were scattered across the boards. Paint had been splashed everywhere although most of it was over Arthur King. There wasn't a drop on Grimble. He smirked innocently into the camera beneath a headline that read: *'DON'T BLAME ME! I'M NOT RESPONSIBLE!'*

The write-up was full of praise for King's act. *'Hilarious! Side-splitting! A comedy genius!'*

Melanie frowned. "It doesn't look that funny to me."

A succession of similar snapshots followed, all with a laughing Arthur King suffering some slapstick mishap while the dummy grinned at the audience and implored them to believe it wasn't *his* fault. The laughter soon ended.

Melanie turned the page. King was shielding his face from objects thrown by an unseen crowd. You could almost hear them booing. The stage lights had come on giving the photograph a severity the others never had.

Arthur King looked scared; it was the first picture in which he hadn't been smiling. But Grimble was, he appeared to be laughing out loud.

His slack jaws had formed themselves into a dead-man's grin. The lidded eyes were wide and crazy. He was leaning away from King, as if whatever had gone wrong was down to the ventriloquist. But there was something else about the dummy's posture; it suggested confrontation. This time he wasn't telling the crowd it couldn't be his fault, he was shouting at them that it was, but that he held King responsible.

The headline read:

'WORLD FAMOUS VENTRILOQUIST SUFFERS BREAKDOWN ON STAGE!'

There were no other details.

"God, I wonder what happened?" Melanie glanced at the head lying on the floor. Its open-eyed gaze seemed fixed on her. She felt her hackles rise.

"Let's find out," her husband said.

But there were no more photographs, only dark spaces on pages where they once had been. Someone had ripped the past from the album, as if looking back had become too hard to bear.

***

Holly Lodge was a big house. Melanie's mother's death had resulted in an inheritance that had enabled them to buy the old red brick mansion. Their decision to purchase such a large property had been based on two reasons: investment and their desire to start a family. Investment had been the only successful part of that decision. Now they longed to fill the silent rooms with the sound of children's laughter.

It was a longing that two years earlier had bred unspoken doubt. Those doubts had turned to worries; the nearer to completion the house became the more concerned they were at their failure to fulfil their dream. Two years seemed a long time to wait for something you wanted more than anything else.

Now the house at the end of Windmill Lane had been fully renovated and there were still no children. If the preliminary reports they'd received from the fertility clinic were accurate it was a possibility there might never be. In an attempt to take their minds away from news they were dreading the couple had decided to empty the one room that hadn't been touched. That was when Christopher had discovered Grimble.

***

Google was all it took to research an old music hall star.

Many years earlier Arthur King had indeed been famous. Wikipedia had preserved the history of a man no longer remembered. Christopher wondered how many other acts had shone for a while in the public eye, performing to sell-out crowds before their light dimmed and then went out completely.

It was a short but detailed piece.

King had been born into an East-End family whose poverty mirrored that of those living around them. His father had seldom worked, preferring to drink away whatever little money his wife brought in. On the frequent occasions when that wasn't enough his anger led to violence, first towards his wife, and then towards the boy he'd never once called son.

Arthur King fled home aged fifteen and never returned.

As a young man new to show business he witnessed first-hand the power of money: how those who could afford the best were treated with a respect not shown to the less fortunate. It was a lesson learned early, one that led him to single-mindedly pursue a career which might lift him out of the ordinary and reward him handsomely.

His reputation as a talented mimic saw him slowly rise through the ranks of others on the same treadmill. But he was impatient and there were few avenues open for a man who could disguise his voice to sound like others. His epiphany came one evening after watching a second-rate ventriloquist receive a standing ovation. The knowledge he could do better excited him. Six months later Arthur King and his dummy, Grimble, were receiving standing ovations themselves.

The doll's name, a hybrid of 'grim' and 'grumble,' seemed a strange choice for something meant to be a comic character.

For the next two years King toured extensively, building a following as he played to sell-out crowds in half-a-dozen countries. But then at the height of his fame something went wrong and he disappeared from the vaudeville scene forever.

His breakdown lacked the sensationalist slant it would have been given by today's paparazzi but must have still raised eyebrows at the time.

King was performing on stage and according to reports of those present began arguing with the dummy. It soon became evident that what, at first, seemed part of the act was in fact an abusive exchange between King and Grimble, as if the operator truly believed the puppet possessed a separate personality. When the crowd showed their disapproval King began cursing at them through the doll. He was heckled from the stage.

What was less apparent was the aftermath of that night. There were vague references to 'personality disorder,' and King spending time in a mental hospital, followed by an even lesser detailed account of his later years. All that was certain was that he became a recluse who rarely left the shelter of the house he bought on Windmill Lane: Holly Lodge.

Christopher and Melanie exchanged glances.

"Bloody hell, he lived here!" The colour had drained from Melanie's face. She chewed on a nail as her husband searched the internet for more information.

There were two YouTube clips of the ventriloquist and his doll; rare footage of an act that had become humourless a long time ago. The ancient black and white Pathetone News recordings lasted less than five minutes each. It was long enough.

Melanie re-ran the clips. "I've never seen a ventriloquist's dummy that didn't look creepy," she said, "but that one's freakier than most."

Christopher agreed. It was like circus clowns. As a kid they'd scared the life out of him. He knew a lot of people who felt the same way. Although reluctant to admit it the dummy brought back those fears. There was something sinister about Grimble. The way he slyly looked into the camera as Arthur King tried to calm the chaos erupting around him; chaos the puppet had caused: his intimidating manner as he threatened the audience into siding with him: *'DON'T BLAME ME! I'M NOT RESPONSIBLE!'* It was a catch-phrase the crowd seemed to find irresistible.

Was that part of the ventriloquist's personality coming through? Christopher wondered. *Did King hide bully-boy traits behind a dummy intent on causing mischief?* A ridiculous thought entered his mind: *Perhaps it was the other way around?*

"I wonder what happened to the body."

Melanie's question wasn't something Christopher had considered. He'd been so engrossed in discovering where the head had come from that the rest of the dummy hadn't entered his mind.

"There's nothing else in the eaves," he said. "Perhaps Arthur King kept the head as a memento." *But why would you want to keep something that destroyed your livelihood and maybe stole your sanity?* It was a thought that came suddenly and went just as quickly.

When they returned to the attic Grimble was still lying on the boards.

For another hour they made a half-hearted attempt at clearing up. In truth all the dummy and a forgotten music hall performer had been was a welcome distraction. Their minds were fixed on the following morning and a visit they had to make. It was then that they'd discover if the family they longed for might be a possibility.

They climbed from the roof space. Christopher followed Melanie down. He had the dummy perched on his shoulder the way a soldier might carry a rifle. When she glanced up it looked as if Grimble was nodding his head and staring at her, smirking in the knowledge that it knew something she didn't.

***

The head without a body was lying on the breakfast table. Neither Christopher nor Melanie had managed to eat anything. He pushed his plate away and picked up the dummy. As he fidgeted with the controls, eyes swivelled and lips moved; Melanie thought it was like watching a demon mouth silent threats.

"Why don't you put it down, Chris?" she snapped, and regretted her anger immediately. She saw him about to argue and then think better of it. He rested the head on a chair and rubbed his eyes

"Come on," he said. "We'd better get ready."

An hour later they left the house, a couple with low expectations and little to say to each other because of that.

It was news they'd been expecting but that still didn't lessen the sting.

When they returned from the clinic Holly Lodge seemed bigger and emptier than ever. Grimble was propped on a dining room chair, staring through a window and grinning at the world. It was a world that had grown darker for both of them.

"What are we going to do, Chris?"

Her husband's stony silence was the only thing keeping his emotions in check. "I'm sorry," he whispered.

The specialist had explained the problem but his words had become meaningless once he'd offered his verdict. Vague phrases kept running through Melanie's head. *Robertsonian translocation: conception unlikely: one in a thousand men affected: a risk of serious disability to the new born.*

In layman's terms what Christopher suffered from was an acute case of genetic bad luck.

Adoption had been suggested. Wheels could be set in motion. Through her tears Melanie had wondered how slowly those wheels turned and if they ever reached their destination.

"It's not your fault," she said, but locked somewhere deep in her disappointment a small rebellious voice told her it was, and she couldn't help but listen.

***

Harold Barker was the man Melanie had been searching for. The master craftsman's website displayed an array of dolls and dummies, which according to the blurb were all made lovingly by hand. It also boasted that a talent for creating those heads and bodies had been handed down from father to son through generations. BARKER'S IMAGES was proud of the fact it was a family business. By luck the workshop was no more than a forty-five minute drive from Holly Lodge.

At first Melanie had been uncertain about her choice of gift. She'd never been particularly fond of Grimble, its troubled history stirred in her an unease she couldn't explain. Sometimes she'd glance at the dummy, sure it was watching her, and then laugh at her stupidity. It was a wooden head and no amount of imagination could change that.

But now she wanted to celebrate Christopher's coming birthday with something out of the ordinary. Ever since their appointment with bad news, heartbreak had hung over Holly Lodge. Her husband had been trying to lose himself in his work, but still walked around looking like a man guilty of a crime he couldn't name. Melanie felt almost as bad for him as she did herself. It was strange how a life could seem emptier when no-one had left it.

She was sure reuniting the head with a body would make him smile, and god knows neither of them had been doing much of that lately. His two day absence attending a sales conference would be the perfect opportunity to plan her surprise.

"Hello, Harold Barker speaking."

Melanie was surprised; she thought the craftsman might have a secretary.

"Hello, Mr Barker," she said. "My name's Melanie Page. I wonder if you could help me."

"Well, my dear, that all depends on what kind of assistance you need." The old man's voice was laced with humour. He laughed, and it was such an unexpected sound she joined in.

"I'd like a body made for a head that I've inherited."

There was a pause, as if Harold Barker was trying to make sense of her request.

"I'm a carpenter, not a surgeon," he answered, and laughed again. For some reason this time the sound brought tears to her eyes. It was like listening to something that had happened long ago and trying to recall exactly when that moment had occurred. *Don't break down on the phone,* she thought, and pulled her frayed emotions together.

When she went on to explain the planned birthday surprise the old man's interest sharpened. Even at the end of a telephone Melanie could sense his enthusiasm.

"Bring it down," he said, when she informed him she didn't live far. "I'll see what I can do."

They arranged a date and time and she replaced the receiver. Behind her Grimble's head was leant against a chair. The dummy's eyes were closed but there was a smile on the painted lips, as if it had been eavesdropping and approved of every word.

***

Harold Barker's workshop looked nothing like the modern, spacious premises she'd imagined. A narrow lane had led her to a barn that stood adjacent to a modest farmhouse. Beyond the garden, fields ran down to a slow moving river. There was a large hand-painted sign hanging above the outbuilding door. *BARKER'S IMAGES.*

The old man who welcomed her was short and stout and wore old fashioned brown overalls. His wire-rimmed glasses were perched so near the end of his nose they might have been a disguise. He shook her hand and smiled. "Come in, Mrs Page," he said, and closed the door behind her.

She could smell paint and glue, wood shavings and varnish. Heads and bodies, all in various stages of completion, hung from the walls. It was like entering a macabre doll's house filled with unborn figures. Harold followed her gaze.

"It's an obsession," he explained, almost apologetically, and gestured to the small case she carried. "So what have you brought me?"

Melanie placed it on a workbench and unclipped the lid. When she opened it Barker's eyes widened in surprise.

"Grimble!" There was wonder in his voice. He gently lifted the head out and held it in front of him. "Where did you get this?" he asked.

Melanie was shocked Barker knew the dummy's name. "In the attic of the house we moved into some time ago. Why?"

He rubbed his chin and studied the head with interest. Then he placed it back in the case and offered her a seat. "Let's have some tea," he said.

There was a kitchenette squeezed into a corner of the barn. As the kettle boiled Melanie Page began to learn the full story behind Arthur King's breakdown and why all that had survived of a famous puppet was its head.

"My grandfather made that doll," Barker said. "That's why I recognised it. The reason I was so surprised was because I didn't think it existed anymore." He gazed at Melanie. "Are you aware of the story behind it?"

Melanie nodded. "Vaguely." She related how they'd discovered the head and a half-emptied photograph album in the attic.

The news interested Barker. "Fascinating, I'd love to see it," he said.

When she described the YouTube clips and Wikipedia's condensed version of events the old man shook his head. "That's only half the story."

The kettle boiled. Harold poured tea and they settled down at the workbench.

"My grandfather met Arthur King on a number of occasions. From what I remember I got the impression he wasn't fond of the man. I often heard him talking to my father about King's ill-mannered ways, and how he would ritually try and beat him down on a previously agreed price." Barker looked at her over his teacup. "I think he was, as the Americans say, *'always chasing another dollar.'*

Melanie grinned; she wasn't sure if that was exactly what the American's did say. The old man continued.

"I believe that was one of the reasons his mental problems began. Overwork, a lack of sleep, the stress of travel, they all take their toll, on the mind as well as the body. Whether it was greed or the memory of the poverty he'd left behind, I don't know, but King couldn't refuse a booking. From what I've been told I also think he spent too much time alone with that dummy."

He looked over to where Grimble's head lay in the case. Melanie could see him reliving the past, picturing a childhood where the seeds of his vocation had been sown. Then he smiled. "Would you like another cup of tea?" he asked, as if an everyday household act might bring back that time.

Harold Barker was a devotee of everything related to his trade; a mine of information that he was eager to share with the woman who had reunited him with a small part of his past.

"You mentioned the report regarding his breakdown," he said, "but there were other occasions when similar incidents occurred that never reached the press." He shrugged his shoulders. "They were different days, times when it was easier to hide your mistakes. Perhaps if a doctor had witnessed those first signs of Arthur's illness he might have gotten help. But that didn't happen and for a while King managed to conceal his mental problems."

The old man went on to tell her how he believed the ventriloquist's upbringing had made him an insular character, someone who could never place his trust in another human being. "His father used to beat him you know." Barker's voice was burdened with sadness. "How could someone do that to their son?"

Melanie didn't know. A child of her own was something she couldn't imagine. Beating that phantom infant was beyond her understanding. If Harold was aware of her discomfort he appeared not to notice. He returned to the past.

"I always remember my father telling me that as a boy how he witnessed King rehearsing a routine with Grimble. There was nobody else in the workshop. The ventriloquist seemed to relish the opportunity at being able to showcase his skills in front of an infant." He shook his head. "Halfway through his performance my grandfather walked in. I think that was the first time anybody realised there was something seriously wrong."

"What happened?" she asked.

The old man gazed into yesterday. "Evidently Arthur hadn't finished the script for his new sketch, a fact that probably didn't worry him, after all he was only showing off in front of a small child. The problem was Grimble didn't see it that way." Harold looked at her and laughed. "Of course, that's if you can believe the dummy had a mind of its own." His laughter died. "I think Arthur did, even then."

Melanie sipped at her tea and waited.

"*'There were two of them there.'* I swear that's what my father said. *'A man and his dummy, but Arthur was arguing with Grimble as if they were a double act.'* Can you believe that?"

Melanie didn't want to but she could.

"With my father and grandfather looking on King suffered a screaming fit, swearing at the dummy as Grimble taunted him. He was forehead to forehead with the doll. My father told me it was like watching a power struggle neither could win. The ventriloquist suddenly seemed to be aware of his behaviour and for a moment fell silent. The doll flopped lifelessly against his shoulder. "Are you all right?" my grandfather asked.

Barker paused, as if he'd been there and was revisiting the scene. Melanie could imagine a small boy's delight turning to horror. She shivered. "What happened then?"

Harold looked at her. "The dummy's head snapped back up and slowly swivelled to face him. My grandfather frowned, wondering what King was doing, and then Grimble spoke.

"Don't blame me," it said. *"I'm not responsible."*

"With that, King started laughing. It was a wild, high sound that soon became a crying fit. As my grandfather went to comfort him King shrugged him off and threw the dummy to the ground. Then he looked at my father, who remember was still a child, and reached out to him. '*It's trying to take over my life,*' he moaned. '*It's trying to take over my life.*' My father burst into tears."

The rest of Harold Barker's story came second-hand.

His family had made and supplied puppets to showbiz clientele for years. Gossip and rumour had always circulated amongst that tight-knit community. Word of mouth was a potent messenger.

"King's mental problems eventually led him to believe the doll was possessed. As his condition deteriorated so it became harder for him to disguise that illness. His final performance proved that.

"When he refused medical treatment and tried to continue touring promoters shunned him. None of them wanted a repeat of the previous debacle, and who could blame them, they were trying to get bums on seats, not frighten an audience away.

"King began drinking heavily, a trait handed down from his father, and the more he drank the worse his paranoia became. One evening, before he shut himself off from the outside world completely, my grandfather received a phone call. The ventriloquist was drunk. It was a rambling, one-sided conversation in which he confided that he'd destroyed the doll's body.

"Why?" My grandfather asked. He was shocked at how rapidly his ex-client was losing touch with reality. In a slurred whisper King explained that he believed separating the head would weaken the dummy's powers. When my grandfather tried to reason with him Arthur hung up. It was the last time they ever spoke."

Melanie pictured King roaming through the rooms in Holly Lodge, searching for an audience he'd never find.

"Why didn't he just destroy the head as well?" she asked.

"That's a good question," Barker said. "Why didn't he? If you want my opinion, I think he'd genuinely come to believe Grimble held power over him. He'd managed to dispose of the body, but his subconscious wouldn't allow him to do the same to the head. He literally talked himself out of the act through the dummy.

"There were rumours he spent nights at home performing his routine in front of a mirror, as if he were attempting to relive days gone by. I understand he took photographs of some of those occasions. I dread to think what those lonely evenings must have been like."

Melanie recalled blank spaces in a photograph album. Maybe they'd been snapshots of those solo performances: a drunken madman staring into a looking glass as his dummy told him how crazy he was. In a lucid moment who wouldn't want to rip out those memories? Harold Barker continued.

"One night King was found weeping, wandering naked along the lanes around Holly Lodge. He was carrying a knife and told the shocked couple who found him that he'd had to get out of the house; that Grimble was making threats and he wasn't safe.

"This time there was no question of him refusing treatment. He was committed to a mental asylum for an indefinite period. Therapy and medication proved unsuccessful. As his condition worsened it was recommended he underwent a course of shock treatment."

'*Shock treatment.*' To Melanie the words conjured up images of leather straps and gagged mouths; of silent screams and bodies arched in agony. "Did it work?" she asked.

Barker ran his fingers over Grimble's face; it was like watching a father caress his son. He shook his head. "Not at all, and then on the day a decision was made to transfer him to a more secure unit, King killed himself."

Melanie rubbed her arms. The workshop had grown cold. Half-formed dolls hung from the walls and listened as Harold's voice grew distant.

"It was after dark, lights out. The broken silence was littered with the sounds of restless slumber. But Arthur wasn't sleeping, not on this night. Orderlies said they heard him screaming, raving that Grimble had appeared in his room and the head was demanding to know what he'd done with its body. By the time they got to him King had somehow managed to force open a barred window, climb across a ledge and fling himself onto railings three floors below."

Harold raised an eyebrow and smiled. "Enough of the horror stories, that was a long time ago. Let's see what we can do about getting your little fellow back in one piece."

Barker made himself busy. He measured and photographed the head, scribbling notes as he studied colour charts and checked records. Melanie watched him and saw a man whose work made him complete; a man doing what God had created him for.

When he'd finished, he rested the head back in the case, clipped it shut and slid it towards her. "I don't need to keep that," he said, "I've got all the details I need."

She accepted the price he quoted and they agreed on a completion date. As he saw Melanie to her car she asked him the question she'd been too embarrassed to voice in the barn. "Do you think the doll's possessed?"

The craftsman looked at her and smiled. "Mrs Page, it's a dummy."

She felt colour rise in her cheeks. They shook hands and he promised to have the doll delivered before Christopher's birthday.

It was only as Melanie drove away that she realised Harold Barker hadn't answered her question.

***

The body arrived in a box slightly larger than the one they'd discovered in the attic. She thanked the delivery man and carried it into the lounge. The suit the child-sized torso wore matched the outfit she'd seen in an ancient film clip perfectly. Harold Barker had crafted an exact double.

Grimble's head was lying on the table. She picked it up and slipped it into the body. Melanie found it hard to believe that an eighty year old prop could fit so easily into a modern replica of a music hall dummy. She slipped her hand into the hollow of the doll's back and swivelled the head to face her. "Hello," she said.

Grimble's sightless stare was watchful. When the phone rang in the hallway she placed the doll on a chair and went to answer it. As the door closed behind her Grimble's eyes opened. The head performed a slow ninety degree turn. "Hello, yourself," it said.

***

The birthday that started so well ended with a drunken confession and a row that was to be the first of many.

The gift had done what she'd hoped it would and brought a smile to her husband's face. His pleasure had been evident. For an hour-and-a-half he'd attempted to master the basic techniques of ventriloquism before giving up and taking her to lunch. It was later in the day when they were halfway through dinner that Christopher dropped his bombshell.

He'd insisted on opening a third bottle of wine, despite Melanie protesting she'd had enough. Perhaps that was what made her bring up the subject they'd barely mentioned since their final visit to the clinic.

"When do you think we should look into the process of adopting?"

He shrugged his shoulders and poured more wine. Something in his manner told her he was reluctant to discuss a question that never left her mind. She could feel anger building. Christ, they had to talk about it sometime!

"Come on Chris," she said. "We need to get this sorted out. Personally, I don't want to wait any longer."

She could see his good humour fading and didn't know why. He placed his glass with drunken care on the table and looked at her.

"I don't think I want to adopt," he said.

For a moment Melanie was dumbfounded. They'd been trying for a child for over two years. It was what they both had wanted. Fostering was their only chance.

"What do you mean? I thought we agreed it was the route we were going to take."

He shook his head. "I've been thinking about it and the truth is I'm not sure I could love another man's child. It would be like bringing up a stranger. I couldn't commit to that."

He smiled, as if his explanation solved everything. She fought an overwhelming urge to slap the expression from his face. *'I couldn't commit to that.'* His confession was like a betrayal.

"You bastard!" she cried, and banged her hip against the table as she stood up. "You know that's all I've wanted. I thought it was all we both wanted!"

He raised his hands in a gesture of apology she could never accept.

"This is all your fault!" she shouted. "If you were anything like a proper man this wouldn't have happened!" Her words cut him. She saw it in his face and was glad. "Happy fucking birthday," she snapped, and threw her wine over him. Then she ran from the room.

Much later Christopher finished the third bottle. He had no desire to climb the stairs and face another domestic storm.

He'd been drunkenly practising with the dummy. There was something therapeutic about working the levers. To see the eyes and mouth open and close was like witnessing a small child waking up: *a child of his own.* It made him sad and wish for things he could never have.

He repeated the procedure until his fingers ached. When he took them from the controls the head spun around so violently it startled him. Grimble's blind gaze seemed to read his mind. Christopher couldn't look away.

"She thinks you're a failure you know." Arthur King's alter-ego sounded just as it had in a 1930's film clip. The dummy's hypnotic stare demanded an answer.

"No, she doesn't." There was a defensive whine to Christopher's voice that he didn't like or recognise.

Grimble laughed, a cynical man of the world I've seen it all, sound. "You're a sap, pal. What's the point of getting it up if you can't finish the job?"

Before it even crossed his mind what he was doing Page rebuked himself. "Shut your mouth!"

But Grimble wouldn't shut his mouth. Christopher's fingers were clenched around the control levers and the dummy was determined to have his say.

"She's going to look elsewhere. A good looking broad like that needs her fires stoked." The doll winked; "Seems to me like you're putting them out, buddy."

Page realised he was voicing what he felt, or at least he thought he was. Speaking through the dummy appeared to be the only way he could face unspoken fears.

"Want my advice?"

Christopher had a feeling Grimble was going to offer it, whether he wanted it or not.

"I'd keep a close eye on her if I were you. Women are fickle. If the klutz they're with can't put a bun in their oven they'll find one who can." The dummy's voice dropped to a conspiratorial whisper. "Trust me; you're going the right way to lose her." Grimble lapsed into silence. His satisfied smile looked almost dreamy.

Christopher placed the dummy back on a seat they'd unconsciously got into the habit of reserving for it. He shook his head. What was he doing talking to a doll? *'She's going to look elsewhere.'* His wife wouldn't do that, he was certain. One way or another they'd sort out their problems: manipulating a dummy wasn't going to solve anything.

When he eventually climbed the stairs to bed he'd almost forgotten how the head had suddenly spun around when he'd released the controls. A short while later drink and sleep buried the memory.

He left for work the next morning without a word passing between them. His hangover didn't ease until after midday: his guilt and unhappiness lasted a lot longer.

Later that evening after a pretence at civility they had a re-run of the row that had taken place the night before.

Now Melanie was alone. The argument had fanned flames of a disagreement that continued to burn. His treachery had led to petty insults and words that couldn't be taken back. When she deliberately brought up the subject of blame her husband had stormed from the house in a childish rage.

She poured another glass of wine and realised she was drinking too much. She raised the glass in Grimble's direction. "Here's to you my little man."

The dummy was slumped in his chair. His eyes gazed at her adoringly. *'Pick me up,'* they pleaded. *'Pick me up.'*

She placed her drink on the table and reached for him. When she folded her hands around the body she imagined she could feel a tiny heart beating beneath them. She slipped her fingers over the controls and turned the head towards her. With her spare hand she picked up the glass.

"What am I going to do, Grimble?" she asked.

The doll's eyes had grown harder.

"Kick him out, he's a waste of space!"

Melanie giggled into her wine and drank some more. "I couldn't do that."

"You could," the doll said. "Who paid for the house?" It was a sly question Grimble answered. "Why, your dead mother, that's who. Wouldn't she have wanted to hear the sound of little kiddies running around?"

Her mother would have but never got the chance.

"Here, put your wine down and lift me up, I need to tell you something."

Melanie did as Grimble said. When his lips brushed against her ear they felt soft and warm: human.

"What you need is a real man," the dummy whispered, "someone who can do the hard end of the business."

It was like listening to a dirty phone call. She didn't want it to end.

"Imagine somebody else running their hands over your body; somebody who could give you what you wanted. Wouldn't that feel good?"

Melanie pictured the imaginary stranger and nodded. A small wooden hand dropped down and rested on her breast. She could feel her nipples hardening.

"Don't rely on that loser." A tongue Grimble didn't possess caressed her ear lobe. The sensation of pleasure travelled to her groin. "Think of all the other men you could have."

As she did she heard the front door open and then slam shut. It was a sound that filled her with guilt. She held the puppet at arm's length.

"I could be your baby." Grimble's voice had slipped into that of a child's, and of everything she'd imagined he'd said that was the one thing that stayed with her when all else had been forgotten.

'I could be your baby.'

***

Christopher had placed the dummy in the attic. He'd told himself it was because he was worried his wife was becoming too attached to it; that she was starting to regard Grimble as a child substitute. But there was also another reason; he resented the time she spent with the doll, after all it was his, what right did she have to covet his possession?

He knew his confession had upset her, but the guilt he'd initially experienced had since been erased by her behaviour. She'd become cold towards him, just because he was reluctant to be the father of another man's child.

They hadn't made love since before the birthday row. He remembered her spiteful words on the one night he had attempted foreplay. *'What's the point?'* The recollection still stung. Well, if he couldn't play with her, she couldn't play with Grimble.

He sat the doll in an upright position and ran his fingers through its hair, the way he might have done to a son he was never going to have. "Sleep tight," he said, and grinned as he realised it didn't sound at all strange talking to a dummy.

He climbed from the roof space, retracted the ladder and pulled the loft hatch shut. Melanie was already in bed, no doubt waiting for another chance to hatch an argument. He remembered an unopened bottle of wine chilling in the fridge and made his way downstairs.

Above him the attic room dimmed. Light faded beyond the bulls-eye window. Grimble gazed into the shadows.

"You're still a shmuck," the dummy said, and laughed.

It was probably the same sound Arthur King had heard before he jumped from a third floor window and impaled himself on iron railings thirty feet below.

***

It was one of those rare summer nights where the humidity of the day had strayed beyond its boundaries. Christopher was snoring, wrapped up in sheets on the far side of the bed. Their sleeping place had become territorial, now there was an invisible line between them that neither crossed.

She was restless. Her thoughts kept straying to a child she'd been denied and a silent house that would always be devoid of the sounds of family life.

As her eyes grew heavy those thoughts were replaced by others. Her weary mind pictured the attic. She could see a cardboard box gathering dust in the shadows and a photograph album containing an epitaph of empty pages. But most of all she saw a severed head. Her dreams were filled with them and they were all wooden; their faces painted with hollow eyes and mad-men smiles.

Before she'd bought the substitute body that's how she'd come to regard Grimble; as a head that would do anything to be reunited with its missing half. But now she felt differently; the doll was a comfort, something to turn to when her husband's betrayal hurt too deeply. She drifted into sleep and followed a dummy down the years.

High in Holly Lodge, beneath where the steep roofs formed peaks and valleys, a shaft of moonlight pierced the bulls-eye window. It formed a hazy spotlight on the doll Christopher and Melanie now called by name. Grimble's eyes were open.

***

Melanie found the dummy soon after her husband left for work. She could only guess the reason he'd placed the doll in the attic was because he was jealous; envious of the attention she gave it and resentful because she refused to share that time with him. And why should she? He was a liar; a man who'd gone back on his word; a husband prepared to see his wife suffer because of his own shortcomings: *'a man who couldn't do the hard end of the business.'*

She climbed into the roof space. Grimble was sitting like an abandoned child in a shaft of sunlight. A tear had traced a long wet stain down his painted cheek. The head turned in her direction.

"He left me here," the dummy said.

Something broke in Melanie's heart. If her husband could discard a precious gift as it were nothing she realised he could do the same to a child. Perhaps that was why he'd never be able to have one; God had seen the cruelty in his heart and cursed him. Well fuck him!

Grimble's arms were open. Hooded eyes shone with childish anticipation. Melanie picked the doll up and held it against her. "There, there," she said.

"Mummy," Grimble whispered, and grinned over her shoulder.

***

The meeting had ended earlier than expected. There was nowhere else to go but home. Christopher opened the front door to Holly Lodge and called out his wife's name. The house was a silent maze of empty rooms. He climbed the stairs.

Above him the loft ladder hung from an open hatch. He could hear whispers. As he climbed towards the opening they stopped. He hesitated. "Melanie? Are you in there?"

There was no answer. He was suddenly afraid to go further. Then he heard the sound of soft laughter. Reluctantly he placed another foot on a rung and slowly raised his head through the gap into the roof space.

Christopher couldn't believe what he was seeing.

Melanie was cradling the doll against her as if it were an infant in need of protection. A dress strap hung from her shoulder. Grimble's head was pressed to her naked breast. She was cooing, offering soft words of comfort as she rocked a dummy into sleep.

"Melanie! What are you doing?"

His words startled her. She backed away and glared at him. Christopher saw suspicion and madness in that gaze.

"Melanie, I said what are you doing?"

"It's your fault!" she spat. "If I'd married someone else, this would never have happened! Well, I have a child now and you can't take him from me, he's mine!"

He suddenly felt a terrible sympathy for his wife and a sad longing for a time he feared he might never see again. It *was* his fault. His refusal to consider adoption had driven her away and now she was visiting a place where comfort and insanity overlapped. Hoarding the dummy had only made things worse.

He climbed into the attic and moved slowly forwards. "Melanie, give Grimble to me and then we can go downstairs. I promise you we can sort things out."

Her eyes momentarily cleared. When she smiled Christopher saw the woman he'd married. He took a step closer and reached out. "Come on, Mel."

He only saw the knife she had concealed beneath the dummy's body as the blade flashed in the shadows. When she thrust it into his stomach the force of the blow pushed him backwards. In a struggle for balance he pulled rubbish he'd never cleared on top of him.

He lay on the floor, stunned. His mind refused to accept what had happened. Zig-zag images ran across his vision: Melanie's Judas smile: the silver blur of steel: a doll's mouth suckling at his wife's nipple. He gazed down and saw the blade embedded in his stomach.

Melanie was grinning, a twisted snarl that resembled Grimble's unearthly smile.

"Why?" he moaned, and coughed up a mouthful of blood. His pain seemed to enrage her. She pressed the dummy harder to her breast and stood over him.

"DON'T BLAME ME!" Melanie screamed. "I'M NOT RESPONSIBLE!"

For a terrible moment, as the life drained from his body, he suspected that maybe she wasn't, but if that were the case, who was? A sudden shaft of pain tightened itself behind his ribs. His eyes refused to focus. Before they closed forever Grimble's head slipped from his wife's breast and lolled drunkenly in his direction. The dummy's dreamy smile seemed to answer a question he'd never get the chance to ask.

THE OTHER SIDE OF THE COIN

It was a cruel game; one that Levi had had no choice in reluctantly becoming drawn into. The boy with the haunted eyes and gaunt face who sat opposite him was trembling. It was like looking into a mirror. Mueller was crouched between them, his boyish grin exposing his tender years.

'He shouldn't be here,' Levi thought. *'He should be at home helping on his father's farm or studying to go to college.'* Another thought. *'None of us should be here.'*

"Come, it is time to play." Mueller pulled a coin from his tunic and held it up to the light. "See," he said, "an English penny." His smile was sly as he turned it in his fingers. "Heads or tails?" He balanced it on his thumb and flicked it into the air, then caught it and slapped it down on the upturned crate they were using as a table. The flat of his hand covered the coin. He stared at the child opposite Levi.

"Rules of the game, visitors go first."

A tear had formed in the corner of the boy's eye. Levi felt a pang of jealousy. He had no tears left, he'd cried the last one a long time ago. No tears and no smiles.

Mueller pushed his handsome farm boy's face into the child's. "Well? Make your choice."

The boy tried to swallow the dryness from his mouth. "Heads," he whispered.

Mueller lifted his palm and laughed excitedly. "Well done little one." He grinned at Levi and raised an eyebrow. "Perhaps Lady Luck smiles on someone else today." He flipped the coin. Levi watched it spin through the air. The sight made him feel light-headed. All he wanted was for the game to be over.

"Heads," he said.

Mueller whistled through his teeth as he exposed the penny. "I should have known better." He turned to the other child. "What is your name little one?"

"David Sir. David Rosenberg."

"Well, David Rosenberg, I must warn you Levi here is my champion." Again he spun the coin. It glittered in the dusty sunlight. "Call," he commanded.

"Tails."

Mueller moved his hand away. The coin was heads up. "Oh dear, let us hope Levi calls wrong also." Levi did. Mueller seemed pleased.

"The game goes on."

This time the penny seemed to tumble in slow motion. Somehow Levi knew David Rosenberg would be wrong again; as if all the bad luck that had led him to this place would have a final sting in its tail. It did.

His turn came and he wished himself into making another wrong call; prayed the coin would land against him. His prayer went unanswered.

"You win again, Levi."

Mueller pulled his pistol from its holster, pushed the end of the barrel against David Rosenberg's temple and pulled the trigger. If anyone saw the boy's body flop to the ground they appeared not to notice.

As he re-holstered the gun Mueller handed Levi a stale bun wrapped in cloth. The bread was stuffed with meat. Levi was powerless to prevent a strand of saliva dribble down his chin.

Mueller stood up and grinned, a smile full of boyish charm. Only his eyes looked crazy. Levi wondered if they'd always been that way or had changed since he'd been posted to the camp. When Mueller patted him on the shoulder he couldn't help noticing how spotless his uniform was; how only the heels of his leather boots were rimmed with dust. The last time he could remember wearing boots was when the soldiers had force-marched his family to the railway station.

"Well done Levi. You are still the champion." He raised a finger and thumb and aimed them at the boy. "We play again next week, jah?"

As the guard walked away Levi bit into the bun and stared through the wire of the perimeter fence. Beyond it, he could see the crematorium. He took another mouthful of food and watched smoke pour like poison into the morning sky.

THE HANGMAN'S CHOICE

Silas Greybourne had watched murderers weep their way to the gallows and felt nothing. The hangman's indifference to the last moments of the condemned was based on the belief those who took life deserved to pay with their own. But this was wrong; the boy was innocent.

Had it not been for the accident, Isaac Miller, the wandering child-beggar, might have passed through the village unnoticed. But he was a stranger and these were dangerous times to be looked on as an outsider. Superstition had gripped the Fens, the isolated flatlands and marshes becoming fertile hunting ground for those who believed evil walked in human form. It was the young boy's misfortune that the girl who died was the niece of Phileas Lacey. Now he was on trial for witchcraft and a bitter man was determined to see him hang.

'The child's in league with the devil!'

Lacey's words stunned the congregation. They listened in silence while the preacher force-fed them his reasons for believing the boy should die. As his voice rose and fell in practised rhythms an undercurrent of unease spread like a murmur through the assembly.

The community of Buxton had been divided ever since the new minister's arrival. His fire and brimstone sermons thrilled and appalled in equal measure. There was only one path to follow as far as Lacey was concerned and God help those he suspected trod another.

But the preacher nursed a secret. Long ago his faith had been poisoned by deformity and the ridicule it invited; since childhood the hunchback's heart had become harder with every slight and insult aimed at him. Yet as he'd grown older something in his appearance and power of speech had silenced those who once taunted him. The frightened child had become a religious bully; a man who used his cover as a servant of the Lord to further his own ambitions.

His transfer to Buxton had suited him perfectly, the rural backwater giving him an opportunity to mould the farm workers and labourers to his will. Now it was time to convince the wealthier of his constituents, the landowners and gentry, to donate more freely to the church: and they would, or face being named from the pulpit as misers and hypocrites.

But first he had to make an example of the boy.

The niece Lacey had raised since her parents died had been taken from him. His grief was gilded with bitterness and frustration. The girl had become a temptation, a filler of dreams, and his desperate prayers for strength to resist her had gone unanswered. On a morning in which a dream of desire and corruption drove him from sleep he came to a decision: the girl would be his or she would be homeless. It was time she paid her keep.

Whether or not his niece had sensed his intentions he had no idea, but the following night she'd fled the house with nothing more than a change of clothes and a handful of coins stolen from his purse. The storm she ran into cost her her life.

Lost in the darkness she floundered into a swollen drainage ditch. Unable to scale the steep banks she became trapped in the rising water. Her cries for help went unheard.

Isaac Miller discovered her body as he was leaving the village the following morning. He pulled the girl from the ditch and laid her gently on the side of the road. That was where Lacey discovered them after he'd realised his niece was missing and had gone in search of her.

The sight of the child cradling the body he'd longed for filled him with hate. The plan slipped easily into his mind. There'd be no awkward questions asked as to why she'd run away if someone, or something, had made her leave against her will.

He climbed down from his carriage, shuffled across the track and accused the boy of murder. Before the startled child could protest Lacey raised his walking cane and beat him unconscious. Then he fumbled in his dead niece's clothing and placed the stolen coins in the lad's pocket. It was clear what had happened.

The devil had called out to her in the shape of a child. She'd been weak, deceived by that treacherous voice, and walked out into a storm from which there was no return. The boy had stolen her soul and then taken her money.

For that he would hang.

An air of superstitious excitement infected Buxton. The news of what happened that terrible evening had spread by word of mouth. Truth and lies became twisted, fact and rumour blurred beyond recognition. But the preacher's niece was dead, of that there was no doubt, and stolen money had been found in the boy's clothing. The one man in possession of the truth spent it in lies.

The trial became a formality, as did the verdict and sentence. Phileas Lacey's testimony carried with it the weight of the Lord, and no judge or jury were willing to question that authority.

The day of the execution was a strangely sombre affair. Excitement had given way to apprehension. A community blinded by the preacher's accusations suddenly seemed to be seeing for the first time where they were being led. When the boy stepped on to the scaffold the hangman gave voice to what he suspected many of the crowd already believed.

"This isn't right! He's only a child! He's sworn he did nothing!"

The gathering fell silent. Overhead, storm clouds broke like waves in the sky. Lacey's eyes narrowed as he turned to the hangman; a thin smile touched his lips.

"Are you saying you're siding with the boy?"

Silas Greybourne immediately realised the implication of the question. He stared into faces he'd known all his life, no-one would meet his gaze; they were as scared of the preacher as he was. Behind him the boy was crying.

"Well?" Lacey's voice was hard; it stole the words from Silas's mouth and the courage from his heart. He hesitated for a moment and then shook his head. The preacher grinned and placed bony fingers on his shoulder. "Do your duty then, hangman."

So to save himself, Silas Greybourne did something he'd never done before; he hung an innocent human being.

The shame of that day loomed large in his past; a terrible mistake cowardice had prevented him from correcting. Phileas Lacey felt no such guilt.

The preacher slammed his fist against the pulpit, daring the congregation to meet his eye. "No-one escapes the Lord's justice! Those who try are already damned!" His words echoed around the church.

"The boy *was* in league with the devil, and believe me, there are others out there performing his dirty work. But we shall search and we shall find them! Now, let us praise the Lord!" He spread his arms in a gesture of triumph, a dark shepherd convinced his flock would follow where he led.

After the service the parishioners filed out into the grounds. They were an uneasy procession, reluctant to voice their misgivings about a man who put death and retribution before compassion and forgiveness. Silas Greybourne walked amongst them, but he walked alone. A line had been drawn. Their silence might have made them conspirators, but they hadn't tied the rope and they hadn't taken a life. If the hangman could live with his deeds they'd decided, then they could live with theirs.

When the last of the worshippers had passed beneath the lych-gate Lacey shuffled back inside and closed the door. The church was silent. He picked up the collection plates, weighed them in his hands and grinned; faith brought its own rewards.

Phileas Lacey never held another service, nor did he get the chance to persecute another innocent. Two weeks after the execution his body was discovered inside the same church he'd used to spread his poisonous sermons. The dead man was kneeling in an upright position with his hands clasped together. Bibles and prayer books had been ripped apart and scattered across the nave. An angry red wheal was imprinted around the preacher's throat. His eyes were locked open. It looked as if he'd been scared to death.

For a man used to forgetting the dead Silas Greybourne was surprised at how easily the image of the boy would slip into his mind. Long after the execution he could still hear him pleading his innocence, begging for mercy as the noose was placed around his neck. Those phantom words never failed to conjure up an image of Isaac Miller's body dangling from the scaffold.

Since that time he always slept with a candle burning and his bedroom door locked. In those dark hours his conscience would haunt him. He'd listen to the wind rattling against the shutters and imagine a dead child trying to gain entry.

Three weeks later, as a new moon rose to meet an empty sky, a dead child did.

The hangman woke to the sound of movement. The candle was out and the door open. A chill clung to the room. He pulled the blankets around him and peered into the shadows. "Who's there?"

A small figure stepped into a shaft of moonlight. Silas moaned. The boy he'd hanged raised his arm and pointed a finger in silent accusation. "I was never in league with the devil," he said. As he spoke his body rose slowly above the bed until he hung over Silas in a shape of crucifixion. A scream locked itself in the hangman's throat; he pressed himself against the wall.

"I know you weren't," he cried. It was a wasted confession. The boy smiled and then his grin twisted into something darker.

Silas was unable to move. He watched with dread as a dead child floated down towards him and then noticed the noose that had appeared in the lad's hand. Isaac Miller hung inches above him, when he spoke again Silas smelt death on the boy's breath.

"I was never in league with the devil," he repeated. He slipped the rope around the hangman's throat and pressed cold lips against Silas's cheek. "But I am now," he whispered.

As Greybourne's scream freed itself Isaac Miller slowly tightened the noose.

Barry John Watson

AHEAD OF THE GAME

Tony Sinclair had been ahead of the game long enough to know a pretender when he saw one. You didn't get to be salesman of the year every year for the last decade without recognising competition, and that's what Rowena Dawson was; competition. Sinclair wasn't stupid. They might work for the same company and be chasing the same targets, but in the dog-eat-dog world of sales he knew the only thing that counted was performance, and those who failed to perform were swiftly trampled underfoot. He'd seen grown men cry like babies after being notified the company no longer required their services. The sight had disgusted him; Sinclair didn't do crying.

He sipped at his beer and watched his rival joking with two of the sales team as they stood at the bar. Alan Banister and Mark Houseman weren't in Sinclair's league, a fact he knew they resented, but there could only be one top-dog and that was a position Tony had made his own. Now Dawson, who was drinking mineral water and listening to her colleagues as if they were two of the wise men, hoped to be the next big thing.

The salesman had heard rumours of the young girl's achievements, successfully gaining contracts where failure seemed the only option; opening up new avenues of business which until then had appeared closed. Tony wasn't worried. He'd seen them come and he'd seen them go and if there was ever a candidate who looked as if she was going to burn herself out, then Dawson fitted the bill: too keen, too energetic and probably too young. She was a looker though, there was no doubt about that, which probably worked to her advantage.

159

A jealous thought entered his head. He could imagine her showing off those long legs, displaying a glimpse of her impressive cleavage and fluttering those big blue eyes. She'd have the contacts he dealt with eating out of her hand. But that was her only advantage. There was no substitute for experience, and to gain that experience you had to pace yourself. It was a lesson he'd learned a long time ago, that was why he was still on the front line and the company were prepared to pay him big bucks. That, and the fact he could squeeze a signature out of a blind man.

As he finished his beer he tried to ignore the cramp in his stomach. Recently it had been returning with depressing regularity and the nagging worry that what might only be indigestion could be the first signs of an ulcer surfaced again. An image of all the late-night dinners and service station fry-ups he'd consumed ran through his mind. No wonder he'd put on weight. But what could he do? That was part of the job; if you worked late you ate late. To wind down you also had a drink, at least Tony did, and you made sacrifices. Sacrifice was something he knew all about.

He'd had a marriage before sales had become his life, and although bitterness prevented him from admitting it, he'd loved that time more than any other. Unfortunately, absence hadn't made his wife's heart grow fonder, Sinclair's punishing work schedules and repeated nights away had led to the longest separation of all; divorce.

He fought the urge to down a quick brandy, to wash away the memory with something stronger than a beer. The company's quarterly assessment meeting was about to take place and he needed to keep a clear head. He knew what was coming; a mind-numbing afternoon dominated by facts and figures, terminating in endless speeches outlining budget and expansion. The only light at the end of the tunnel was the free bar and evening meal to follow.

Sinclair picked up his briefcase and grinned. They could talk all they liked about targets and performances, but he'd already excelled on both counts, *and* it was only August. The ache in his stomach flared briefly and then subsided. "Bring it on," he muttered under his breath, and joined the queue of employees filing into the conference room.

Ridgemont House was a lot plusher than the kind of establishments Tony was used to, the days of inflated expenses and lingering business lunches were long gone. He'd seen the inside of more cheap hotels than he cared to remember. How many lonely evenings had he spent listening to the sound of main road traffic disappear into the night as he worried himself sleepless over another unsigned contract? Yet no expense was spared when it came to discussing the gravy train. But that was the way of the world, something he knew and accepted. You listened to the bullshit, you shook hands and smiled and then you went out and did what you had to do. Only you did it your own way and you accepted the consequences; there were no parachutes.

The conference room felt airless and too hot, as if someone had switched on the radiators and forgotten to turn them off. Sinclair loosened his tie and found himself seated between Banister and Coleen Gorman, head accountant of sales. That was when he knew it was going to be a long afternoon.

He'd never seen eye to eye with Gorman, not since she'd overheard him talking to a colleague, accusing her of being a ball-breaking man-hater. It was an observation he'd based on the fact she'd once double-checked an expenses sheet he'd submitted and deducted what she construed were personal allowances. Sinclair hadn't been able to believe it. The meeting he'd claimed for had netted the company a record profit and yet she'd quibbled over a few lousy drinks and a couple of hefty fuel receipts. (Okay, maybe they *hadn't* been company expenses, but he wasn't going to admit to that, was he?) The stand-up row that followed was still talked about. Needless to say Tony had received his expenses and Gorman had received a dressing down.

It paid to stay ahead of the game.

Eventually the meeting drew to a close with reports on how the sales team were progressing, and then came the time to name who would be receiving a bonus for best quarterly results. Tony turned and grinned at Banister, who ignored him. Alan was struggling, that was evident. He hadn't reached his targets, existing clients were unhappy and leads were drying up. The disappointment in the managing director's voice had sounded like a death sentence. The room stilled as the assembly waited for the successful agent to be announced.

Sinclair anticipated his name being read out and prepared himself for the inevitable round of applause. What he didn't prepare himself for was the shock of hearing Rowena Dawson being named sales person of the quarter. Banister looked at him and smirked. From the corner of his eye he could see satisfaction written all over Coleen Gorman's spiteful face. It was then he realised he might have to be very careful with the next expenses form he submitted.

As Dawson made her way to the podium he joined in the applause but his fingers stung every time they met.

***

It was early evening when Sinclair came down from his room. He'd been surprised when Dawson's name had been announced but now he'd composed himself. They were only a quarter of the way through the year; it'd be interesting to see how the girl was shaping up by late October. Traditionally that was the time sales dropped, the following winter months could be harsh: *a period that sorted the men from the boys - and the women.* He smiled at the thought.

Houseman was at the bar, a sickle-shaped grin splitting his face. "Pipped at the post," he said, "you must be slipping, Tony." He laughed and Sinclair fought an urge to swing his fist through the sickle. Instead, he shrugged his shoulders and ordered a beer.

"I'm in it for the long haul, Mark. As you well know, as long as the management are happy, that's all that matters." He lowered his voice in affected sympathy. "I see you only just made your targets this quarter."

Houseman's grin disappeared. In its place appeared the expression of a worried man, a man who knew that his next mortgage payment, his kid's private school fees and his wife's over-indulgent spending all depended on how well he could handle the next three months. Sinclair didn't rate his chances. A woman's voice interrupted them.

"Mr Sinclair? We haven't met but I believe we're batting for the same team. I'm Rowena Dawson."

He turned around. Close up she was even more stunning. She smiled and offered a neatly manicured hand. As he took it he realised he'd been wrong and right about her; she wasn't a pretender but she *was* competition; more than that, she was a threat.

"Please, call me Tony, and by the way congratulations on your award."

"Thanks," she replied. "I'm hoping it's the first of many." He realised then her eyes had parted company with her smile. They stared at each other for a long moment. He saw the ambition in her gaze and recognised the challenge in her words.

"That might be harder to accomplish than you imagine." His voice had dropped a little, as if he were sharing a secret. Their hands were still linked; they looked like old friends bidding each other farewell rather than rivals staking out territorial boundaries.

"We'll see, won't we?" Their fingers parted and the smile returned to her eyes.

"Are you two having a drink or are you going to talk shop all evening?" Mark Houseman's sickle grin had reappeared. He'd witnessed the confrontation with interest, but it was only with the interest of a spectator, not a competitor.

***

The following three months passed in a frenzy of meetings and telephone calls; of late nights and early mornings; a never ending round of hearty back-slapping and time spent laughing uproariously at humourless jokes. The fake banter came with the territory, but Sinclair could handle that all night and all day, just as long as the end result meant a sale. It usually did.

Halfway through that period he heard Alan Banister had left the company, a departure that hadn't been from choice. Sinclair recalled a saying that did the rounds when he first joined the sales team: *'Make the grade or don't get paid.'* It was as true now as it had been then. Evidently Banister was currently filling shelves in a local supermarket; his house had been repossessed and his wife had left him, taking with her their two kids. A reconciliation wasn't on the cards.

Tony could sympathise with his ex-colleague; hadn't he lost a wife himself? But that was where his sympathies ended, in this line of business you either swam or you went under. Banister had gone under. He pencilled in another appointment and closed his diary. He was ahead of the game.

***

It had to be today of all days that the stomach pains felt worse. The meeting had gone on far longer than he'd anticipated and as finalising the details went down to the nitty-gritty he'd found it almost impossible to concentrate.

"Are you feeling okay, Tony?"

William Marshall's look of concern surprised him. Up until then the head of Marshall Enterprises only looked concerned if he suspected he was getting a raw deal. Now he was staring at Sinclair with something like alarm in his eyes.

Tony was hot, too hot. His heart was racing and the ache in his stomach felt as it was trying to win a prize. Sweat formed on his forehead. He pulled a handkerchief from his pocket and ran it over his brow. He couldn't quit now, not when a contract that Rowena Dawson could never hope to match was within his grasp. If only he didn't feel so faint.

"I'm fine, thanks," he said, and poured himself a glass of water. His hand was shaking. "Now, are you satisfied with all the relevant points in our agreement?"

Marshall smiled and suddenly didn't appear like a multi-millionaire with the welfare of his company on his mind. He looked like a human being who cared about someone else.

"Tony," he said, "when I do business with you I know I have nothing to worry about. I just hope you're going to make an appointment to see a doctor."

Sinclair tried to grin and shrugged his shoulders, as if feeling under the weather was an occupational hazard, and what could you do but get on with it?

They shook hands and as Tony handed Marshall a pen that would seal the transaction he realised the world was slipping away. His last glimpse of it seemed to be from the wrong end of a telescope. William Marshall said something, but the words were coated in cotton wool. As Sinclair tumbled from the chair and slipped into unconsciousness he briefly wondered why it felt as if someone had kicked him in the stomach.

***

"How are you feeling, Mr Sinclair?"

He opened his eyes. Sunlight flooded a single bed ward. The nurse looked young enough to be the daughter he'd never had. Her professional smile could have hidden anything. He felt helpless and it suddenly seemed terribly important to know if William Marshall had signed the contract.

"How long have I been here?" He didn't recognise his own voice, it sounded weak and breathless, like an old man's. There was a tube running from his nose. He saw the drip in his arm and wires running from his chest to a monitor parked by the side of the bed. He could hear a steady beep that sounded like sonar.

The nurse rested her hand on his forehead and checked her clipboard. "Three days," she said. The beep that sounded like sonar picked up speed. *Three days!* All he could think of was missed appointments and lost opportunities. He could imagine Rowena Dawson taking advantage of his absence. The sooner he got out of the hospital the better.

The nurse removed her hand. "You've been sedated since the operation," she said.

Her words stunned and scared him. "Operation? What operation?" Before she could answer, the door was opened. The man who entered saw Sinclair and smiled.

"Here's Doctor Lessing," the nurse said. "He'll tell you everything." As she left the room Lessing folded his frame into a bedside chair and ran his eyes over the clipboard. Then he shook his head and looked at Sinclair.

"Well, Tony, what I see here is proof that you haven't been looking after yourself."

'Here we go,' Sinclair thought, *'it's bloody lecture time. Get it over and done with and then tell me when I can leave.'* What Lessing said next shocked him.

"Do you realise you almost died three days ago? If it hadn't been for Mr Marshall's quick thinking in calling an ambulance you wouldn't be here now." The doctor let his statement hang in the air. Tony swallowed and realised he owed his client a big one, but still he couldn't help himself, his mind kept running over the question of whether Marshall had signed the contract or not.

Lessing leant back in his chair, steepled his fingers beneath his chin and closed his eyes. "Let me make a guess," he said. "You're in a stressful job. You eat the wrong things, you drink too much and you don't exercise." He opened his eyes and gazed at Sinclair. "Am I right so far?" Tony nodded. He didn't like the way the beep that sounded like sonar seemed to pick up speed and then slow down. Lessing leaned towards him and carried on.

"You sleep irregular hours, you live alone, your work's your life and you never switch-off." The doctor raised a questioning eyebrow and again Sinclair nodded agreement. Lessing tapped the clipboard and lowered his voice. "Tony, you've got to slow down. The burst ulcer you suffered, and which thankfully we managed to sort out, was just a warning. Your blood pressure and cholesterol are sky high, and your heart-beat is erratic. It's your body's way of telling you it's had enough." His tone was serious. "You're heading for a stroke or a heart attack if you carry on the way you have been."

His warning knocked the resistance out of Sinclair. He laid his head back on the pillow. "What do you advise?"

Lessing counted out recommendations on his fingers.

"One, cut down on the booze. Two, eat more fruit and vegetables and take regular exercise. Three, change your sleep pattern, someone your age needs at least seven hours a night. Four," he said, and hesitated. Tony frowned.

"What?"

"Get out of that job." Lessing stood up to leave. "If you don't, it's going to kill you."

The door closed behind him, leaving Sinclair with the lonely sound of the monitor tracking his over-worked heart. That was when he noticed there were no get well cards on the bedside cabinet and suddenly understood his job had made him more of a loner than he'd realised.

When the door opened again he expected to see Lessing returning to issue another warning. Instead, Mark Houseman's face appeared. It was the only time Tony could remember ever being pleased to see him. "Hello buddy," he said, and fought an irrational urge to give the man a hug.

Houseman entered the room and took the seat Lessing had vacated. He ran his eyes over the monitor and tried unsuccessfully to look Tony in the face; his attention kept wandering back to the drip and the wires.

"How are you feeling?"

Sinclair gestured towards the monitor. "I've been better."

Houseman nodded understanding. Two sentences had passed between them and already the silence was uncomfortable. Then the question that begged an answer resurfaced in his mind.

"Mark, did William Marshall sign the contract?"

Houseman hesitated. His gaze slid to the corner of the room and stayed there. "He did."

The sonar beep sped and slowed, as if it were celebrating. Tony grinned. "That's great!"

His colleague didn't seem to share his enthusiasm; Houseman's fingers were twisting themselves into knots.

"Mark, what is it? There's something you're not telling me."

Houseman was still staring into the corner of the room, as if it was the most interesting place he'd ever seen.

"Rowena Dawson's taking over your client base."

"What!" For a moment the sonar sounded like an alarm call. Tony forced a deep breath and waited for it to settle. His colleague took advantage of the pause and squeezed words into the gap.

"Tony, I've been selected to pass on information. The management realise how ill you are and so have rescheduled your appointments. They're setting up a considerable compensation package so you'll have no worries on that score. I'm taking over Rowena's clients, which hopefully means the transition will go smoothly."

Sinclair was reeling. Houseman had been *selected,* not asked. Mark and Dawson were on first name terms, and Houseman's professional life had taken an upturn with the acquisition of the girl's portfolio. Everything was just rosy; for them. A bitter consolation thought came to mind.

"I bet the Dawson girl was upset when she discovered I won the Marshall contract and made salesman of the quarter."

Again Houseman couldn't look him in the eye.

"Well, that's not exactly true, Tony. Yesterday she clinched the Maddox deal. It's the biggest in the firm's history."

The monitor rate sped up but Tony didn't hear it. He was trying to take in the fact Dawson had won a deal he'd been trying unsuccessfully to get for years. Houseman was eyeing the heart monitor with alarm.

"Tony, I'm going to get help."

He rushed from the room and as the door slammed shut Sinclair felt tears roll down his cheeks. He should have been disgusted with himself but he was more worried by the fact the sonar beep wasn't slowing down.

REMEMBERING JACK

My name is James Henry Driscoll and my story is a confession. It concerns events that occurred in the days when the back-alleys of Whitechapel and Spitalfields were best avoided after dark.

Why tell it now? I'm old and the past lies heavily on my conscience, it's a burden I'm unwilling to take to the grave; besides, the others involved in that silent conspiracy are long since dead. I doubt they rest in peace; we're all as guilty as the murderer.

***

The East-End was then much as it is now, a place of over-crowded humanity, hard friendships, rough justice and an underbelly of society with a weakness for drink. Yet, I loved it. To walk those teeming streets was to experience life with all its earthy good-naturedness and lively danger. Then Jack the Ripper struck and the lanes and blind alleys became an invitation to a terrible death.

Two years as a member of her majesty's constabulary hadn't prepared me for my first sight of the Ripper's handiwork, I do believe nothing could. To this day I still see that poor lass walking through my nightmares. I knew her well, a good time girl who'd plied her trade on the streets of Whitechapel and been warned of her behaviour on a number of occasions. But what use are warnings? She made her living the way a lot of girls with little choice did, and I knew as soon as my back was turned she'd be on the streets again. Who knew then that her good times would end on the blade of a madman's knife?

A murdered prostitute wasn't an unusual occurrence in those harsh back lanes but the manner of her killing was; she'd been ripped open and sliced to pieces. It was as if her assailant had begun his attack and discovered he enjoyed it so much he couldn't stop.

For days fear and suspicion rose with the moon and hung like a death sentence in the shadows. No trace was found of the monster whose crime had become headline news, but someone walked in those dark places and he was soon to unleash a butcher's storm.

I wasn't working the day the next mutilated body was discovered and for that I'm eternally grateful. By then the East-End had become a place of haunted faces and backward glances. There was a killer on the loose, yet still the girls walked the streets and wore their painted smiles, as if lipstick and rouge were protection from the kiss of a scalpel.

***

I remember as if it were yesterday the September morning my life changed forever. Bad luck saw me on duty, covering for Tom Hillier, injured while attempting to break up a pub brawl. How different my future might have become had he been the one assigned the task that fell to me.

I was one of a number of officers called to Mitre Square in the early hours. Another street walker had been brutally murdered. I have no need to go into detail of what Jack stole from her body, it has since been well documented. The horror of that discovery was heightened by the shocking news she was his second victim of that blood-stained morning. Shortly after, I was ordered to Goulston Street where I became a victim myself.

I remember walking the deserted pavements and turning into a roadway sided by sprawling, run-down tenements. A figure stood silhouetted beneath a gas lamp. He was huddled into his overcoat, fighting a chill that had nothing to do with the weather.

As I approached I recognised him as Detective Inspector Moss. He looked up and then checked the street, as if he wanted to be certain we were alone.

"What's your name, constable?" he asked. I could hear tiredness in his voice, but also something else; looking back I think it was guilt. I answered and then he gestured towards a wall. Graffiti had been chalked across the brickwork, below it lay the remains of a blooded apron. "It seems our killer has been putting in overtime." His laugh was bitter and full of secrets.

I wasn't listening. My eyes had been drawn to the words so obviously scrawled in haste. He saw me staring.

"Wash it off, Driscoll," he said.

I looked at him in amazement. "But sir, there's a strong possibility this tells us who the murderer is."

He pulled out his pocket-watch and checked the time, as if he were eager to be away, then leant his face into mine. I could smell drink on his breath.

"Don't tell me my job, constable," he hissed, "Wash it off or I'll see that you're out of the force before this week ends. I decide what is and isn't evidence and I won't tolerate interference from a man who walks the beat." He was angry but I could also tell he was scared, why, I had no idea.

I tried to make sense of his command. Why on earth would a senior officer order me to wash away our only known link to the man calling himself Jack: the man proud enough of his dirty work to brag about it in a note sent to taunt those hunting him?

"Now do as I say," Moss barked, "or before you know it you'll be living in these slums."

He was right and we both knew it. How would a discredited police officer find work in this crowded city of half-starved families, where men fought each other for jobs paying a pittance?

When he looked at me he must have seen the confusion on my face. He smiled, and then patted me on the shoulder as if we were friends. "You're a good man Driscoll. We need men like you on the force."

He picked up the apron and then turned and walked away. As I listened to his footsteps fade into the night I rubbed a rag across a murderer's message and realised the future wasn't mine anymore.

***

The Juwes are the men That Will not be blamed for nothing.

That was the message Police Commissioner Sir Arthur Welby, claimed was written on a tenement wall that still builds itself in my dreams. He defended his decision to have the words erased by stating he feared they might incite anti-Semitic riots. Other darker reasons that couldn't be defended he kept to himself.

Nobody doubted the content of the message, why would they? But I knew the truth. So did Inspector Moss and a thin line of important people with reputations to protect.

The jury are the men that will not blame me.

Those were the real words. How clever it was of the Ripper's uncle to twist them into a racially motivated message and claim they were written by a semi-literate madman. Jack wasn't semi-literate; he was an educated man with a fondness for drink and a hatred of women; a young man who happened to be related to the most powerful police officer in the country. He was also insane.

Thirty-six-year-old William Bell was the man who murdered those women. I knew it and yet could do nothing. If the true message had been revealed his guilt would have become obvious to a lot of people, all of them policemen.

Three months earlier at just after midnight on a Sunday morning Bell had been dragged drunk and abusive into Whitechapel Police Station. He'd been caught beating a prostitute into unconsciousness, claiming the filthy whore deserved everything she got.

All those present heard the words he shouted.

"The jury are the men that will not blame me!"

In his drunken state Bell believed everybody held the same poisonous attitude towards women as he did. He was charged and thrown into the cells; at that point no-one knew of his connections but they soon became apparent.

The following midday he was a free man and the charge sheet destroyed. Word was passed down from above that we were to forget the incident. I was the one person who knew of the connection between his drunken boast and a written confession wiped from time.

I've lived with that secret for over forty years and it's followed me like a shadow. I've woken with it on my mind and slept with it in my dreams and it's stained my soul with shame.

***

Five weeks later in a run-down room off Dorset Street, Jack killed again. He took most of the girl's insides with him.

Newspaper headlines grew ever more hysterical. *'HE ISN'T GOING TO STOP!'* the press proclaimed, but they were wrong; he did. As the East-End shivered its way towards Christmas the Ripper's activities mysteriously ceased; a community that had been living on the edge of fear waited for another murder that never happened.

Had Sir Arthur's conscience finally told him it was time to act, or did he panic, worried that sooner or later his secret might be revealed? Whatever his motives, I believe William Bell was incarcerated, perhaps as a punishment or maybe in the hope his confinement might lead to a cure. Who knows, but by then it was too late. If Welby had imprisoned Bell after the double murder and the discovery of the incriminating message Jack would never have had the opportunity to kill again. His lack of action drew me into a conspiracy from which there was no way out.

I've often wondered what his reasons were for doing nothing. For years I suspected a misguided man had sheltered his damaged nephew in order to protect a reputation. It was only much later, in the early days of my retirement, that I learnt of rumours which led like stepping stones to an unproven truth.

Those rumours suggested a Masonic connection bound Welby and his nephew, as well as Inspector Moss and other influential men who thought themselves above the law: *A protective circle whose ancient traditions demanded they take care of their own even at the expense of truth and justice.*

How true were those insinuations? I washed a wall clean and listened to a drunken madman's accidental confession: any doubts I once harboured have vanished with the passing of time.

At some later date I believe that protective circle gave permission for Bell to be released. I also believe he murdered more girls; you only need to look at the reports of that time to see a list of victims who never gained the notoriety of those slain earlier. But he was clever, he'd curbed his appetites and refined his techniques; no blame ever travelled in his direction.

Then one day, soon after Sir Arthur Welby retired from office, William Bell disappeared from the face of the earth and the killing stopped. No doubt important men in high positions could have explained that disappearance. If only it had happened sooner.

The jury are the men that will not blame me.

I hope the judge I have yet to face is as lenient.

Author's note:
Although based on well-known factual events the names of the police commissioner and detective inspector have been altered for the sake of story-telling.

THE LATE ARRIVAL

"Can't you go any faster?"

The cabbie turned around and looked at him. His expression told Patterson he'd probably heard that question a thousand times.

"If I could, sir, I would." He put his hands back on the wheel and lapsed into a sullen silence.

Lewis Patterson stared out of the window and swore to himself, it was taking an age to get to the docks. He'd never seen so many people. They crammed the road and pavements and whatever accident had occurred up ahead was only making matters worse. He checked his pocket-watch and wished he'd left his apartment earlier. If it hadn't been for the unfortunate incident with Fisher he would have. It didn't even make him feel any better knowing Fisher was dead. The ship sailed at noon, if he wasn't on board he might well end up the same way. Maynard had traced him to Southampton and suddenly England wasn't big enough. He remembered Fisher's warning.

"Didn't think we'd find you, did you? Mr Maynard wants his money. If you don't pay up now you're going to be in a lot of trouble."

Fisher was red-faced and overweight, a big man who loved making threats. It boosted his self-esteem and gave him a false perspective of his own importance. Patterson laughed at him.

"You're a weasel Fisher. Get out of here and tell Maynard it's my money, not his."

Fisher bridled at the insult and pulled a cosh from beneath his jacket.

"Weasel, am I? You've become too big for your boots, Patterson." He raised his arm and took a step closer. "I've been waiting to do this for a long time."

Patterson moved backwards and realised Fisher wasn't going to stop with words of warning, he wanted to kill him. As he swung the cosh Patterson ducked and felt the blow brush the side of his head. Fisher lunged again. Patterson grabbed his wrist and twisted his arm in the opposite direction. They stood locked together, each of them straining to force the other off-balance. Fisher's eyes suddenly clouded. He dropped the cosh and clutched at his chest; as he fell backwards Patterson landed on top of him.

"Fisher?" His assailant didn't move. Patterson felt for a pulse and realised the big man wouldn't be making any more threats.

He got to his feet and dragged the body to a chair. When he placed Fisher in an upright position it looked as if he were asleep. Patterson hoped the effect would convince whoever discovered the body that the big man had died alone. He picked up the cosh and realised Maynard was serious, his accomplice wouldn't have acted that way unless ordered. It appeared he was leaving the country just in time.

He was already behind schedule when he climbed into the cab. As it crawled towards the docks his mind went back to the beginning of a partnership that had quickly soured.

He'd met Lionel Maynard through a friend of a friend: discreet enquiries, guarded answers; the way he often made business contacts in his line of work. The diamond necklace he'd wanted moving on had belonged to a duchess and was priceless. He doubted she'd even realised it was missing; the expensive copy he'd left in its place had been an exact replica. And that was how he worked, charm his way into wealthy company, decide what to steal and then replace it with a lookalike. It was a faultless operation.

Maynard had sold the jewels for a sum exceeding Patterson's expectations and gradually won his trust. Then he'd suggested a partnership: he'd sell whatever Patterson supplied. It had been a good idea; some of the valuables he stole were so instantly recognisable they were hard to shift. A professional fence would be the ideal solution. He agreed to the proposal.

At first, things ran smoothly. Money and valuables changed hands, business boomed.

Maynard proposed they set up a joint business account. *"To make our activities appear legal,"* he said. Again it had been another good idea. Fake invoices were printed for imaginary goods and their rapidly expanding bank balance took on a veneer of respectability. But then Maynard became greedy.

It took Patterson a while to realise the funds in the account were slowly being drained. Not large amounts, just small, steady drips that at first glance weren't noticeable. It was only when he added them all up that he realised his partner was siphoning away a lot of money.

He decided to confront him but then changed his mind. Maynard was a volatile character with a penchant for violence. Patterson had heard about the justice he'd dispensed to two men he'd discovered skimming profits from one of his other operations. Their bodies had been found floating in the Thames. No, there was another way. He smiled. It was time to dispense his own brand of justice.

***

The tiara was a magnificent fake. It fooled Maynard; his eyes glittered with greed when he saw it. Patterson told him he needed cash up-front, there were a number of people he needed to pay for services rendered. His partner fell for the lie; his contacts would be more than willing to forward the amount on his say-so. Patterson was suddenly the recipient of an enormous amount of money. Then he withdrew half of the funds from the account. It was time to disappear.

America seemed like a wonderful opportunity. A man with money could do well in that country. His one mistake had been staying too long in England; if Fisher had found him Maynard couldn't be far behind.

***

The driver pulled up and took the luggage from the boot. The quayside was crowded with well-wishers and sightseers and to Patterson's horror he saw the gangways had been retracted. He paid the cabbie, found a porter to look after his luggage and struggled through the throng to the booking office.

The clerk looked at him from behind his desk. "Can I help you, sir?" he said.

The ship's siren sounded. Through the window Patterson could see passengers waving from the decks.

"Is there any way you can get me aboard that ship? My cabin's booked and I've paid my passage." Even as he spoke he realised he was too late. The clerk was professionally sympathetic.

"I'm sorry sir, she's already cast-off."

Patterson cursed and slumped into a chair. Outside, he could hear people cheering. He wondered if Maynard was in Southampton yet. The clerk stood up, walked around the desk and placed a hand on Patterson's shoulder. When he spoke his voice had lost its official tone.

"Don't worry sir, I can understand your disappointment but we'll get you on another ship."

Patterson suddenly realised that might not be a bad thing. Maynard would assume he'd already sailed, if he kept his head down until the company found him an alternative berth there'd be no trail to follow. He smiled and glanced at the calendar hanging behind the desk, little knowing it was a date he'd never forget.

Through the window he could see the Titanic sailing into the horizon.

HAVEN REST

On a rain swept November evening, a fortnight before Haven Rest was officially due to open; Adam Hooper left the site after meeting late with his colleague, Neil Furlong. The unlit roads were wet and dark. Clouds had covered the moon. Somewhere along those deserted lanes Hooper lost control of his car. The crash had been fatal.

***

"Although you probably read the details in the brochure I'd like to reiterate the fact we don't accept children." Neil Furlong smiled; a tight expression that thinned his lips and concealed his teeth.

The salesman was tall with the build of an ex-rugby player. He leaned back in his chair and folded his arms, as if he expected his statement to be challenged. Behind him an image of Haven Rest stretched from wall to wall and floor to ceiling. The aerial view looked down on a development of up-market lodge homes. The gated site was bordered by woodland that ran into the distance. To the rear, beyond the boundary fence, was a lake. It looked as if the surface had been polished blue and reflections painted on later. The strategic angle of the camera shot made the development look larger than it truly was. Furlong had supervised the shoot himself.

Simon and Patricia Ruddock had no intention of challenging Furlong, from the moment they'd viewed the Haven Rest video they'd known their search for a new home had come to an end. The fact children weren't accepted was an added bonus.

"It's wonderful." Patricia Ruddock's hands were clasped prayer-like against her mouth. Her husband grinned in silent agreement.

Neil Furlong smiled and unfolded the barricade of his arms. "Please excuse my defensive manner," he said. "We've had a couple of adverse reports from journalists who don't seem to appreciate what we've achieved here. They claim Haven Rest is a development without a soul." He licked his lips, as if the words left a bad taste in his mouth. "As founder of this project I tend to take criticism to heart."

The Ruddock's nodded their heads in a sympathetic gesture of support.

Furlong pushed back his chair and stood up. "Let me give you the guided tour," he said. "You can have a good look around the property and get a feel of the place." He beamed at them. "You're lucky. We don't often get homes coming up for sale. Believe me, you won't be disappointed."

Neil Furlong knew he wouldn't have to hard sell Haven Rest to the Ruddock's; the location sold itself and their eagerness to buy was transparent: he was preaching to the converted. Miles and Rosemary Sutton had been the only couple who'd needed his persuasive charm to edge them into a purchase otherwise his sales patter had become a redundant side-line. But now the Sutton's were dead and the home he'd talked the old couple into buying was up for sale. The Ruddock's were unaware of its history; Furlong was certain they'd like it; the Sutton's had.

Simon and Patricia Ruddock's inability to produce offspring had left them with a deep-rooted mistrust of those who could and an aversion to the thing they'd once wanted most: children. The solitude of Haven Rest was an opportunity for them to leave that mistrust and aversion behind. They held hands as Furlong ushered them through the office door, a couple attempting to defy the disappointment of the past as the unknown territory of old-age beckoned.

"As you can see it has its own veranda and patio area."

Furlong was pointing in the direction of the nearest building. "There are only twenty-five lodges here," he said, "so there's plenty of room for everybody." He looked at the Ruddock's. "It's an exclusive location, that's one of the reasons why it's so expensive." He nodded towards the lake. The white hull of a sailboat was just visible through the trees. "Do you own a boat?" he asked.

Patricia shook her head. When Simon Ruddock explained that most of their budget would be swallowed up on the property, Furlong grinned.

"I may be able to help you there, then" he said. "Miles and Rosemary Sutton, the couple who used to live here, asked me if I might be able to sell the Sunray for them." He winked at Patricia. "It's on offer at a ridiculously low price."

Simon Ruddock looked surprised. "Didn't they want to keep it?"

Neil Furlong's sympathetic expression was partnered with a shake of his head. "They did," he said, "but unfortunately circumstances beyond their control meant they couldn't."

The Ruddock's glanced at each other; the agent's meaning was clear. Furlong had been professionally tactful, he didn't want to spell out the fact some kind of financial difficulty had led to the Sutton's having to leave their boat as well as their house behind.

"Still," Furlong continued, "their loss could be your gain."

Simon Ruddock squeezed his wife's hand; things were getting better and better.

When Furlong stopped abruptly the couple almost walked into him. He turned to them; a serious look had replaced the one of sympathy. "There is one problem though," he said.

"What's that?" Patricia asked; she'd had a feeling this was all too good to be true.

Furlong hesitated and then smiled. "If you do buy the Sunray I insist you treat me to a free trip around the lake." His laughter was infectious. "It's a perk of the job!"

The sound of their good humour carried across the site. Furlong led them along the pathway, remembering another trip he'd taken around the lake; a voyage from which the Sutton's hadn't returned.

Patricia was still laughing as Furlong unlocked the door of the property they hoped would soon be theirs, unaware of how right she'd been: it was all too good to be true.

The inside of the lodge was bathed in sunlight. Carefully positioned windows boasted views of either the lake or woodland. Beyond the lounge, patio doors opened onto a decking area.

"It's beautiful." Patricia gazed out at the water and watched a heron rise lazily from the branches of a distant tree.

Furlong smiled. "I can honestly say there isn't one resident here who would argue with you."

"What kind of age group does a place like this attract?" Simon Ruddock had taken off his jacket, as if he couldn't wait to make himself at home. Again Furlong smiled.

"As a rule our clients tend to be in the older age bracket; those who either don't have children or whose offspring have flown the nest. Sixty upwards is the average." He pointed to a lodge situated in the shade of a cluster of beech trees. "The Whiteheads live over there, and they're in their mid-eighties. They've been here for three years and they told me there's nowhere else they'd rather end their days!" He laughed. "You can't get a better recommendation than that."

"So Haven Rest is a retirement complex?"

Furlong frowned at Simon Ruddock's suggestion and adopted a serious manner.

"To me the word retirement, brings to mind the end of something," he said. He gestured towards the lake. "I prefer to think of Haven Rest as a beginning, another chapter of people's lives waiting to unfold in these blissful surroundings." His self-satisfied smile became dreamy. "That was one of the reasons I built it."

There were other reasons, but he couldn't possibly tell the Ruddock's those.

Furlong and his business partner, Adam Hooper, had been responsible for the creation of Haven Rest. Furlong had scouted the location, drawn up plans, cherry-picked the workforce and generally worked his backside off making sure the construction of such an expensive undertaking ran smoothly.

Hooper's sole contribution had been the one that made the whole project possible; he'd financed it, and with that influx of capital came a demand he receive the lion's share of future profits. *'After all,'* he reasoned, *'without my money there would be no Haven Rest.'*

Furlong's unspoken opinion was that his partner was a greedy bastard intent on making money off the back of someone else's hard graft, namely his, but Hooper had him over a barrel and they both knew it. The contract he reluctantly signed stipulated earnings to be split sixty-forty in Hooper's favour.

And that would have been the case if it hadn't been for his partner's unfortunate accident. Police came to the conclusion heavy rain and poor visibility were the reasons Hooper skidded off the road and ploughed into a flooded ravine. Only Furlong knew better.

As a mark of respect to his late partner Neil delayed the opening of the complex until after the funeral. As he watched the coffin being lowered into the ground, he was amazed to feel tears running down his face. He wiped his eyes and thought of the way death can rob one man of a lion's share and yet gift another everything.

As the Ruddock's made their way out onto the veranda their excited chatter brought a grin to Furlong's face. He decided to talk about the clause in their contract as soon as they were back in the office; the clause he hadn't yet mentioned.

"Come and meet your neighbours," he said, and pointed through the trees. "It'll take us a few minutes to get there. That's part of the beauty of this development; everybody's got their own space."

Ted and Barbara Chambers answered their door together, as if they were a double act and had been rehearsing the moment. Their matching smiles and toned bodies bore tribute to the advantages of private dentistry and flirtations with plastic surgery. Ted and Barbara were in their early-sixties, still vainly pursuing their long lost youth. They greeted Furlong as if he were an old friend.

"Neil!" Barbara Chambers air-kissed her way around their visitor. "How lovely to see you."

Her husband bear-hugged Furlong and then his gaze fell on the Ruddock's. "And who have we here?"

Neil Furlong pulled himself free and made the introductions.

A short while later they were seated on the Chamber's veranda, sipping wine and admiring the view as the Ruddock's listened to Ted and Barbara shower praise on Haven Rest. Furlong gazed into his glass and let their words wash over him; he was silently working out how he was going to kill them.

The Chambers might have looked artificially healthy but Furlong happened to know Ted's pacemaker wasn't doing what it was meant to. Consequently, his heart wasn't either, and the pills he was taking to combat the problem were known to cause various side effects. Furlong had seen a medical report that should have been confidential.

To make matters worse, Ted's wife had problems of her own. She was drinking far too heavily; a lifetime's habit had become a necessity. There was a lake nearby. Who knew, one evening she might wander out drunk and accidentally slip into deep water? What if her husband was incapacitated at that very moment, struggling for breath as her cries for help went unheard? It was an interesting scenario, and one that could so easily occur; especially if Ted had been unable to find his pills.

He tuned back into the conversation to hear Patricia saying she just *had* to live here. He grinned to himself. The Ruddock's were a little younger than most of the other residents, a fact that had initially deterred him from interviewing the couple. But then he'd realised he wasn't looking at the big picture: they were an investment; an accident waiting to happen. In this business he'd learnt it was sensible to have something to fall back on.

Ted and Barbara stood on their veranda, arms linked, and waved them goodbye. As Furlong led the Ruddock's back to his office his mind returned to Miles and Rosemary Sutton.

They'd been the ideal couple; old, childless and with few friends. Any relatives who might have become suspicious at their untimely deaths were long gone. Their health had also been suspect, but that was no surprise, people grew old and became ill; it was the natural way of things. Why let them suffer? Not so long ago he'd made the decision that if he could hurry along their passing then surely he was only doing what a vet might do to a sick animal. Of course, a vet was rewarded for his expertise, surely, Furlong reasoned, he was entitled to the same benefits?

Old people needed someone to rely on, somebody they could trust; it was an opening Neil Furlong was made for. He found honesty and discretion easy to fake; after all he was a salesman; a salesman with inside knowledge.

The residents of Haven Rest were unaware that every detail kept on their computers was illegally monitored and stored on his own. The discreet payment he'd made to the engineer who set up the system had been lost in expenses. Ever since the site opened he'd had a fool proof way of keeping track of things that had nothing to do with him. Now he knew everything: business transactions; bank account information, health records, a long list that included personal trivia certain residents might hope never saw the light of day.

For instance: Barbara Chambers was having sex with one of the grounds men employed to look after Haven Rest. Furlong had intercepted explicit emails and then secretly filmed the boy who was young enough to be her son doing things to Barbara her husband was probably no longer capable of. Furlong had been amazed at how a woman of her age could be so athletic and keep going for so long. He also wondered how Ted's heart would cope with the news.

Then there was Len and Colleen Bartlett. They lived like hermits in the lodge nearest the lake; a couple who rarely went out and kept themselves to themselves. Furlong couldn't remember once seeing them out walking, but that didn't surprise him, they hid secrets that could ruin them.

Len had once run his own insurance company. Colleen had been his secretary. It had been a perfect set-up for the couple to sell over-priced policies to people who had no idea that the agreements they'd signed were worthless. When they did find out it was too late.

The Bartlett's had left a lot of unhappy customers in their wake, but Len and Colleen had been clever; they'd covered their tracks and pleaded innocence. Now they'd retired to Haven Rest with their ill-gotten nest-egg.

Unfortunately, they hadn't been clever enough. Furlong was in possession of certain documents, copied illegally, that proved beyond doubt the Bartlett's were guilty of serious fraud. Sooner or later he was going to use that information or be well paid not to. It was a win-win situation.

Furlong smiled to himself as he led Simon and Patricia into his office; it was time to bring up the matter of a significant clause. This was always the moment where he'd know how badly his prospective customers wanted the property. It was also when his well-practised sales-patter normally made them see the sense of donating part of any future selling fee to Haven Rest Holdings.

"Twenty-percent?" For the first time that day Simon Ruddock's smile faltered. "Isn't that a lot higher than the average? I thought ten-percent was the norm?"

Furlong laughed, as if *'ten-percent'* was the funniest line he'd ever heard. "There's a lot more to take into consideration, here," he said, and laughed again.

The Ruddock's didn't seem to appreciate the humour of the situation. Patricia looked close to tears. Neil stopped laughing and became sincere; it wasn't hard, he'd rehearsed the emotion. He leaned towards them in a confidential manner, his body language suggesting this was more than a business transaction, this was a lifestyle choice, and that's all he was there for, to give them that choice.

"Look," he said. "I'm not going to beat about the bush. I'm up-front with all my clients." He nodded towards the window. "Ask anybody who lives here. I've had this very same conversation with them and often got the same reaction. I can understand that, but as I told them, this is an exclusive development, probably the only one of its kind. It's taken a lot of investment, investment that to this day continues to pour in." The lie slid off his tongue with practised ease. "There needs to be a balance," he added. "That's where that twenty-percent comes in."

He paused and then looked each of them in the eye. "I want the best for my clients," he said, and rested his hand on the corner of the desk as if he had a confession to make. "If that means charging slightly above the average, so be it, I'm not prepared to let standards drop!"

Patricia Ruddock's expression betrayed her. She'd mentally accepted the fact they'd lose twenty-per-cent when they came to selling their home and didn't care. Her husband hadn't and did.

"But surely ground-rent and maintenance fees cover any cost incurred in keeping Haven Rest up to standard?"

Furlong saw Patricia glance at her husband and noticed a faint scowl form on her lips. He smiled at Simon Ruddock and wondered if the man suffered from any health-related issues. He also wondered if Ruddock could swim; it was a deep lake.

"If only that were the case," he sighed, and reached for a folder conveniently positioned on the desk. "Let me show you something."

He pulled out a sheaf of papers and spread them across the work surface. "I know this may seem inappropriate," he said, "but I'd like to show you these." His tone became confidential. "The details are personal so I'd appreciate it if the information went no further than this office."

Ruddock suddenly looked embarrassed, as if he realised he'd pushed Furlong into a situation that needn't have arisen. His wife's scowl grew darker.

"These are bills and invoices related to Haven Rest. I won't bore you with all the unnecessary details, but as you can see I'm working on a narrow profit margin. The only way I can keep Haven Rest operating as a viable concern is to ensure sufficient funds come in at the end of a client's tenure."

Simon Ruddock scanned the paperwork. The facts and figures told their own story; the development was making money, but only just. What he didn't know was that none of the accounts he held were genuine. Furlong had drawn up false papers a long time ago especially for moments like this. Patricia refused to look.

"Mr Furlong," she said. "That's your business; it has nothing to do with us, and I for one am perfectly happy to accept your terms." She stared coldly at her husband. "What about you, Simon?"

His nervous cough signalled a climb down.

"Well, it does seem a large amount to lose, but I can see why it has to be done."

Neil Furlong held out his hands. "It's perfectly legal," he said, which was one of the few statements he'd made that day that wasn't a lie. The contract *was* perfectly legal, but weighted so heavily in favour of Haven Rest Holdings that any impartial lawyer would have advised them against signing it.

The Ruddock's didn't have an impartial lawyer, and even if they had Patricia wouldn't have listened to him. Haven Rest was soon to be their home and nothing was going to spoil that. Which was exactly what the Sutton's had thought.

Furlong waved the Ruddock's goodbye and locked up his office. Hands had been shaken and agreements made. They could move in almost immediately; a fortnight from now Haven Rest would be welcoming its latest residents.

Showing them around the lodge had brought back memories of another couple. As he climbed into his car, his mind went back to the Sutton's and a rainy night his journey from businessman to killer had begun.

The late Adam Hooper had been too greedy for his own good, and the bitter prospect of profit unfairly shared had led Furlong to take action. He remembered stepping out of the trees bordering the hairpin bend and aiming the spotlight into the windscreen of Hooper's car. His partner hadn't stood a chance.

Ever since that fateful evening Furlong had come to realise there were all kinds of accidents, and if properly arranged those accidents might benefit him immensely. He'd also come to the conclusion he'd misjudged his dead partner. Greed wasn't a bad thing; which had led him onto the Sutton's; an old couple with too much money and a limited amount of time in which to spend it. How limited they'd had no idea.

He'd glossed over the facts when explaining to the Ruddock's why the Sutton's home had come on the market. He'd had a feeling the truth might have put them off buying the property. He decided he'd explain it all at a later date, after they were well and truly settled in.

Their deaths had been the result of another tragic accident. Rosemary had slipped overboard as they sailed the Sunray across the lake; something Furlong had warned them against in view of the breaking bad weather. Miles had drowned in a valiant but doomed attempt to save his wife.

'Why didn't they listen to me?' he'd tearfully asked the police, before testifying they were a lovely old couple but like most people of that age, very stubborn. *'Perhaps that was the reason they hadn't worn life-jackets,'* he'd suggested.

What he hadn't told them and they'd never discovered, was that he'd persuaded the Sutton's to make that trip. Not only that, he'd also been on board. Rosemary hadn't slipped, she'd been pushed. Her husband's attempts to get her back to the boat had been hindered by the fact Furlong hadn't let him.

He remembered the old man's disbelieving stare as he steered the Sunray further out of reach. Sutton's faint cries for help had gone unheard. Furlong had watched as the old man tried to support his wife while the chill water froze what little resistance he had from his body.

It hadn't taken them long to disappear beneath the surface of Haven Lake.

The life-jackets that might have saved their lives were still locked away in an office drawer. Neil made a mental note to return them to the Sunray as soon as possible

The publicity the accident attracted was minimal; an old couple attempting to defy their years by sailing into a storm. *'They should have known better,'* had been the general consensus, which in Furlong's view was an insensitive and unsympathetic judgement. It was a view gilded by the acquisition of twenty-percent, a sailboat and an illicit transfer of a large amount of money: all in all not a bad return for a damp afternoon's work.

***

Neil was there to greet Simon and Patricia on the day they moved in. After the removal van had left and he'd helped them settle he went to the fridge.

"What have we here?" he asked, in mock surprise, and pulled out a magnum of champagne.

Simon and Patricia laughed as he corked the bottle and handed out glasses.

"Here's to many happy years at Haven Rest!" he offered, and grinned as he realised it was the same toast he'd made to Miles and Rosemary Sutton. The

Ruddock's smiled at each other, their disagreement over twenty-percent long forgotten. They drank to the sentiment and Furlong refilled their glasses.

He left the Ruddock's lodge an hour later in good humour. He'd allowed the husband to beat him down on the price of the Sunray, and why not, he could afford to be magnanimous; he was still making a lot of money. Now he was looking forward to getting back to the office and monitoring their internet traffic, certain that anything he might have lost in the transaction could be more than recompensed in the near future.

As he left the private walkway he saw a car parked outside the gates. A man was leaning against the bonnet. When he caught sight of Furlong he waved.

Neil walked over. "Can I help you?" he asked. "If you're looking to buy I'm afraid you'll have to go on the mailing list. This is a popular development."

The man told him he wasn't looking to buy. His name was Gary Dawes. He was an insurance investigator and what he *was* looking for was a chat with a certain Mr Neil Furlong. Could he come in?

The good humour drained from Furlong, disguised by the same smile that thinned lips and concealed teeth. He opened the gates, shook hands and led Gary Dawes into his office.

"This looks like a wonderful place." The investigator was examining the blow-up photo of Haven Rest. Furlong glanced at his watch and offered the man a seat.

"It is," he said. "Now, how can I help?"

Dawes sighed, as if he already knew he was wasting Furlong's time, and pulled a photo from his jacket pocket. He laid it on the desk. "Do you recognise this couple?"

Furlong picked up the snapshot and stared into the faces of two of his residents. They'd aged considerably since the picture had been taken.

"Why, yes," he said. "That's Len and Colleen Bartlett. They own the lodge nearest the lake."

Dawes shook his head and took back the photograph. "Those aren't their real names," he said, "but I'll explain that later. How long have they lived here?"

Furlong was shocked but his good humour was edging its way back. He'd initially suspected Dawes might be snooping around for details of the Sutton's deaths. He was relieved that wasn't the case. "Just over two years," he said. "May I ask what this is about?"

Gary Dawes leaned back in his chair; Furlong noticed how tired he looked.

"Their company sold a number of dud policies to clients of mine," he said. "It cost them a lot of money. I was hired to gather proof of fraud and build a case against them. Unfortunately, it's taken longer than we all expected. To make matters worse the couple I was representing died in an accident."

He looked at Furlong and leaned forward; his smile was grim. "Of course, you knew them," he said. "They lived here."

He pulled out another photo and handed it to Furlong. Neil felt the colour drain from his face. Miles and Rosemary Sutton stared accusingly into the camera. The picture slipped from his grasp; his fingers were shaking.

Dawes picked it up. "I'm sorry," he said, "I didn't mean to upset you."

Furlong didn't hear him; his mind was working its way back through the times he'd trawled through the Sutton's accounts. He couldn't recall ever coming across any insurance details under the name of Bartlett and suddenly realised why; Bartlett wasn't their real name.

"Mr Furlong, Are you okay?" Gary Dawes saw how the news had affected Furlong and guessed how close Haven Rest's owner must have been to the old couple. The investigator's question dragged Neil back to the present.

"I'm fine," he said. "It's just a lot to take in. Are you trying to tell me the couple who ripped Miles and Rosemary off lived here as well, less than half-a-mile away from their victims?"

Dawes nodded. "The Sutton's didn't even realise," he said. "I can't believe they never ran into each other."

Furlong could. It was clear now why the Bartlett's, or whatever their name was, had shunned any kind of social activity. Their lodge was situated on the edge of the development and closest to the lake. A natural screen of trees and bushes offered a privacy some of the other homes lacked. He wondered how many hours they'd spent peering from behind half-closed curtains, worrying away their old age in the fear their bolt-hole might be discovered. They must have been petrified when they discovered who their neighbours were.

"Neither can I," he said, and shook his head in a gesture of deliberate bewilderment.

"They're crafty, though." Dawes had taken the photo back out of his pocket. He gazed at it with distaste. "If they wanted to stay hidden they would. Look how long it's taken me to find them."

"That's not your fault." Furlong had relaxed. He was thinking of the twenty-percent coming his way when the

Bartlett's were forced to swap their lodge for prison cells. "But why are you still on the case?" he asked. "With Miles and Rosemary gone, what's the point?"

Gary Dawes was still staring at the picture. Neil thought there was something unnerving in that gaze; he looked like a dog refusing to surrender a bone.

"They paid me to do a job and I'm going to see it through," the investigator explained. "Besides," he said, "I'm working on a theory."

"What theory is that?" Furlong asked.

Dawes leaned in closer and dropped his voice.

"I know you believe the two couples were unaware of each other's presence, but I'm not so sure," he said. "I suspect the Bartlett's might have known about the Sutton's."

Neil thought of reclusive residents and half-closed curtains. Dawes was right and this was getting interesting. The investigator continued.

"Not only that," he said. "I think they knew if Miles and Rosemary discovered who their neighbours were then they'd blow the whistle." He looked at Furlong. "That's why they killed them."

Neil suppressed a smile. "But the Sutton's deaths were an accident," he said.

Again Dawes shook his head.

"I don't think so. Why would an old couple like that take their boat out into a storm?"

Furlong could have answered that question but chose not to. He feigned ignorance. "I don't know."

Dawes did, or at least thought so.

"Well, I do. They were forced out there, and once far enough away from land Len and Colleen made sure they never came back." He paused. "I'm certain of it, I just need proof."

A mental image of two bright yellow life-jackets lying in a locked drawer drifted into Neil's mind. That was when he realised he might be able to help Dawes find that proof.

Furlong watched from his office as the couple he'd come to know as Len and Colleen Bartlett were ushered handcuffed into the back of a police van. Hours earlier officers had surrounded their lodge after Gary Dawes had called and told them of what he'd found buried behind the Bartlett's home. Once he'd explained who he was and what he was investigating they'd arrived in minutes.

Furlong grinned as he remembered the conversation he'd had with Dawes the day before. His suggestion that the investigator take a look around the place under cover of darkness had given him time to conceal the life-jackets where he knew they'd be discovered.

The old couple had denied any knowledge of the jackets or the murders. *'But they would, wouldn't they?'* Dawes had said; a statement that silenced the Bartlett's and drew knowing looks from the assembled force.

As the police convoy drove away from Haven Rest, Gary Dawes made his way back to the office. He shook Furlong's hand.

"I have to go to the station now," he said, "but I just wanted to say thanks. Without your help that wouldn't have been possible."

Neil smiled. Dawes didn't know how right he was.

* * *

Furlong passed Barbara Chambers another drink. She'd already had too many; twice she'd left her hand on his thigh when her husband had left the room. Now Ted was asleep and Barbara's fingers were exploring further.

Earlier her husband had seemed to be having breathing difficulties. He'd been unable to find his pills and his inhaler hadn't helped. Furlong knew why; he'd hidden the tablets and replaced the medicinal spray with water. When Ted had slumped into an armchair Barbara had mumbled something about how some people couldn't handle their drink. Neil had laughed: soon Ted wouldn't be capable of handling anything. Now he had to get her out of the house before her husband stopped breathing.

"Shall we take a walk beside the lake?" he whispered. "We can bring this with us." He picked up an almost full bottle of wine and pressed it to her mouth. Barbara sucked at the neck greedily. Wine ran down her chin and into the furrow that lay between surgically enhanced breasts. She was wearing a blouse meant for someone thirty years younger. Furlong forced himself to lick her throat; she moaned with pleasure. "Let's take that walk," he said, and helped her up.

"You're so strong," she slurred, and ran a hand over his backside.

By the time they reached the lake the bottle was almost empty and Barbara Chambers was drunkenly groping him. He steered her closer to the water. Fifty yards away the Sunray lay moored in the darkness.

"Isn't it a beautiful evening?" he said, and pushed her backwards. She hit the water at the same moment a torch beam blinded him.

"Is that you, Neil?" It was Simon Ruddock's voice. Furlong could see him standing on the deck of the boat. Then he saw Ruddock's wife; she was pulling on clothing. He momentarily pictured the romantic interlude that had been taking place on the vessel they'd recently purchased. Barbara Chambers surfaced and began screaming.

"Oh my God," Patricia cried, "there's someone in the water!"

That was when Neil heard undergrowth being flattened and saw Ted Chambers lumbering towards him. "I found my pills!" he shouted, and pointed at Furlong. "That bastard hid them!"

Barbara was still screaming. Furlong was just considering the idea of diving in to save her and then possibly trying to talk his way out of the mess when he saw the flashing blue light of a police car. It pulled up next to the fence. Gary Dawes climbed out followed by the Bartlett's and two officers. One of them was holding the life-jackets. Neil realised his idea wasn't going to work.

He took a deep breath and jumped in anyway.

SMOKE AND MIRRORS

On the evening I was due to leave London Town I gazed from my apartment window and watched the dying sun silhouette Tower Bridge. It transformed the river into a snakeskin of burning amber, throwing into shadow the towers and spires that broke the horizon. Even then, as I climbed into the horse drawn cab that would take me to the station I felt a sense of foreboding I couldn't shake off.

How many charlatans and tricksters had I exposed up to that point? More than I could remember. All of them fakes, the only difference between them being that some were more sophisticated than others. And yet as I sat back in the shadows of the cab I had an unexplainable feeling that this time might be different. Perhaps the words I'd first read two days earlier had some bearing on my mental state.

The letter had arrived early morning, a handwritten plea for help. Mrs. Dawson, my housekeeper, had left the envelope on my breakfast tray. Picking it up I noticed it carried a Sussex post mark. I remember as I read, the sounds from the river seemed to diminish, almost as if a thick fog had layered itself over the waterway. The shouts of the tugboat men slipped into whispers, the blast of a steamer's horn turning into nothing more than a distant echo. It was as if my room had closed in on me and the rest of the world had slipped away.

Josephine Grant
Haywood Manor
Lowford

Sussex

Dear Sir,
Please excuse this intrusion into your privacy but I have reached a point of desperation. I know of your work and I am praying you may be able to assist me in dealing with a matter that is not only both mysterious and frightening, but also I fear life threatening.

My husband and I, along with our two children, moved into Haywood Manor just over three months ago. Shortly afterwards he sailed for India where he is engaged in the business of trade and will not be returning for a further three months. (Perhaps if he were here now this message might not be necessary.) Now to the reason for my letter.

Since my husband left, this beautiful old house has changed beyond all recognition. I no longer feel safe here, a situation made worse by the terrifying events that now seem to occur on a nightly basis, each one more frightening and hostile than the last. It is impossible to go into detail about these happenings, mere words cannot convey the horrors I and my children have been experiencing.

I know of your reputation as an honest and decent man, one who has solved many strange cases, and I believe you are my last hope.

I fear for my sanity and the lives of my children. I beg for your help and would be forever in your debt if you would grant me that assistance.

I pray to hear from you soon,
Josephine Grant.

In all my years of investigating what others might call the paranormal I had never received such a desperate letter. How could I refuse this woman's pleas?

Sitting at my desk by the window the sounds from the river gradually filtered their way back into the room. I sent a telegram that morning. I would be in Sussex by Thursday.

***

The children were asleep, now they lay in her bed, a look of exhaustion ingrained on their faces. Rising from the chair she walked to the mirror and stared into her tired reflection. The constant tension and sleepless nights of the last three weeks had worn her down.

The silence was broken by the landing clock striking twelve. From the hallway beyond the door Josephine Grant heard the sound of footsteps. Two sets pacing slowly along the corridor, stopping now and then, as if whoever walked there was searching for something. It was starting again. The cry that threatened to escape her lips silenced itself as her eyes fixed on the door handle that began to slowly turn.

***

I watched the darkening landscape rush by, a jumble of silhouette and shadow broken by the occasional glow of a distant light. The rhythm of the speeding train served to relax me and as I unintentionally let my guard down thoughts I'd kept at bay for a long time slipped treacherously into my head.

"I'm sorry Mr Crozier there was nothing more we could do."

The doctor's words fell like stones. For seconds nothing seemed to register. My mind felt as if it had been wiped clean of any emotion, a blank canvas where even insanity might be welcome. The midwife guided me to a chair but I neither felt her arm on mine nor heard the words she said.

My wife, my lovely Ilene, had died in labour, our baby son stillborn. All I could think of were the wonderful months leading up to that terrible moment. The happiness and excitement that had infected the two of us, the plans we'd made and the dreams we'd nurtured. And now the woman I loved was gone, along with the little boy I'd never see.

The months that followed were dark ones indeed.

Grief can hang like a millstone, poisoning your thoughts and taking your mind to places where no sun has ever shone. I do believe for a while I was on the edge of madness. I never want to visit that place again. I still remember the moment purpose returned to my life, little realising the direction it would lead me.

It was a warm June morning, a day for lovers. Blossom hung from the trees, the river shone and overhead the sky was cloudless. I saw none of it then, only the passage of time has opened my eyes to the beauty of the past.

I'd sold my house and bought an apartment close to the river. I wanted to be surrounded by people, stupidly believing I might be able to lose myself and my loneliness by being part of that crowded city.

I saw the advertisement as I sat on a bench on the embankment, idly flicking through the pages of a newspaper I wasn't going to read. My eyes were drawn to the words that would shape my future.

Barry John Watson

HAVE YOU LOST A LOVED ONE RECENTLY?
LET NATASHA MILVERN HELP YOU THROUGH
YOUR LOSS
Miss Milvern, respected psychic, will be conducting a spiritualist
evening at Cloverley *Hall on the 21ˢᵗ of June from 8pm onwards.*
The after-life awaits us all.

I knew of Cloverley Hall. It was a theatre two miles west of my apartment. I briefly wondered why a psychic would be appearing in a building normally home to the acting fraternity. Little did I realise then that by the time the evening finished I'd have reached the conclusion there was no difference between her profession and theirs.

My grief was still raw, I must have read those lines a dozen times but my eyes were continually drawn to the same sentence. *Let Natasha Milvern help you through your loss.* I decided to visit Cloverley Hall. I think I was clutching at straws.

The evening was warm, the streets crowded with people eagerly making the most of the fine weather. I took a cab part of the way and finished my journey on foot, enjoying being part of that bustling throng. I do believe then that I thought I could discard my grief; how foolish I was. I joined the line of people awaiting entry and as we filed into the theatre the good-natured banter that had developed amongst us gradually stilled. It was as if the expectation of the evening was slowly rendering everyone speechless. Once everybody was seated the lights dimmed and a murmur ran through the crowd.

209

Natasha Milvern walked onto the stage, unannounced and seemingly oblivious to the rapturous applause that greeted her arrival. A single spotlight followed her movements. She was dressed completely in white. A black jewel shone from the turban she wore. It was as if her appearance was calculated to give the impression of a messiah. She pointed into the darkened theatre and said five words. "I know who you are."

It was a theatrical statement. She pressed fingertips against her temples and closed her eyes. The audience were suddenly hushed. My heart sank. Was I the only one in that auditorium who could see how staged her actions were? I knew without hesitation she was a fraud, a lady who would say anything to profit from other people's grief: from *my* grief. The anger I felt was almost uncontrollable. I realised I'd been a fool to even contemplate attending the meeting. I sat there as the evening passed with Miss Milvern reassuring members of the audience that their dead loved ones were still with them. I was surprised at how many people would grasp at lies to be convinced of an after-life.

Half-way through the evening there was an interval. *"I need to re-charge my spiritual batteries,"* she explained, and I heard a sympathetic murmur travel around the theatre. Why did I stay for the rest of the evening? To this day I'm not sure. I think I was hoping someone might expose the woman for what she was, little realising that in the end it would be me.

As the evening drew to a close she invited people to raise their hands, asking if they'd like to take part in a séance on stage. Her two assistants would then walk around the audience and pick six people to share the experience. A lot of hands went up, mine included, although probably not for their reasons. One of her helpers, an old lady in a shawl, walked past staring at the patrons as if she were trying to make her mind up who to choose. She picked someone to the rear of the auditorium and asked them their name. There was a small burst of applause and then she came back down the aisle. She stopped at the end of the row where I was seated and looked at me. I returned her gaze. Maybe she saw a desperate man, I don't know, but she pointed at me.

"You sir, what is your name?"

"Adam Crozier," I replied. She beckoned for me to stand, and another ripple of applause went around the theatre as I made my way up onto the stage.

The curtains had been closed, a table placed at the edge of the dais. Natasha Milvern seated us and asked the audience to remain silent. The lights were lowered. She knew how to build an atmosphere.

We spread our hands as directed, on the table-top, fingers touching those who sat either side, and then she laid hers down last. "I'm completing the circle." Her voice carried over the soundless crowd like a warning. For long moments we sat that way and then she spoke into the darkness.

"Is there anybody there?"

I could feel the tension building in the audience. Her head suddenly slumped forward and she seemed to go into a trance. From the hall there was an audible intake of breath. The woman should have been an actress. Her head tilted back and when she spoke again her voice was that of an old woman's.

"Do you still visit my grave, Thomas?" An elderly man sitting opposite me let out a moan.

"Elizabeth! Is that you?"

Smoke drifted into the air behind Natasha Milvern's head, forming ghost shapes against the drapes. I couldn't believe how staged it all was. The old man spoke again and the pain I heard in his voice made me feel sick at the way he was being duped.

"Elizabeth! If it's you, please show me a sign."

The hall was silent, every single person waiting for proof of an after-life. Somewhere in the darkness there was a nervous cough. Natasha Milvern's head slumped forward again. An empty chair on the other side of the stage slid across the boards towards us. Someone in the audience screamed. That was when I saw the wire, almost invisible in the half-light, attached to the chair leg. I couldn't take any more. I stood up and thumped my fist on the table.

"You're a fraud!" I cried. Before anyone could react I pulled the curtains back. The lights suddenly came on. People began voicing their displeasure, and with good reason. Behind the curtain and now clearly visible to everybody stood Miss Milvern's assistants. The old lady who had picked me from the audience held some kind of device. Smoke wafted from it, only now it didn't drift into the air, it poured across the stage. The other women stood frozen in the lights, one end of a length of wire in her hands, the other end attached to the chair. As the crowd jeered she unconsciously pulled her arm back and the chair fell over. There was almost a riot. Without knowing it that was the evening my life changed.

The next morning I opened my newspaper and was shocked to find my name in an article on page two.

MEMBER OF THE PUBLIC EXPOSES HOAX MEDIUM!

212

Until now, Natasha Milvern, a young lady who claims Russian descent, has been regarded by a large number of the public as one of the few genuine psychics operating today. Her legion of followers were left angry, disgusted and disappointed when last night a member of her audience, a Mr Adam Crozier, exposed her for what she really is, a liar and a fraud!

Miss Milvern, who has given readings to royalty and prominent government figures, will today find she no longer commands the large fees or respect she was once accustomed to."

As I read on there was a knock at the front door. Mrs Dawson answered. I heard muffled conversation and then she entered my study.

"Mr Crozier, there's a gentleman at the door who wonders if he might have a word with you."

I looked up from my paper. "On what business?"

She came into the room and lowered her voice. "He's from the press, sir."

I couldn't help smiling, Mrs Dawson was clearly impressed. I was curious to see what he wanted. "Send him in please Mrs Dawson, and would you make a fresh pot of tea?"

"Of course, sir." She said it as if it would be an honour.

I stood up. The man who entered my study was tall and well built. He was smartly dressed, his face intelligent his handshake firm. Behind his eyes I saw inquisitiveness and humour. I liked him straight away.

"Mr Crozier, thank you for seeing me. My name is Michael Shaw and I'm editor of The View." He glanced at the paper I'd placed on my desk. "I see you have impeccable taste."

I smiled and offered him a seat. "I was surprised to see my name mentioned in your hallowed pages." Before he could reply the door opened and Mrs Dawson entered with a tray. As well as a pot of tea she'd also laid out a small plate of her home-made scones. Mr Shaw was indeed a favoured guest.

"Thank you very much," he said. I swear my house-keeper blushed as she left the room.

I poured tea and handed him a cup. "So how can I help you?" He became serious.

"Mr Crozier, I was at Cloverley Hall last night, I witnessed what you did and I want to thank you."

I was puzzled. "Why would you want to thank *me*?" He put his cup down.

"Mr Crozier, I'm a man who deals in facts, it's my business. My readers want the truth and I like giving it to them. They trust me and I try to live up to that trust. I was there last night preparing material for an article we were soon to feature on Natasha Milvern. If it hadn't been for your timely intervention I'm afraid this old hack you're looking at would have been completely taken in. Can you imagine it, me endorsing that woman, a charlatan dealing in smoke and mirrors? I would never again have been able to hold my head up in Fleet Street."

We laughed and I poured more tea. "Well, I'm glad to have been of service."

"May I ask you a personal question?" he said.

I nodded, suddenly unsure where the conversation was leading.

"Why were *you* there?"

I hesitated, not certain I could bear the telling. The newspaper man looked at me and I could see he saw something in my face that made him regret asking. Perhaps it was that expression that prompted me to tell him everything. When I'd finished there was a moment's silence.

"I'm so sorry," he said, "I'm thoughtless. Here I am worried about my pride when that woman betrayed your grief."

"You weren't to know," I said. "It just sickened me to see the way she tried to profit from other people's loss."

Shaw leant forward in his seat and rested his hands on his knees. "Adam, I'd like to offer you a job."

His words surprised me. "A job? Doing what?"

He grinned. "Please, hear me out. What happened yesterday evening gave me an idea. When I arrived at the office this morning I spoke to Lord Morley, the paper's owner, and told him what I had in mind. He was as excited about it as I was, and when two veterans of the news business feel that way about something then you know you're on to a winner!"

His enthusiasm was infectious but I still had no idea what it was leading to. He must have seen the confusion on my face because he grinned again.

"What we'd like you to do is become a roving reporter. Go out and investigate claims of the after-life, second-sight, the paranormal, in fact anything strange. The spiritualist movement is a rapidly growing phenomenon and we want someone to cover it. Find out the truth and bring it back to us. You'll get a weekly column, an excellent wage and all-expenses paid." He sat back in his chair. "What do you think?"

What did I think? I thought he was crazy. "That's ridiculous."

He laughed. "That's exactly what I thought you'd say. Now tell me why."

I held up my hand and ticked reasons off on my fingers.

"One, I've got no journalistic skills. Two, I've no experience of the paranormal. Three, I know nothing of the spiritualist movement, and four, why me?"

When I looked into his face I saw he already had the answers.

"Adam, you don't need to be a journalist. You're intelligent and you have a keen mind. That showed last night. As for no experience of the paranormal, answer me this, who has?" Before I could say anything he carried on, probably deliberately, I was to find out in later years that Michael Shaw knew when to leave gaps and when to fill them.

"As for knowing nothing of the spiritualist movement, you don't need to. You'll be going in with an open mind. Once word gets around of what you'll be doing," he looked at me and corrected himself. "What we *hope* you'll be doing, you'll be inundated with requests from people wanting you to investigate their *'powers.'* He snorted on the last word. "You'll be surprised at the amount of ego you'll find when someone thinks their name might be appearing on the front page of a newspaper." I went to speak but once again he filled the gap.

"And I'll tell you why I think you're the perfect choice. Your honesty! You hate the fact vulnerable people can be taken advantage of, and that honesty is something that can't be bought." He leant towards me and patted me on the shoulder. "So what do you say to my proposition?"

I could have said a lot of things but nothing came to mind. He stood up and held out his hand. As I took it I was surprised to hear myself accepting his offer.

Michael Shaw had been right. The more I exposed frauds and fakes the more they queued to prove their authenticity. As I gained experience my job became easier.

I investigated supposed hauntings, imagined sightings, genuine people worried about circumstances they couldn't explain. In every case I looked into I was able to prove a more mundane reason for the events that had been troubling them.

Now I was on my way to Sussex to a haunting of a different kind.

***

The train pulled into Lowford at just after nine. A porter carried my bags to a waiting cab. I climbed in and as we left the station the sound of the steady clip-clop of the horse's hooves drifted into the night air.

Before long we turned into a gated entrance. Up ahead I glimpsed Haywood Manor. Lamps burned in a number of rooms.

As the driver helped me down the front door was opened and a woman stepped onto the porch. "Mr Crozier, I'm so glad you came."

Josephine Grant was slim and attractive but in the light of the hallway I could see dark smudges under her eyes.

"It's a pleasure to be here," I said. As she ushered me in a young girl appeared. She smiled at me and spoke to Mrs Grant.

"Goodnight Ma'am."

I watched her climb into the cab and then Mrs Grant closed the door.

"That's Polly," she said. "She used to be the live-in maid, but now she refuses to stay in the house over-night. Her mother lives in the village so she sleeps there and then returns in the morning." She sighed. "I used to have six full-time staff working here."

"What happened to them?"

When she smiled I could see how tired she looked. "Mr Crozier, come into the kitchen. There's tea and a warm supper waiting for you. You can meet my children and then I'll tell you everything."

Sophie and Robert were the image of their mother. They were polite if a little withdrawn, and once the introductions had been made they ran off up the stairs.

After I'd eaten, Mrs Grant offered me a glass of wine and as we sat in front of the fire she told of the strange events that happened nightly in Haywood Manor.

"Mr Crozier, I know what I am about to tell you will sound ridiculous but I give you my word it's the truth." She took a sip of her wine.

"When we moved here Peter and I thought it the most beautiful house we'd ever seen. The children loved it and we felt at home immediately. For the first few weeks everything was wonderful, right up until the day he left for India. Since then I've come to dread the nights."

The kitchen was warm. I could hear the children playing upstairs. It seemed hard to imagine that there was anything to dread in this lovely old building. Josephine Grant carried on.

"The first night Peter was away I thought I heard footsteps on the landing. I wasn't worried, the staff still lived-in then; I thought it was probably Polly turning out the lamps. Then Sophie began screaming. I rushed along the landing and saw her door was open. From inside her room I heard a voice, a man's voice, and just before I entered the room I caught the words he said to my little girl." She looked at me and her face had paled. "Get out!"

As she took another sip of wine I saw her hand was trembling. "Who was in there?" I asked.

She shook her head. "Nobody. When I'd calmed Sophie, she told me she'd woken up and thought she'd seen the shadow of a man standing at the end of the bed. She'd been too scared to sit up so she'd lain there hoping she was imagining things. Then the shadow began talking.

"You don't belong here," it said. "Get out while you still can. GET OUT!"

"That was when I entered the room and found my daughter alone and petrified." A log popped in the fireplace and I saw her jump. "That was only the beginning."

She went on to tell me of a similar incident that happened with her son two nights later. After that the children had been sleeping in her room. Things had gradually become worse. She'd hear two sets of footsteps walking the corridors, always just after midnight. Sometimes the bedroom door handle would turn, as if someone were trying to enter.

"And has anyone ever come into the room?" I asked.

"No," she said. "And whenever I plucked up courage to open the door there was nobody there." She fell silent for a moment; thinking. "It's strange. After the door handle turned I'd always hear the man's voice somewhere in the house, repeating the same words. 'Get out!' It sounded as if whoever was saying them was beating his fists against a wall."

She stared into the fire. "The staff wouldn't stay in the house after that and I can't blame them. If circumstances were different and my husband wasn't so far away I'd have moved out as well." She looked at me. "Mr Crozier, you're my last hope."

I stood up and smiled, certain I could solve the mystery of whatever had been causing Josephine and her children such distress. "Well, Mrs Grant, I shall do my best."

She showed me to my room and I told her of my plans.

"Tonight, if you don't mind, I'll take a chair and a lamp into the corridor and do what I always do on the first night of an investigation. I'll watch and wait." I saw the look of concern on her face. "Please don't worry. You haven't been harmed since these disturbances started so I don't think I will be either." I smiled again. "Now try and get some sleep."

I positioned a chair at the end of the corridor allowing me a clear view of the landing, hung the lantern on a wall hook, wrapped a quilt around me and listened to the house. And there I sat all night. When the hallway clock struck midnight, I tensed. The last chime faded away and I waited. Nothing happened.

At four in the morning I retired to my room.

The following day the house was bustling. Polly was busy in the kitchen, two other girls were cleaning the rooms and outside I saw a young lad helping an older man tend the gardens. It seemed as if everybody was eager to complete their chores during the daylight hours.

I found Josephine Grant and her children in the dining room taking breakfast. One night of uninterrupted sleep had made them all look a lot better. Mrs Grant bade me sit down and plated me some food.

"A quiet night," I said. She shook her head.

"I don't believe it. I can't remember the last time it was this peaceful."

I laughed. "You'd be surprised at the number of disturbances I've investigated where nothing at all has happened."

"Do you think it'll be the same here?"

I thought of how exhausted the family had looked the previous evening. How none of the staff would stay in the house overnight. I thought of her letter. "No, I don't," I said, and although a number of possible causes ran through my mind I was certain of one thing. It wasn't a ghost: there was no such thing.

The day passed quickly. Mrs Grant gave me a tour of the grounds, I checked the house from top to bottom and later in the afternoon I laid a fine powder over corridor floors, as well as tying cotton line across door openings and open spaces. Simple precautions, but ones I've found extremely effective. Then I did what I'd done the previous evening. I waited.

I must have fallen asleep. In my line of work that often happens, sleepless nights and boredom are a tiring combination. The clock struck twelve and woke me. I realised I felt frozen. When I exhaled my breath drifted like a small cloud into the light of the lantern.

That was when I saw the old couple moving slowly along the corridor. They left no footprints in the powder I'd spread, the cotton line they stepped through remained unbroken. For a moment I was transfixed, more scared than I had ever been in my life. Just as I'd known instantly that Natasha Milvern had been a fake, so I knew immediately what these two figures were and the truth shocked me: ghosts.

My past beliefs were suddenly rendered meaningless. There were no tricks here.

They stopped outside Josephine Grant's room and the old lady rested her fingers on the handle. She nodded at the old man and they smiled. I forced myself to stand up. When I reached for the lantern it trembled in my hands. "Who are you?" I called. (How pathetic that sounded!)

They looked at me as if they'd known of my presence before I'd even woken. The old man bent over, rested his hands on his knees and blew soundlessly into the powder. Letters formed on the floor.

PROTECTORS

I raised the lantern and tried to make sense of the word. "Protectors? Protectors of what?"

The old man exhaled again and stood up. At his feet words formed themselves.

THE CHILDREN

They looked at me as if I should understand. Somewhere in the house a floorboard creaked, as if an unseen weight were pressing down on it. The lamp flickered and I noticed the old couple cast no shadow.

"Who are you protecting them from?"

A look of alarm appeared on their faces. The woman raised her arm and pointed to the far end of the corridor.

A man stepped into the half-light. I have no idea how I knew he was dead, but he was, of that I was certain. I almost cried out in fear when I saw the look of hate in his lifeless eyes. An angry red wheal patterned his throat; it looked like a rope burn. He drifted towards me and I felt the malevolent aura surrounding him. I took a step backwards and knocked the chair over. It was then he seemed to notice the old couple and stopped. He turned to face the wall and began beating his fists against it. His mouth didn't move, but I heard words, so loud they sounded like thunder caught in the narrow hallway.

"GET OUT! GET OUT! GET OUT!"

It was like being bludgeoned by a blunt weapon. I fell to my knees and pressed my hands to my ears. Just as I thought I could bear it no longer the noise ceased. For a moment the silence seemed to toll along the landing like the ringing of a bell. I looked up into a deserted corridor. There were fresh words in the powder.

ALL IN THE PAST

As I gazed down a faint breeze came from nowhere and blew them away.

No-one in the house stirred.

***

"Who lived here before you?"

Once again I was seated at the breakfast table with Josephine and her children and once again they'd had a peaceful night. Not one of them had heard a thing. I could see from their faces they thought I'd performed some kind of a miracle. I hadn't told them what I'd witnessed. I could imagine their reaction if I confessed to them that I believed Haywood Manor was haunted.

She placed her cup on the table. "The agent told us it belonged to an old couple by the name of Hall."

'An old couple.' I felt the hairs on the back of my neck rise. The image of a man and women patrolling an upstairs corridor forced its way into my mind. My discomfort went unnoticed; Josephine continued.

"It's a sad story. They lived here for over forty years, just the two of them in this big house. They were childless and enjoyed holding parties for the village children."

'THE CHILDREN.' Again, I saw words in the powder: phantom letters spelling out a mystery. My hostess poured tea.

"Church-groups, classes from the local school, they'd invite them for the day and give them the run of the house and gardens. It was a treat greatly looked forward to by both the children and the Halls." She looked at me. "Then the accident happened and no parties were ever held here again."

"What accident was that?"

Josephine smiled at Robert and Sophie. "If you two have finished your breakfast you can go and play." They scampered from the room and she lowered her voice.

"It was a summer's afternoon. Trestle tables had been laid out for tea, coloured bunting hung from the trees. Suddenly two children ran screaming and crying from the gardens. They claimed a man they'd never seen before had pushed a child into the boating lake." She looked at me. "It's not there anymore but it used to be situated behind that line of conifers". She pointed to a row of trees visible from the window.

"Two of the grounds men raced down to the bank and were met with the sight of a little boy's body floating face-down in the water. They jumped in and pulled him out but they were too late; the poor little mite was dead.

"The two lads who raised the alarm were questioned but they both told the same story. A man had stepped from the bushes, grabbed their friend and pushed him into the water. The lake was deep there and as the child floundered the stranger stepped back into the undergrowth. Of course the police were called and the grounds searched, but no trace of the mystery man was ever found. The Halls' were distraught and blamed themselves. They had the lake filled-in and never held another party."

Josephine's story sent a chill down my spine. I had no doubt who I'd seen in the corridor the previous night. Even in death, Mr and Mrs Hall were still trying to take care of the little ones. But who was the man, the man who'd looked at me with hate in his dead eyes, and why did he wish the children harm?

I excused myself. I was tired and I needed to think. I had a feeling that the man I'd seen in the corridor and the long ago incident at the lake were connected. I decided to take a walk in the gardens and see for myself the scene of a long ago tragedy.

It was a hot morning. I wandered down the flagstone path that led to the line of conifers and made my way around them. A wide area of lush grass gradually thinned as it neared the surrounding wooded area. It was clear to see where the lake had been, easy to imagine what happened on that terrible afternoon.

I sat down with my back against a beech tree and listened to the sounds of a peaceful summer's day. The garden seemed to fall silent and as sunshine filtered through the branches I closed my eyes and fell asleep.

When I opened them a little boy was standing at the edge of the trees. He waved to me and then disappeared behind the line of conifers. I got to my feet and felt my vision swim, as if I'd risen too quickly. I stumbled across the clearing and gazed towards the house. The little boy was standing by the back-door. He looked at me and then stepped inside.

As I followed I realised I felt feverish. The sunlight seemed too bright and made my eyes ache. I could hear sounds in my head but had no idea where they were coming from. I reached the door and leant against the frame to catch my breath. The boy stood at the top of the back stairway and beckoned to me.

The sweat on my body suddenly chilled and I shivered. Small, wet footprints led up the stairs. I followed them with a feeling of dread. The outer door opened into shadow. I stepped inside and waited until my eyes adjusted to the gloom. Another door led onto the landing. As I closed it behind me I realised how cold this part of the house felt. Halfway along the corridor a bedroom door swung open.

My feet felt like lead, every footstep was an effort. It seemed to take an age to reach the doorway. I paused and listened. A voice drifted from the room, too soft and full of cunning to be properly heard. Like a man in a trance I stepped inside.

That was when I discovered the secret of Haywood Manor and why the dead man would never leave Josephine and her children alone.

From the shadows a hand reached out and touched my shoulder.

"Mr Crozier, are you alright?"

I looked up into the face of the young boy and as I went to scream I realised it was the gardener's son, the lad I'd seen the previous morning. Behind me, I could feel the trunk of the beech tree digging into my back. The sun had risen high above the clearing. It must have been past midday.

"I'm fine," I said, and rubbed my face. "I think the heat must have got to me."

He grinned and handed me a water bottle. "Here, have some of this, it'll make you feel better." I thanked him and took a long drink. The water tasted cold and sweet, it refreshed me, but it didn't make me feel better.

As I made my way back to the house I tried to make sense of what had happened. I knew I'd fallen asleep but what I'd seen then was more than a dream. I'd witnessed something from the past, a terrible thing, and I had a feeling it might be able to affect the future. I needed to speak to Josephine Grant urgently.

***

We were seated in the drawing room, staring out through the open French doors at the sun-washed gardens. She'd poured us each a glass of sherry and as we sipped at our drinks I told her of some of the things I'd witnessed. She looked scared and I couldn't blame her; I felt the same way.

"Don't ask me how," I said. "But I know who lived in this house before the Halls'."

I half expected her to scoff, to question how I, a stranger, could know such a thing. I was wrong. Her expression was one of trust.

"Who was it, Adam?" she said, "And what bearing does it have on what's been happening here?"

For a moment I didn't know what to say. How could I tell her the ghost of a little boy had shown me the past? Sometimes the truth makes itself unbelievable.

"I'm not sure of the man's name," I said. "But I do know he killed his pregnant wife and then committed suicide in the bedroom above us."

"Oh my God!" Josephine's hand went to her throat. "Why?"

"Because he found out the baby his wife was carrying wasn't his."

I remembered again what I'd seen in that room. I'd watched the man stabbing his wife as she pleaded for mercy. I'd seen his arm rising and falling as he tried to rip the unborn child from her womb and then heard him choking to death as he swayed from the rope strung up by his own hand.

I told these things to Josephine but I used gentler words, as if there *are* gentler words to describe suicide and murder. She was silent for a while.

"But why does his spirit mean my family harm?"

The answer to that I could only guess at but I was sure I was right.

"He doesn't want women or children in this house," I said. "After he found out his wife was unfaithful and carried another man's child, he hates them. I think the only reason he left the Halls' alone was because they were unable to have children. Then when the little boy was drowned they realised there was something wrong with the house. That was another reason they stopped holding parties." I looked at Josephine; her face was a mask of grief and fear. I continued.

"I believe that when the Halls' died they couldn't let go. They knew something evil would be left here. Somehow I think the old couple are preventing whatever that is, from harming you. For how long they can do that I don't know."

She looked at me, her face was pale. "What should we do?"

That was a question I'd been tormenting myself with ever since I woke up beneath the beech tree.

"Do you attend the local church?" I asked.

She frowned at the question and nodded. "Every Sunday."

"Do you know the vicar very well?" Before she could answer I carried on. "Well enough to bless this house?"

She thought for a moment and then smiled. "He's a good man," she said.

Josephine refilled our glasses. The sun had edged shadows into the room. We sat in silence and listened to the carefree sound of Robert and Sophie playing hide and seek in the gardens.

***

Josephine had the young lad I met earlier, run a message to the vicarage. He returned an hour later, the Reverend Adrian Giles would be able to visit at nine the following morning.

Later, after our evening meal, I returned to my room. Through the window I watched the dusk turn to cloudy darkness and listened to the breeze stir the trees. It sounded like a threat.

That night was the worst I spent in the house, I also think it was the most terrifying the Grant's had experienced although they never remembered a thing. It was as if the murderer's spirit knew it was running out of time.

It was also the night we lost Sophie.

Josephine had gone to bed with her children tucked up beside her. Again, I'd decided to keep vigil in the corridor, I was scared and anxious. The whole atmosphere of the house had changed. Outside the sky had lowered, compressing the day's heat into a confined flat area. There wasn't a cool shadow to be found.

As soon as the clock struck twelve I knew something would happen. I heard a sound and before I could react the bedroom door flew open. The man I'd seen in my dream was standing in the doorway. He held the body of a little girl in his arms. Sophie was unconscious. Never in the whole of my life have I been so afraid. I sensed movement behind me and turned around. The old couple were drifting along the corridor. They might have been phantoms but I saw tears in their eyes. It was those tears that brought me to life. I barred the way of the man who'd murdered his wife and unborn child and held out my arms.

"Give her to me," I said.

We stared at each other and I swear I saw the devil in his eyes. He snarled a warning and before I could wrest Sophie from him he walked right through me. For a second my whole body seemed to be made of ice: it was like being torn apart from the inside. I staggered and leant on the door frame. By the time I recovered and turned around he was gone. In the bedroom Josephine and her son slept on as if they were drugged.

Powder and cotton, what kind of misguided defence is that against a soul bound for hell?

I ran down the stairs and saw the back door was open. What could I do? How could I live with myself if I did nothing? I stepped outside.

High in the sky the clouds had parted to reveal a half-formed moon. I ran down the pathway and even before I skirted the line of conifers I knew what I would see. The clearing wasn't there anymore. A lake that had been filled-in years before reflected the past. At the water's edge were two silhouettes. One belonged to a little girl, the other to a dead madman. For a second my senses seized-up, reality drifted away. And then I heard Sophie crying; the sound of a little girl who needed her mother. I thought of my wife and the son I'd never seen, and a strange thought slipped into my mind. *How do you kill somebody who's already dead?* I realised I didn't care.

I sprinted towards the water's edge. The man turned and saw me. His rage expressed itself in a howl of frustration. He picked up Josephine Grant's little girl and held her above his head. Before he could let her go I lunged at him and everything changed. The man vanished, the pond disappeared and Sophie lay in the grass fast asleep.

I climbed to my feet and as I caught my breath I realised that somehow I'd prevented a vengeful dead man from committing another murder. Years ago he'd drowned a small child and no-one had disturbed his dirty work. This time he hadn't been as fortunate. I wondered if he'd ever get another chance.

I picked Sophie up and looked around. There was no movement in the shadows, no sounds from the woods, no dead little boy with wet footprints to disturb the silence. And yet I felt as if I was being observed. I turned towards the house. In an attic window a small figure appeared to raise his hand and wave, and then the shape slowly dissolved and turned to shadow.

I smiled and made my way through the gardens. Above the tree-line a thousand stars winked softly in the sky. My head was clear. As I carried Sophie back to her mother's room I prayed that was the end of it all. But it wasn't.

Josephine had woken up confused and panicking, sure her little girl was gone forever. I laid Sophie in her arms and reassured her everything was fine. It was as if she were drunk. She mumbled something and then fell back to sleep, her arms around her daughter. As I made my way along the corridor I realised what she'd said: *Thank you.*

The seat on the landing was uncomfortable and as I closed my eyes in search of sleep the clock struck one. I heard a baby cry, a small, helpless sound coming from the room where I'd witnessed a dead man kill his wife. I couldn't move. I watched the door creep open and wondered how much more I could stand. There was movement in the shadows and just as I felt a scream rise in my throat the old couple appeared in the doorway. They were smiling. When the woman beckoned to me her hand seemed to move in slow motion.

I rose from my chair and walked slowly along the landing. All I could picture was the terrible sight that had greeted me the last time I'd entered that room. When I reached the door the old couple stood aside. Reluctantly, I went in. For a moment I was stunned. Then I began to cry.

My wife, Ilene, was seated on the side of the bed. In her arms she held our beautiful little boy. I could hear his breathing and his small contented sighs. My wife looked at me and smiled. Through my tears I smiled back and as my vision blurred I watched the outline of my lovely wife and child fade.

A ghostly hand rested gently on my shoulder. I turned and looked into the face of an old man who had loved children, but never been able to have any of his own. He smiled and then blew softly against the window pane. Words formed on the glass. *THEY ARE SAFE.* It was the most wonderful thing I'd ever read. I wiped my eyes and the old couple were gone.

***

"Mr Crozier, it's a pleasure to meet you. I admire the way you exposed that Milvern woman as a hoax." The vicar shook my hand and laughed at my expression. "It's not often we get someone famous in this neck of the woods."

It came as a shock to discover the Reverend Adrian Giles was an avid follower of my adventures. As Josephine made us tea we sat at the kitchen table discussing cases I'd investigated.

The vicar was as appalled at the number of charlatan's plying their dubious business as I had been. After all the talk of fakes and frauds I wondered how he'd feel about my request. We sipped at our tea and I told him of the events I'd witnessed and what I hoped he might do. I expected him to be sceptical. His reaction surprised me. He looked at Josephine.

"Mrs Grant, are you happy for me to conduct a service here?"

I could see the look of relief on her face. She nodded and smiled.

Adrian Giles stood up and clapped me on the shoulder. "This is a lovely house," he said. "Let's make it a lovely home."

KEEPING WATCH

Those who know, the fishermen and the old-timers, say Echo Cove is full of voices, that they belong to every soul that ever walked its desolate beach. They say the rocks and gullies have trapped those voices and when the wind blows in off the sea and twists its way around the lonely stones they speak again. They also say if you stay there long enough you'll hear them all.

***

I persuaded Rebecca to move to Hope Bay in the spring of ninety-four, when our son, Peter, was still a baby, and the future a thing of promise. I dreamt of raising him in fresh air and open spaces, and if my wife's dreams didn't match my own she was willing to bury hers for the sake of our child. I remember the look in her eyes on the day we left the city; the smile that couldn't hide her longing to stay where she felt we belonged. It was the one and only time I glimpsed that expression, yet it's stayed with me through the years like a reminder of how things could have been.

We discovered early on that Bay people liked to keep themselves to themselves; if you weren't born inside the invisible boundary line that ran from the Cove to Hope, you were regarded as an outsider. It took us a long time to wear down the subtle barriers they erected, to form friendships based on more than just a smile and a wave, but wear them down we did. The years passed, our son grew tall and strong and we came to love Hope Bay more than we ever thought possible.

But then Peter went missing and from that day on my wife's love for me and the bay slowly died.

***

The crew of a homeward bound fishing boat discovered my son's skiff drifting out to sea, pulled by the evening tide like a ghost vessel with a phantom at the tiller. It was the calmest day of the year. On board they found a first-aid kit, a lifejacket and the remains of a half-eaten meal. What they never found was my son. *"The boat was empty,"* the captain said, but he was mistaken; it was full of memories.

I only realised something was wrong as I made my way down the narrow streets that led to the harbour. I saw the knot of people clustered on the pier and recognised the boat they were crowded around. A butterfly of fear settled in my stomach. It seemed to take an age to reach them. They looked up and fell silent as they saw me walk slowly towards them like a man lost.

I stepped into the skiff and ran my fingers over the weather-worn sail. Images of trips we'd taken flickered through my mind. A young boys' delight as he reeled in his first catch. The wonder in his eyes as a dolphin leapt from the ocean and twisted its sleek wet body through the air. Broken fragments of a past that would never be pieced back together. "Where's my son?" I asked. "Where's my son?"

Their silence held the answer I dreaded, and yet even then, numb with shock, I wondered how I would ever be able to break the news to the woman who I'd persuaded to leave the life she loved behind.

When your only child disappears without trace the least you expect is answers. For days an army of volunteers combed the shoreline and tidal backwaters without finding a thing. It didn't make sense. My son had grown up on this coastline; he knew where the dangers were and what to stay away from. Whatever trouble he'd run into hadn't been of his own making.

A search of his room uncovered only more heartache. Invitations yet to be sent lay at the bottom of a set of drawers; a surprise party planned to celebrate a wedding anniversary that became a wake. There'll be no more of those now, the marriage crumbled when my wife and I discovered our son was the foundation on which it was built.

Rebecca's parting words will follow me to the grave. "It's your fault," she said. "I'll never forgive you."

Grief makes people act in unexpected ways; heartbreak prompts them to say things they later regret. Whether Rebecca regretted the leaving or the words she spoke I won't ever know. The city reclaimed her and left no trace of the woman who'd once sacrificed her dreams on the altar of mine.

'I'll never forgive you.'

And why should she? I'll never forgive myself.

***

On a clear spring morning, Herbert Jennings, a born and bred Hope Bay man, took his boat out. He'd gone to check on lobster pots he had strung along the seabed beyond Echo Cove, and to catch the shellfish he sold from his harbour road stall. By the time the sun was going down he still hadn't returned. I watched search boats sail into the sunset in the futile hope they might find him and felt a cold certainty they wouldn't.

Two days later, when no trace of him had been found, I came to the belief there was something out there, something in the ocean, waiting for its chance to drag another unsuspecting victim to a saltwater grave. I was laughed at when I voiced my suspicions. What did I know? I'd only lived in Hope Bay twenty years; I was still almost a newcomer. People went missing at sea.

I wondered if those who made their accusations would have done so if my son hadn't disappeared and my wife hadn't left me. I could read their thoughts; I was a broken man clinging to anything that might make sense of the wreckage of my life. I wasn't to be listened to, I was to be pitied.

Perhaps they were right.

A single man's loneliness is a strange thing; the hours are too long and his thoughts too loud, there's no hiding place. For years I've been accustomed to the comfort of company and the sound of friendly voices. The new found silence I'm forced to endure feels worse than the burden of guilt my wife's blame loaded me with.

Now the television set that's become my only company throws out a clue, a crumb of hope.

'There was something in the water; a shape I couldn't recognise. It moved like a shadow beneath the waves. I thought I saw someone struggling, as if they were being dragged towards its centre. When I circled back they'd disappeared.'

The pilot of a light aircraft had been flying above Echo Cove and was the sole witness to a man's last moments. When interviewed he gabbled nervously, a strange look of dread and excitement on his face.

'*Perhaps I was seeing things,*' he said, and laughed, but his words carried the hollow ring of desperation and were edged with fear. Now I wait. As yet no-one's been reported missing, although a shoe was found washed up on the beach. It wasn't my son's.

Since that broadcast I spend my days at Echo Cove, keeping watch. The grey and creamy waves are full of secrets. They wash against the shore and whisper their lies while I listen to the cry of the gulls and the sigh of the wind.

I thought I saw a dark shape floating just below the surface of the water yesterday, a shape far too large to be any kind of fish. It drifted with the current like a cloud caught in the breeze. By the time I fetched my binoculars it was gone. I sat on the rocks above the shore-line and felt like the loneliest man in the world.

Now Edwin Marshall has disappeared, an old man whose one joy in life was fishing from the end of the disused jetty that enters the water like a broken spine. His rod and line were found scattered across the weather-beaten boards, along with the backpack containing a lunch that would never be eaten. Since daylight the coastguards have been searching for his body, but I fear they search in vain.

Hope Bay doesn't feel like home any more. It's become a place of suspicion. I hear the gossip and see the sideways glances aimed in my direction: the lowered voices of accusation disguised behind covered mouths, as if it were my fault people are living in fear. All the old barriers have been raised; the time I've spent here means nothing.

Freda Jennings stopped me in the street yesterday morning and in a voice filled with angry grief blamed me for her husband's death. People I've known for years stood and stared. What could I say?

"I've lost my son."

I don't think my words reached her. She hurried away from them as if leaving my heartache behind might bring her husband back. The bystanders shook their heads; whether in sympathy or disgust I have no idea. I was left standing there alone like the stranger I've become.

The rumours grow. People have seen things, or so they say. Fishing boats remain moored in harbour; the beach is deserted. Nobody any longer dives from the rocks above Echo Cove.

"What's out there?" I've heard them ask.

There are some questions that have to be answered whatever the cost.

Tomorrow I'll sail the skiff to the mouth of Echo Cove. I'll moor beneath the cliffs where the water's deep and throws no reflection. From there I'll watch the tide break against the shore. I'll search every wave and I'll listen to the voices the wind blows in off the sea. Maybe they'll tell me of the secret that Echo Cove guards so jealously. Maybe they'll tell me what happened to my son.

DAMAGE

Relocating hadn't been the nightmare Millie French imagined, unlike the events leading up to her departure. But now it was done, she'd closed a door on the past and there was no turning back. The removal men had left and shortly afterwards her new neighbours, Lee and Stephanie Ward, had called and introduced themselves. Their warm welcome had only served to remind Millie of all the things she'd missed.

She wandered through the rooms, enjoying the luxury of solitude. The house was hers, a home she was no longer forced to share with a partner whose true colours had lain dormant beneath good looks and easy charm. Although Craig Manderly had no idea of where she'd moved to she thanked God the restraining order was still in place. As she began unpacking, the doorbell rang.

"We meant to give you this." Stephanie Ward had returned, there was a bottle of wine in her hands. "Once again, welcome to Churchway Close."

Millie took the gift and thanked her neighbour.

"Remember; if you need anything, just give us a call. We know what it's like when you're new to an area."

Millie watched Stephanie cross their shared driveway and marvelled at the woman's appearance; she looked as if she'd just stepped from the pages of an upmarket fashion magazine. When her neighbour returned her wave and closed her door Millie couldn't help noticing how the house matched the owner. Both the building and the woman looked as if they'd had a lot of time and money invested in them.

Back inside she leaned against the hallway wall and closed her eyes. Things were good and could only get better. The bottle was ice cold. It was time for a celebratory drink.

***

Craig Manderly's transformation from doting partner to control freak had been so subtle that at first Millie hadn't even realised it was happening. The good-natured accusations and smiling criticism accompanied by a patient tolerance, had initially filled her with guilt. How could she be getting things so wrong? Her efforts to right those wrongs only seemed to antagonise the man she thought of as the love of her life.

But as those mistakes gradually became more frequent so his reprimands grew harsher. *What was she, stupid? Couldn't she do anything properly? How many times did he have to tell her?* Abuse that soon became more poisonous and personal. *Don't wear that dress, it doesn't suit you. You've put on weight. Who was that guy you were talking to? Why are you so late back from work?*

Then it got physical.

And still she was apologising, blaming herself for faults that didn't exist while covering the bruises with make-up and excuses.

Things looked set to continue on that downward spiral, a wearing away of her spirit until the girl she used to be was left behind like a faded memory. But then one evening she overheard him bragging on the phone, telling someone she'd never met how he had sad little Millie exactly where he wanted. That was the moment a cloud cleared and she saw for the first time what he really was; a spiteful bully filled with a loathing for women.

She also saw what she'd become and the sight scared her so badly she knew she had to get away.

***

Sunshine flooded the bedroom and woke her from a dream in which Craig had been telling her how special she was; how much he needed her. *How no-one could ever love her the way he did.* His smile had been full of the things that had first attracted her before she found out what went on below the surface. Then the smile had disappeared. He'd laced his fingers around her throat and squeezed. As she fought for breath his lips brushed against her ear. She heard the menace in his voice.

"Don't leave me Millie," he said. "I can do a lot of damage."

It was a relief to open her eyes and find herself alone, to discover she was safe in the sanctuary of Churchway Close. Last night's wine had left the ghost of a hangover and bad memories etched in her dreams.

She climbed out of bed and stretched lazily. The sun threw warm patterns across her skin. She closed her eyes and linked her hands behind her head, basking in its warmth. When she opened them she saw Lee Ward staring from his bedroom window. Her new neighbour appeared to be enjoying the view and she realised how she must look, as if she were parading herself. She fought a ridiculous urge to wave and as casually as she could took a dressing gown from the bed. By the time she'd pulled it around her shoulders he'd disappeared. She didn't know whether to feel flattered or mortified and made a mental note to hang curtains as soon as possible.

Downstairs there was an envelope on the hallway mat. *'To our new neighbour,'* it said. Inside was a note.

Dear Millie,

Lee and I would like to invite you round for dinner tonight. It would be lovely to get properly acquainted and we could also give you a few pointers regarding the neighbourhood. We'll expect you at eight.

See you then,

Stephanie.

Millie grinned; the Ward's didn't beat about the bush. There was no, *'can you make it?'* or *'is it convenient?'* Just, *'we'll expect you.'* But that didn't matter; she had nothing planned, apart from spending the rest of her life as far away from Craig Manderly as she possibly could.

The Ward's were almost the same age as her; it'd be an opportunity to make new friends. God knows she'd lost contact with most of her old ones since her ex had put up fences and kidnapped her personality. She made her way to the kitchen and switched on the kettle. Outside, Churchway Close was Saturday morning silent. The sound was like music to her ears.

Far away Craig Manderly was listening to a different tune.

***

There'd been no need for the restraining order; that was something he could never forgive. Now he was an outcast, labelled with titles he couldn't shift. Stalker: Control Freak: Bully. Work colleagues either shunned him or treated him with contempt; telephone calls to old friends went unanswered; e-mails were ignored. And it was all Millie's fault.

Didn't she realise she'd made his life unbearable? Each day was a collection of pointed fingers and sideways glances; of whispered comments no-one had the guts to say to his face. Now he was forbidden to go within five-hundred yards of her. Why? Because he loved her and she'd broken his heart: because he'd followed her and tried to persuade her to come back: because he'd lost control and hit her when she refused. And hadn't she deserved it?

He grinned; she wasn't going to get away that easily. What was the law going to do, follow him wherever he went? He was prepared to let the rumours settle and wait for the gossip to die; to carry on with his life as if Millie French had never existed. But then he was going to track her down, find out where she'd run to and watch her as she attempted to rebuild her pathetic little life.

Then he was going to tear it to pieces.

***

"Have some more." Stephanie Ward refilled their glasses. Dinner was over and they were all pleasantly mellow. Earlier Millie had noticed how the interior of the house matched the outside; pristine; just like Stephanie. She couldn't help thinking her neighbour was a woman trying too hard.

Her husband seemed more relaxed. He'd given no inclination he'd seen Millie that morning and what could have been an awkward moment passed easily. Lee was charming and polite, his ready smile and good looks caused her to feel a twinge of envy towards his wife. *Why couldn't she meet someone like him?*

"So what brought you here?"

Lee's question caught her off-guard. Earlier in the day she'd been wondering how much of her past she should share. Would the Ward's really want to hear of the troubles she'd gone through with her ex? Now she discovered she wanted to tell them, to shed the invisible load Craig Manderly had burdened her with.

"I had to get away from someone," she said. "I needed to make a new start."

Her words drew Lee and Stephanie Ward closer.

"How do you mean?"

Millie took another sip of wine and as the candle on the table burned lower she made another trip into the minefield that was her past.

"What happened when you left him?" Stephanie was topping up their glasses again.

Millie had told them the whole story: the physical and mental abuse; how she'd come to believe everything was her fault. She'd described Craig's controlling personality and how she'd secretly fled the house one morning and moved into rented rooms.

"He kept phoning me," Millie said, "and then leaving text messages when I wouldn't answer. At first he begged me to give him another chance, promising me he'd change. But I'd seen too much of the real person to know that wasn't possible. Besides, after what he'd put me through I never wanted to see him again.

"Then the messages became threatening. It didn't take long for the old Craig to surface. I remember the last one he sent before he found out where I was staying. *Don't leave me, Millie,* it said. *I can do a lot of damage.*"

Stephanie Ward gasped and put her hand to her mouth.

"You poor thing; did you call the police?"

Millie nodded.

"I did, but they said all they could do was warn him. Craig hadn't done anything; they regarded it as just another domestic incident."

She looked at them both.

"That changed when Craig turned up on my doorstep and beat me black and blue."

The Ward's appeared stunned. Millie continued.

"I was lucky a neighbour heard the commotion. He came out and dragged Craig off me. That was when he suddenly changed tack, trying to blame me, saying I'd betrayed him and then provoked him when he'd called to beg me to come back."

Lee Ward shook his head in disgust. "What did the neighbour do?"

"He held onto Craig and called the police." Millie managed to smile at the memory.

Then she told them what else had happened. How Craig Manderly hadn't been such a big man after that: crying in court when the poisonous text messages were read out in evidence; pleading to be given another chance: begging for forgiveness. Millie had seen that act too many times to be fooled. Unfortunately the judge hadn't. Her ex had been handed a suspended sentence, along with a heavy fine and an order to keep away from her.

She was the only one who'd seen him smirk at her when he left the dock. That was when she suspected it might not be over.

"Do you think he'll come looking for you again?"

Lee Ward's question scared her.

"I don't know," she whispered, He put his arm around her and she wept into his embrace.

***

Craig Manderly's contract had been terminated. *'Attitude problems,'* his supervisor had explained, without making eye contact. His reply hadn't done him any favours.

"Whose? Yours or mine?"

She did meet his gaze then. They stared at each other and he saw the animosity in her eyes. He also saw the fear that lay just below it. She was scared of him. She had good right to be.

"That's exactly the sort of ignorant response that's led to this moment. The company was prepared to give you a chance after the unfortunate incident with your partner. " He saw a spiteful smile touch her lips. "Obviously we were wrong."

She was trying to bluff it out, he could tell, vainly attempting to keep up the pretence she was the one in charge. He leant across the desk and saw her flinch. His voice dropped to a whisper.

"Don't patronise me, you stupid cow. Keep your fucking job and just pray we don't meet on the street one evening." He stood up and ran his hand in a sawing motion across his throat. "Know what I mean?"

"Get out!" she said. "Get out of here before I call security." She wasn't scared now, she was terrified.

His grin was like a snarl. He sauntered across the office and paused at the door. She'd picked up a pen. He could see her hand shaking.

"Remember what I said." He winked at her. "Have a nice day."

There'd been no collection or farewell drink, just a minimal compensation package and a less than flattering reference. Millie French had a lot to answer for.

***

She lay in bed and ran her mind back over the evening. It had been a relief to pour out her troubles and the Ward's had been sympathetic listeners. Churchway Close felt like a good place to be.

Lee's question returned, casting a shadow over her good mood. Would Craig try and find her? Surely he'd learned his lesson? If he tried anything else he'd end up behind bars, would he be foolish enough to risk that? She remembered his threat: *I can do a lot of damage.* The words still had the power to send a shiver through her. The past was something she didn't want to dwell on. Instead her thoughts kept returning to Lee's reassuring goodnight hug and the look of concern she saw in his eyes.

Now she couldn't sleep.

She climbed out of bed and made her way to the window. The glass felt cool against her breasts. As she watched the moon climb into the stars she saw movement in her neighbour's bedroom. A shape melted into the shadows.

She wasn't sure but she thought it might be Lee Ward. Watching.

She stayed at the window, staring into the night until a cloud covered the moon.

***

"Is that Mr Beale? Mr Harry Beale?"

"Yes?"

The voice sounded as if it were a hundred years old. Craig Manderly grinned into the phone; he didn't think this was going to be a problem.

"I wonder if you could help me. I'm trying to trace a school friend I haven't seen for years. I heard she used to rent one of your properties."

He'd thought about visiting Millie's old landlord but then decided against it. He wasn't sure how much the man knew regarding the circumstances of her departure. A phone call seemed the best way of keeping his true identity hidden.

"Well, I'll help you if I can. What was your friend's name?"

"Millie," Craig said. "Millie French."

There was a pause, as if the old man was running a list of half-remembered lodgers through his tired mind.

"What did you say your name was?" Beale's voice was sharper. Craig realised the old duffer wasn't as dead as he sounded.

"I didn't, but its Gerald Simpson." He decided to embroider the lie. "She might have mentioned me. We used to be very close."

Another long pause; Manderly could imagine the old boy croaking it, standing there with the phone locked against his ear as rigor mortis set in.

"No, she didn't. May I ask what school that was?"

This time it was Craig's turn to let the line hang silent. *Crafty old bastard,* he thought, and rested the handset back on its cradle. Harry Beale could smell a rat. He drummed his fingers against the wall. It would have been so much easier to conduct this business over the phone. Now he was going to have to pay a visit; sort things out face to face. Gerald Simpson wanted to know where his old school friend had gone and one way or another Beale was going to tell him.

Craig Manderly pulled into an overgrown driveway and wondered if the properties Harry Beale rented out were as run-down as the one he lived in. It was a big house that needed a lot of attention.

He climbed from the car and knocked on the front door. When nobody answered he knocked again and then knelt down and peered through the letterbox. A figure was shuffling along the hallway. Craig stood up as the door was opened.

Harry Beale was leaning on a stick and looked as if he'd been asleep. He also looked as if he needed a bath and a change of clothes. Behind him bundles of newspapers were stacked in a hallway badly in need of decoration.

"Hello, Mr Beale, my name's Gerald Simpson. We spoke earlier on the phone. I was enquiring about an old school friend."

The hand Craig offered was ignored. Beale's rheumy eyes gazed at him from behind rimless glasses. The corners of his mouth were folded down in a permanent expression of distaste.

"Don't lie to me, young man," he said. His voice sounded dusty, as if his vocal cords had been damaged by a lifelong smoking habit. "I may be old, but I'm not stupid. I know who you are; you're Craig Manderly, the bully who terrorised that poor girl. I saw your picture in the local paper. You should be ashamed of yourself."

Craig smothered an urge to hit the old man; to show him how much terrorising a bully could do. Instead he smiled and raised a hand in apology. It was a convincing gesture.

"Look, I'm sorry," he said. "I shouldn't have lied to you and I *am* ashamed. Believe me there isn't a day goes by where I don't regret my behaviour. Now it's too late to take it back. I made a mistake and now nobody will give me a chance." He let the words catch in his throat; it was an effect he'd rehearsed.

"The truth is I wanted to tell Millie how sorry I am and return some belongings she left behind. This was the only way I could think of doing it."

He rubbed his eyes, as if he were fighting back tears. It was an act that had fooled a courtroom judge. "I realise I shouldn't have troubled you, Mr Beale. I'll leave now. Please forgive me."

He turned and walked slowly towards the car; a man with the weight of the world on his shoulders and no-one to share the load. As he opened the door Beale called after him.

"Mr Manderly! Wait a minute!"

Craig grinned to himself and then looked up. Harry Beale was waving him back. He crossed the driveway and wiped an imaginary tear from the corner of his eye. The old man had no idea how close he'd come to a beating.

***

There was another envelope on the hallway floor. Millie was amused at the way the Ward's communicated; most people would have picked up the phone. Through the porch window she could see Lee stripped to the waist, washing his car in the sun. Beads of sweat had formed on his back. She was embarrassed to find herself momentarily wondering how they'd taste. The thought left her feeling guilty. She opened the envelope and unfolded the note. There was a single sentence printed in capital letters across the paper:

I CAN DO A LOT OF DAMAGE.

The day suddenly darkened. As the note floated from her fingers she groped for the front door and heard someone screaming.

It was her.

She was sitting in the Ward's kitchen with no recollection of how she'd got there. A mug of steaming coffee was on the table. Lee and Stephanie were crouched in front of her exchanging worried glances.

"Millie, are you okay?"

Stephanie Ward's voice seemed to come from far away. Millie couldn't answer; her thoughts were somersaulting over each other in a mad scramble to be heard.

Get away! He's found you again! You'll never be safe! And the one that concerned her the most. *How?*

"Millie?"

Lee Ward rested his hand on hers. His touch was like the breaking of a spell.

"What happened?" she asked.

"Don't you remember? You almost fell out of your front door. You were screaming that Craig Manderly had found you. I managed to calm you down and brought you in here. Stephanie made coffee while I checked your house." He handed her the note. "There was nobody there but this was on the floor."

Millie didn't need to read it again; she thought the words would stay imprinted on her mind forever.

"Oh God," she said. "He must have come to the house last night." The thought sent a chill through her.

She could imagine her ex prowling around in the darkness, checking the doors and windows, searching the building for a weakness. Perhaps he was even watching now. She couldn't stop shaking.

"What do you think I should do, call the police?"

Stephanie handed her the coffee. "Definitely, they need to know. But listen, Millie, don't read too much into that note, he's probably only trying to scare you. He knows if he breaks that restraining order he'll go to prison. Why would he risk that?"

Millie knew the answer to that question, had known it from the moment she'd read his threat: because Craig Manderly had lost the control he'd once had and would do anything to get it back.

The police arrived later in the day; an older officer accompanied by a rookie. *A routine call* they said. She guessed her problems weren't a priority. A question and answer session followed.

"How long have you been separated?"
Six months.
"Have you been in touch with Craig Manderly?"
No.
"Has he been in touch with you?"
Only by the note I found this morning.
"How do you think he managed to find you?"
I have no idea.
The policemen glanced at each other.
"Why would he risk breaking a court order to threaten you?"
They didn't know him like she did.
"Do you think it was him who left the note?"
Who else could it be?
Again, another glance.

"Could we take a look at your computer?"

The inference was obvious: they suspected she might have printed the note. God knows why. Did they think she was doing it for the attention? That was when Millie lost her temper.

I was the one he beat up. I was the one being followed everywhere.

"Did you enjoy that?"

What?! She couldn't help thinking that maybe the younger officer believed some women asked for it. It took all her self-control not to tell him to fuck off.

They left with a promise that an officer would visit her ex-boyfriend and have a quiet word.

"It normally does the trick," the older man said, as if he was a magician and Millie's stalker was nothing more than a rabbit he might pull from a hat.

***

The evening sun had draped shadows over Churchway Close. The flowers Millie held as she crossed the driveway had taken half the afternoon to purchase. When she'd attempted to leave her house earlier, traffic beyond the cul-de-sac had formed long lines in either direction.

"A head-on collision," a passer-by informed her as she sat waiting for a gap to pull into. The sound of sirens confirmed the pedestrian's message. It had been late in the day by the time the road had cleared.

She went to knock on the Ward's door and hesitated. Through the glass Millie could see Lee and Stephanie, they appeared to be arguing.

Lee's wife had a finger pointed in his face, waving it back and forth like a weapon as she emphasised a point. Millie could see her mouth working, a constant barrage of words played out like a silent movie. Their disagreement seemed to be serious. She wondered whether to call back in the morning. Lee raised his hands in a mime of explanation and as Stephanie went to shout him down she caught a glimpse of Millie. The anger on her face instantly transformed itself into a smile. She glanced back at her husband and then opened the door.

"Why, Millie, we didn't hear you knock."

Was there an undertone of accusation in her words? If so, Millie could understand why, she'd obviously caught them at a bad time.

"I'm sorry if I'm interrupting anything," she said, and handed Stephanie the bouquet. "I wanted to give you these as a thank you for what you did for me today."

Her neighbour's smile turned warmer. "They're lovely. Look, why not come in and have a glass of wine?"

Millie glanced from Stephanie to Lee. "Are you sure I'm not intruding?"

It was Lee's turn to act as if their argument had never happened. "Of course not," he said. "Anyway, we want to hear how your visit from the police went."

Millie stayed longer than she planned. The evening disappeared as one bottle of wine led to another. It was almost midnight by the time she left.

She was pleasantly drunk, a feeling that clouded the misgivings she'd had since finding Craig's note.

Perhaps she was over-reacting, hadn't Stephanie almost convinced her that was the case? Even the police didn't appear to think it was a matter of great concern. Still, she wasn't sure. In a week's time she was due to start a new job; she didn't want the thought of leaving the house empty all day playing on her mind.

As she made her way upstairs she remembered watching Lee Ward washing his car. She could still see the beads of sweat clinging to his back and recalled how she'd longed to run the tip of her tongue across his skin. Was he watching now?

She switched on a bedside lamp; soft shadows patterned the walls. Millie walked across the room and stood in front of the window. Across the driveway the Ward's house was in darkness. A silhouetted figure stood behind half-closed curtains. She smiled to herself and very slowly slipped out of her clothes.

***

Someone was thumping their fist against the front door. The sound was like thunder as it broke into her sleep. She sat up and clutched the sheets to her. The bedside clock said 7a.m. *He's come back to finish what he started!* Fear drained her of the will to move. When she finally gathered the courage to leave her bed the noise abruptly stopped.

She tip-toed down the stairs and peered through the hallway window, certain she'd see the figure of Craig Manderly standing on the porch step with a triumphant look on his face. She could even hear his voice. *Open up, Millie, I've come to do the damage I promised.*

No-one was there.

Another note lay on the hallway floor. This time there was no envelope. Millie could read the message from where she stood.

IT'S ALL YOUR FAULT. I'M GOING TO MAKE YOU PAY.

She let out a cry and picked up the telephone.

The policewoman who answered her call seemed reluctant to talk over the phone. Millie explained who she was.

"I've got your records," the officer said. "What's the problem?"

"Craig Manderly's been to my house again," Millie was close to tears. "I want something done about it." She could hear the woman tapping details into a computer.

"Someone will be round," she said, and hung up without waiting for a reply. Millie held the dead phone in her hand and wondered what she'd do if Manderly came back before the police arrived.

Thirty minutes later a patrol car pulled into the close. Two officers climbed out; a man and a woman; Mille was relieved it wasn't the young rookie.

She opened the door as they walked up the pathway. Neither of them smiled as she invited them in and both refused her offer of a hot drink.

"I'm Officer Hendricks," the woman said. "This is Constable Appleby." The man nodded. "Can you tell us what happened?"

Millie produced the note.

"He's come back again," she said. "Craig Manderly was here last night." She ran a hand through her hair. "This is only the beginning, I know it. He's going to keep on harassing me until I can't stand it any longer."

There was an awkward silence. Officer Hendricks spoke.

"Miss French, I'm sorry to be the one to break the news, but your ex-boyfriend was killed in a road accident yesterday afternoon." She gestured out of the window. "It happened five-hundred yards away on the main road. We believe he was on his way to see you. What time did you get the note?"

Millie didn't hear the question, she was still trying to take in the fact Craig was dead. An image of traffic queued up as she tried to leave Churchway Close the day before entered her mind; a passer-by informing her there'd been a head-on collision.

"That's impossible," she whispered. "He was knocking on my door this morning."

The officers swapped a glance similar to one another police team had exchanged.

"Whoever that was, it wasn't Craig Manderly," Hendricks said.

Millie stared at them. "Then who could it be?"

Appleby spoke for the first time. "We were hoping you'd be able to tell us."

Their attitude towards her thawed as the interview went on; perhaps due to the fact they could see the state she was in, or maybe because they sensed she was telling the truth. Either way, this time there was no request to look at her computer or the vague insinuation she had somehow encouraged Craig Manderly.

Millie's relief at knowing she was free of her stalker was tempered by the realisation someone else was posting poisonous mail through her front door.

"So it couldn't have been him who left the first note, either?"

Hendricks had told her they'd managed to track Manderly's movements up to the moment of the crash. Harry Beale had phoned them; he'd had second thoughts after revealing Millie's new address and decided to clear his conscience. That call had come long after her first warning.

"We think maybe Manderly did intend to harass you but he never got the chance. Is there anyone else you can think of who might bear you a grudge?"

Appleby's question echoed the one she'd been asking herself.

"Nobody," she said, "nobody at all."

But Millie French was wrong. Someone did hold a grudge against her. The proof was printed in capital letters on the note she held in her hands.

It was only after the officers had left and Millie was running events through her head that a suspicion wormed its way to the front of her thoughts. The neighbours: Lee and Stephanie Ward. Since she'd relocated they were the only people who knew of Craig's threats. She remembered being invited over the evening after she'd moved in. The first note had even been a word by word copy of the line she said her ex had used. *I can do a lot of damage.* It was ridiculous. All they'd shown her was kindness.

She recalled the row she'd witnessed, the way a smile had draped itself over Stephanie Ward's angry face when she'd caught sight of Millie. But surely that meant nothing, it was only an argument; a married couple's domestic. Anyway, why would her neighbours dream of doing such a thing?

She didn't know, but it was a question that left her feeling uneasy.

The plan came to her as she worried the day away. It would mean lying and keeping the truth from her neighbours, but she needed to gauge their reaction. Millie stared at the Ward's house and hoped her suspicions were ill-founded.

***

"I saw the police here earlier. Is everything okay?"

Stephanie Ward was at the door; her look of concern could have hidden anything. Millie stared into her neighbour's face and smiled.

"It was just another routine call," she lied. "They were checking to see if I'd had any more threatening notes delivered."

The look of concern had become rigid, as if Stephanie Ward was afraid to try another expression. Her eyes searched Millie's.

"Have you?"

"Not yet," Millie said. She paused. "The police told me they'd warned Craig and that they're keeping an eye on him. What good that's going to do, I have no idea."

Stephanie Ward's features eventually broke into an unconvincing smile. "As long as you're sure everything's okay." She turned to go and looked back. "It's just I thought I saw someone on your driveway earlier this morning and wondered who it might have been."

Millie frowned. "What time was that?" She watched her neighbour pretending to mentally tick off the hours.

"I think it was about seven o'clock."

"I didn't hear anything," Millie said.

Stephanie Ward's eyes gave her away. The smile strained to stay in place.

"I must have been mistaken," she said, and hurried back across the driveway.

Millie watched her go. They'd told each other lies and had both known it.

She spent most of the night staring at the bedside clock, unable to sleep as Stephanie Ward's visit re-ran itself through her mind. The lies had become clearer with every sleepless moment.

Stephanie's fake smile when Millie told her she hadn't received another note.

The invented visitor: 'I thought I saw someone on your driveway.'

The look of disbelief her neighbour couldn't disguise after Millie said she'd heard no-one.

She knew now Craig Manderly had never been anywhere near her house – apart from on the day he died. Stephanie Ward was the mystery stalker, the person attempting to make her life a misery. She couldn't make sense of it. Why would the woman want to play such an evil trick? Before she eventually drifted into sleep Millie decided she needed to talk to Lee Ward, and she needed to talk to him alone.

***

The next morning she witnessed another altercation between the Wards; one stranger and more violent than their previous row.

She'd got up and made her way downstairs, relieved to find nothing more than a couple of circulars lying on the hallway floor. As she bent to pick them up she saw Stephanie Ward fling open her front door. There was a bucket at her feet and a cloth in her hand; she was still dressed as if she were on the catwalk. Her face was like thunder. She picked up the bucket, slammed the door shut and walked around to her kitchen window. From where Millie was standing she could just see what was happening.

Her neighbour slopped the cloth into the bucket and began furiously rubbing the wet rag against the glass. There was a blemish spoiling Stephanie Ward's perfect property and she was determined to remove it.

Then Lee appeared. He seemed to be trying to coax her back inside. When she ignored him he took the cloth from her fingers and smiled, and then pointed through the kitchen window. Whatever remark he made enraged his wife further. Her face grew darker. She picked up the bucket, barked something at her husband and then threw the dirty water over him.

Millie watched her storm back into the house and felt sorry for Lee. He stood there soaked with a look of despair on his face. Then he shook his head and reluctantly followed his wife indoors.

Twenty minutes later Stephanie Ward drove out of Churchway Close. Millie watched her leave with a sense of relief. Now was her chance to get to the truth.

"Could I come in for a moment?"

Lee Ward held the door ajar; he seemed guarded, on edge. Millie couldn't blame him, after his wife's earlier performance she wondered what other behaviour he was forced to endure.

"Sure." He pulled back the door and beckoned her in.

"What's wrong?"

They were seated in a kitchen that belonged in a show home; Lee Ward looked as if he already knew the answer to his question.

"Look," Millie said. "I know you're going to find this hard to believe but Stephanie is the one who's been posting those threats. I've thought it through. The police told me Craig was killed in a car accident and yet I still received another note. It was your wife."

Her neighbour didn't even appear surprised. "I knew she was up to something," he said. "Ever since the morning she caught me watching you she's been acting strangely." His face coloured. "It wasn't deliberate. I just happened to catch sight of you in your bedroom." He looked at his hands. "The sun was shining. I knew you hadn't realised you could be seen and I couldn't stop staring."

It was Millie's turn to be embarrassed. Lee carried on.

"She went berserk and accused me of being unfaithful." He sighed. "As if that would matter, our marriage has been over for a long time, although Stephanie would insist that isn't true. We sleep in separate rooms. We only have civilised conversations when someone else is present. She doesn't want me; she just wants the trappings that come with a relationship."

"Lee, why don't you leave her?"

He rubbed his eyes. Millie realised how tired he looked.

"I've tried to, but Stephanie's manipulative. She's threatened to kill herself. She said she'd never be able to stand the shame, as if a broken marriage was the worst thing that could possibly happen to anybody. *'What would my family think?'* she said. *'What would our friends say?'* Millie, she fell out with her family a long time ago. Now they don't speak. As for friends, we haven't got any."

He looked around the kitchen.

"She's obsessed with perfection. That's all she cares about; the things that don't matter."

Millie placed her hand on his and remembered Lee once doing the same to her. They stared at each other. It was so quiet they could hear each other breathing. When he kissed her she didn't pull away. It might have been wrong but it didn't feel that way.

The front door burst open.

This time there was no false smile camouflaging Stephanie Ward's features. The woman looked crazy.

"What are you doing in my house, you slut? Trying to seduce my husband?"

Millie pulled away. Her neighbour slung her bag on the floor and closed in on her.

"I knew something was going on. Don't you think I haven't noticed the way you stare at my husband; all those lingering looks and come-on smiles? You must think I'm stupid. I've seen you walking around your bedroom with nothing on, trying to entice my husband. Well I'll tell you this, he's mine!"

As she spat the words into Millie's face Millie realised a terrible truth. The other times she thought Lee had been watching from the window it had been his wife. Guilt and anger curdled in her stomach.

"Is that why you've been posting those notes?"

Millie's question silenced her neighbour. Stephanie Ward glanced at her husband; for a moment Millie thought she was going to deny it; plead her innocence and try to win back Lee. Then she saw the twisted grin on Stephanie's face.

"You deserved it. No wonder your ex wanted to harm you, I know how he must have felt."

"Stephanie, shut up!" She flinched at her husband's words. "Our marriage breakdown has got nothing to do with Millie and you know it. It's been over for a long time."

"HAS IT? HAS IT?" Stephanie Ward screamed the words. Millie saw flecks of spittle form at the corners of her mouth. "Perhaps it has for you, but I've been the one working to mend what she's broken."

Lee shook his head. "What are you on about?"

Stephanie jabbed a finger in Millie's direction. "You know exactly what I mean. Her! Well listen to me," she shouted, "I'm not having my perfect life ruined by a whore and a husband who can't keep his hands off other women. Do you hear me?"

She backed into the kitchen and wrenched open a drawer. Her eyes were unreadable; blank discs with insanity written invisibly across them. She pulled out a knife and held it in front of her.

"I'm sick of trying," she said. Her voice had dropped to a whisper. Expression had returned to her eyes. It looked worse than the dead stare it replaced. "Sick of working on things that don't deserve the effort and sick of trying to mend things other people have broken." Stephanie Ward laughed, as if she found the thought of sickness and broken things unbearably funny. Then she took a step across the kitchen and raised the knife.

***

It seemed to Millie that Churchway Close had been as much a temporary address as the rented rooms she'd moved into in her attempt to escape Craig Manderly. Now Mulberry Crescent was home, another peaceful backwater she hoped would become a more permanent abode.

As she cracked two eggs into a frying pan Lee wandered into the kitchen. He was dressed in a pair of jog-bottoms and Millie was reminded of the morning she'd seen him washing his car. He kissed her on the neck.

"Breakfast is almost ready," she said.

His hands moved up her body and cupped her breasts. She laughed.

"I think you ought to get some food down you before I wear you out completely."

Lee grinned. "We'll see who wears who out first," he joked, and sat at the table.

It had been almost six months since they'd moved in together and they were happy. It was a new feeling for both of them.

They'd agreed leaving Churchway Close had been the right thing to do. The image of Stephanie wielding a knife in their faces as the police pulled up outside was a memory that needed distance. They'd been lucky, if the officers hadn't been making a routine call Millie dreaded to think what the outcome of that particular morning might have been.

She remembered them dragging a kicking and screaming Stephanie from the house: the knife lying on the kitchen floor: Lee's arms around her.

Now his ex-wife was detained in a secure hospital. *'A mental breakdown,'* doctors had diagnosed. Millie couldn't help thinking it was more than that. There was something bad inside Stephanie Ward, and she had a feeling it would take more than psychiatric help to get rid of it.

She placed Lee's breakfast in front of him and heard the sound of the paper being delivered.

"I'll get it," she said. As she made her way into the hall the phone rang. Lee picked up the handset at the same moment she lifted the paper from the floor.

Beneath it there was an envelope. Millie felt her heart miss a beat.

"MILLIE!"

Lee was calling. His voice sounded close to panic. "MILLIE," he shouted again. "That was the police. Stephanie's gone missing. They think she escaped from the hospital last night."

Millie walked into the kitchen and stared at him. He was still holding the phone.

"I know," she said and handed him a piece of paper. On it were seven words neatly printed in capital letters.

I CAN DO A LOT OF DAMAGE.

ONCE IN A LIFETIME

Henderson longed to be back in the city; to feel himself a cog in something vital, to be part of a creative process that long ago had enthralled him. Most of all he longed to be the journalist he once was.

Over the years his fondness for the bottle had become an irresistible attraction. It was a love affair that had gradually led to missed deadlines, rejected copy and apologetic dismissals. Now his work as a small time reporter on an even smaller publication had brought him to Cotters Grey. If ever there was an end of the line, a last chance saloon, Richard Henderson had surely reached that point.

Yet even in this remote outpost of the English countryside someone had recognised him. He'd entered the Haymow, and as he ordered a drink the barman had asked him the question that had stalked him through time. *'Aren't you Richard Henderson?'* Twenty years after he'd made headline news his fleeting brush with fame still followed him like a shadow.

***

It had been a routine press investigation involving a gang passing counterfeit notes. Henderson had questioned an old man, Michael Alford, who'd happened to find himself in possession of a small amount of the illegal tender. Although innocent of any involvement the old boy's behaviour had aroused suspicion. He'd been evasive, his answers erratic, stumbling over sentences as he altered irrelevant details. Henderson realised Michael

Alford had been frightened, as if he clung to a secret and was afraid he was slowly losing his grip.

In those days Henderson had been keen, full of youthful exuberance and a wide-eyed determination to get to the truth. Most of all he'd had a nose for a story. He scented one and began to dig. The details he eventually uncovered led to a once in a lifetime scoop.

Alford, the old man eking out an existence as a night-watchman, had once been Reinhardt Braun, a prominent Gestapo member and a war criminal the world believed dead. The story had been a sensation. The reporter became the reported. Suddenly everybody wanted to hear about the undercover Nazi and the man who'd tracked him down.

But Braun had managed to kill himself after being taken into custody, hanging himself by his bootlaces in his cell. With the media cheated of their prey the spotlight of celebrity switched back to Henderson. How he'd bathed in its glow.

That story had cemented his reputation as a promising investigative journalist; a reputation he'd spent the last twenty years trading on until it had become worthless.

***

"Same again, Mr Henderson?" The barman pushed a pint across the counter. "It's on the house." The drinkers crowded around the bar nodded their approval. Henderson had long ago realised once people discovered you were a reporter they all had a story to tell and were prepared to buy you drinks until their chance to share it came.

"Thanks," he said.

"So why are you here?" the barman asked.

Henderson could have said. *'Because I drink too much: because I've wasted what little talent God gave me. Because as a young man I took a wrong turn and never found my way back.'*

Instead he smiled and raised his glass. "I believe you're in the middle of a mini crime-wave," he said. "I've come to put Cotters Grey on the map."

A couple of the locals cheered at his statement, the others laughed. Henderson hoped they weren't expecting him to make them as famous as the late Reinhardt Braun.

Cotters Grey had suffered a spate of burglaries, an unusual occurrence in such a small community, and one of those robberies had led to tragedy. Barry Morgan, a man regarded locally as a recluse, had been found lying dead on the hallway floor of his ransacked cottage. Cause of death had been a head wound. The police concluded seventy-two-year-old Morgan had disturbed the intruders and attempted to fight back. It was a case that had resulted in a brief flurry of publicity, along with the local constabulary pleading to hear from anyone who might be able to help them with their enquiries.

Morgan had no family and few friends; public response had been lacklustre. Since then the burglaries had stopped, investigations had hit a dead-end, and now the case was slowly gathering cobwebs as it sat on the back-burner.

Henderson had been sent to Cotters Grey to put meat on the bones of an old story; to interview the locals and cobble together an article on how crime was affecting rural areas. It was an assignment he could have carried out in his sleep. Through the years he'd perfected the art of transforming the used into something resembling the new. His conscience told him it was a lazy man's way to earn a living, but no-one had ever accused him face-to-face of plagiarism, although he suspected many of his critics privately voiced that opinion.

It was those suspicions that occasionally made him wonder where the young man he'd once been had gone. When the hour was late and the bar closed he'd stare into the bottom of an empty glass and see a future made up of second rate copy and time spent quibbling over expense claims.

"The budget's tight," his editor, Philip Morley had told him, just before Henderson left for Cotters Grey. "Please don't abuse it, Richard."

Henderson knew Morley could have been a millionaire and the budget would have still been tight. He was an old fashioned newspaperman who believed in dotting the I's and crossing the T's before a story went anywhere near print. His request had carried a weight of meaning. *'Please don't abuse it.'* It was a plea the reporter found difficult to grant and also made him feel guilty: he owed his boss.

Morley had hired Henderson when every other door the journalist knocked on had been closed. Perhaps it was due to the fact the editor had once conducted a similar affair with the bottle but managed to break it off before it became serious. That or maybe he remembered the impact a young Henderson had made and hoped his paper might benefit from that distant connection.

The time bell rang. Henderson looked at his watch, finding it hard to believe a pub would close on a Sunday afternoon. His longing for a return to the city increased.

A while later he climbed the stairs to his room. As he lay on the bed and closed his eyes the voices from the bar followed him into sleep, each of them eager to share a story he could never possibly print.

***

It was late afternoon when he woke. The pub was still closed. To kill time he decided to drive out and take a look at the house where Barry Morgan's life had been so brutally ended. It'd also give him a chance to get a feel for the area. He left the Haymow, pulled out of the car park and drove into unfamiliar countryside.

It took him longer than expected to locate Morgan's cottage. Twice he became lost and had to retrace his route. When Henderson did eventually find the ramshackle dwelling he could see how the murder victim had gained his reputation as a recluse. The house was in the middle of nowhere, stranded between a maze of overgrown lanes and thick woodland. He missed a turn-off almost obscured by untidy hedging and low hanging branches and pulled onto a grass verge.

The mild spring evening still held daylight. As he walked back to the driveway he thought the silence was something he'd never get used to. He'd been brought up with the sounds of the city and the fond memory of them had stayed with him through his long exile.

The narrow entrance that led to the late Barry Morgan's cottage ran between an avenue of hawthorn and cherry laurel before emerging into a front garden that resembled a scrap yard. The rusting skeleton of a derelict car stood propped on bricks, as if forever waiting to be driven away. A washing machine lay on its side in the mud. Someone had dumped a mattress in the long grass that had once been a lawn.

He shook his head and turned his attention to the house. The boarded windows were the only clue to the fact it had once been a crime scene. Henderson found it hard to believe the old man had lived in such squalor.

The front door was locked. Another area of overgrown garden ran down the side of the house. He stepped over a low fence and pushed his way through a screen of tangled shrubbery.

The back of the cottage resembled the front; a jumble of discarded rubbish half-hidden by wild bramble and uncut grass. When he crossed a flagstone patio and pushed against the back door it swung open into shadow. Thin shafts of light forced their way through gaps in the boards.

Barry Morgan's house was testament to the frugal life he'd lived. The kitchen cupboards looked as if they dated back to the 1970's; much like the grease smeared gas cooker and an old fridge that stood with its door hanging open. In the corner a Formica-covered table completed the depressing scene.

The kitchen door opened into a hallway. To the left a lounge-diner was home to a faded three-piece suite and an old-fashioned television set. Motorbike parts were laid across the floor where a dining table should have stood. The place smelt of damp. Henderson wondered why anyone would want to burgle such a run-down hovel and also kill the owner while doing it.

There was no carpet on the stairs. The bare boards creaked as he made his way onto the landing. Not all the first floor windows had been boarded and the upstairs was bathed in half-light. He glanced back down and imagined a dead body lying on the hallway floor.

Morgan's bedroom was another mirror that reflected how the man had lived: a stained mattress covered with blankets; old clothes strewn across the floor. A bare bulb hung from the ceiling like an afterthought.

The spare bedroom was empty. Only the bathroom gave any indication that someone had once lived here. There was a lump of soap and a razor in a dish on the sink. A toothbrush lay between the taps. Above the basin was a shaving mirror, its surface smeared with dust. When Henderson rubbed the glass the frame came loose. Before he could catch it the mirror fell and smashed against the sink. He swore, and as he bent down to pick up the remnants he saw a yellowed fragment of paper that had been tucked between the frame and the glass.

Henderson carefully unfolded the page and held it up. Daylight slanted through the boards, picking out a headline.

WAGE SNATCH GANG ESCAPE WITH FORTUNE.

He read further.

Today police are hunting for a number of men who held up and robbed a security van after ambushing it in the back lanes of Cotters Grey. Once they'd forced the driver to unlock the rear of the vehicle they bound and gagged him before escaping with wages bound for Mentor, the engineering company based two miles from the town of Shaftbourne.

As we go to press Mentor have yet to release details of how much was stolen, but taking into account the holiday period was due, it's safe to assume the amount would be double that of an average week's payroll.

There was no date of when the robbery had occurred but judging by the colour of the paper Henderson guessed it must have been years ago.

Someone had penned four initials across the bottom right hand corner of the page. Although the ink had faded they were still visible: CGMB. He stared at them and frowned; was it a code? He guessed the first two letters stood for Cotters Grey, but what the M and B meant he had no idea. He carefully folded the paper and slipped it into his pocket. Perhaps Barry Morgan's murder hadn't been as random as first suspected. There was a story here, he could smell it; it was a scent that many years ago had excited him.

When he made his way out into the back garden dusk had fallen. Again he found the silence unnatural. A breeze scattered leaves across the no-man's land Morgan had once called home. Henderson buried his hands in his pockets and hurried down the driveway. He needed a drink.

***

The Haymow was busy. Word had spread that a reporter was staying, and in a small community like Cotters Grey, Richard Henderson was a celebrity. He enjoyed the attention, in some ways it reminded him of the days when he could be guaranteed a welcome in every drinking establishment from Fleet Street to Soho.

"What was Reinhardt Braun really like, Richard?"

How many times had he heard that question? He longed to tell the truth: a sad, frightened old man whose loneliness clung to him like another skin. A man who seemed relieved to have finally reached the point in his life he'd always dreaded. But people didn't want to hear that. They wanted the villain of their imagination. He gave it to them.

"Braun?" Henderson shook his head, as if the mere mention of the name disgusted him. "Arrogant," he said; "cold beyond belief. When he looked you in the eye all you could see was hatred. I'm sure he'd have killed me if he could. He was like a cornered animal without the strength to fight his way to freedom."

His answer seemed to thrill Valerie May, the woman whose question had taken him back to a different time. Her husband was at the bar refilling their glasses. She rested her hand on his. "Will you be staying long in Cotters Grey?" She stared at him and smiled, a woman approaching her early forties, attractive and obviously bored. If she hadn't been married he might have been interested.

"I'm afraid not," he said, and withdrew his hand as her husband placed their drinks on the table.

"So what did you think of Barry Morgan's place?" Gerald May had rescued him from a session that had threatened to get out of hand. The crowd at the bar had been determined to see if their visitor could match them drink for drink. Henderson suspected he wouldn't have found it a problem but Philip Morley's words kept coming back to him. *Please don't abuse it.*

He raised his glass. "He wasn't one for home comforts."

May laughed. "I've only seen his cottage from the road," he said, "but even from there you could get an idea of the way he lived."

"Did you find anything of interest?" Valerie seemed to have taken his rebuttal gracefully. By the way one or two of the regulars glanced in her direction he suspected Gerald's wife was a woman who became bored easily.

"I was surprised," he said. "The back door was open."

The May's looked at him, as if expecting to hear a headline-grabbing story. He shrugged his shoulders.

"The place was a mess but I did find a piece of paper that intrigued me."

Henderson didn't mention the fact it was an old newspaper cutting, or that it had been concealed behind the bathroom mirror; he still possessed a journalist's instincts. Gerald and Valerie were waiting for him to continue.

"It had CGMB, written on it; does that mean anything to either of you?"

Husband and wife looked at each other and burst out laughing. Henderson grinned. "What am I missing?" he asked.

"It's no big mystery, Richard." Gerald had recovered his composure. "The letters stand for Cotters Grey Military Base."

Henderson was surprised. "Military base? Here?"

It was May's turn to shrug his shoulders. "Not anymore," he said. "At least not one that's operational. It was closed down before we moved here." He looked at his wife. "How long is that?"

Valerie thought for a moment. "Over twenty years," she said, and suddenly seemed to remember something. "Wasn't there talk of a body being discovered on the site shortly after the military pulled out?"

Her husband nodded. "That's right," he said. "As I recall nobody knew who it was or where they came from. I don't think the police ever found out either."

Henderson took a long draught of beer and placed his glass back on the table. Behind him the crowd at the bar were getting louder. He didn't hear them. *Robbery and murder:* the scent was getting stronger.

Eventually he'd joined the boisterous crowd at the bar. Once Gerald and his wife had left he'd been unable to refuse their repeated invitations. The night ended late.

Henderson had been right; matching them drink for drink hadn't been a problem.

***

Black coffee took the edge off a headache that sat above his eyes like an old friend. He skipped breakfast and called his way through a short list of telephone numbers. Four out of five answered; victims of burglary eager to tell their side of the story.

'Will we be in the papers?' one of the women had asked, as if breaking and entering and the robbery it led to were some kind of reality show that guaranteed fame. Henderson had lied and assured her she would. He remembered a time when the public would have been reluctant to see their names mentioned in the press, now it seemed they couldn't wait.

He spent the morning drinking tea and listening to each of the victims' tell a familiar story.

'My wallet was on the side, they must have missed it.'

'Michelle was fortunate they didn't take her jewellery.'

'When we looked the cash was still there.'

Henderson couldn't understand it; why risk breaking into people's houses and then leave valuables behind? None of those he spoke to had suffered serious loss. It was only Barry Morgan, the man with least to lose, who'd had something stolen from him that could never be replaced.

By the time he left the last house he'd already sketched out in his mind how his article would fit together. Some of the facts might need spicing up a little, but blurring the line between fact and fiction was a talent he'd developed through the years.

Cotters Grey military base had been on his mind all morning. Ever since he'd found the newspaper cutting and discovered what the initials stood for he'd known it was a visit he had to make. He fought the urge to stop for a lunchtime pint and made a call to the office. Philip Morley half-heartedly agreed there might be a story but Henderson could hear the doubt in his voice. When the call ended he could imagine the editor wondering how much more his reporter was hoping to claim on expenses.

Gerald and Valerie May had given him rough directions for the base. He drove out of the village and watched the midday sky cloud over.

Forty-five minutes later he swung off a road that looked like all the rest and pulled onto another.

There was a rusted chain strung between two posts, hanging waist height across the lane. He pulled up and climbed from the car. Beyond the barrier stood a weather-faded sign; Henderson could just make out the lettering.

MINISTRY OF DEFENCE

PRIVATE

KEEP OUT

The chain was only hooked into a cleat. He unclipped it, climbed back into his car and made his way slowly forwards. Weeds had forced their way through the tarmac. Clumps of nettle and bramble spilled into the lane. Beyond the verge, where the woods grew thick, treetops swayed silently in the breeze.

A quarter of a mile later the undergrowth thinned. As Henderson turned a bend he saw a disused security hut standing next to a pair of open gates. A rusty, six-foot-high fence flanked the entrance. Barbed-wire ran along the top of the chain link. In the distance he could see a compound framed by a cluster of single storey buildings.

He pulled up and climbed from the car. Behind the fence was another sign, it's worn out lettering stating he was entering COTTERS GREY MILITARY BASE, and it was a RESTRICTED ZONE. He doubted that was still true.

Henderson gazed into the empty camp and felt uneasy; beyond the clearing clouds had formed banks that towered into the sky as if trapped. A plastic bag flapped noisily in the breeze, caught on the fence like a lost kite.

He rested his hands against the wire. *Why had Barry Morgan scribbled initials on a newspaper cutting concealed behind a mirror?* As he drove through the gates another thought entered his head: *What am I doing out here?*

The base was larger than it appeared from the entrance. Behind the main quarters stood two lines of huts; he parked in the slip-road that ran between them and climbed out.

It was hard to imagine the deserted walkways had once echoed with the sound of marching boots. Dust-coated windows revealed nothing more than forgotten shadows and empty rooms. The sound of a car engine distracted him as he was trying to force open a door.

From behind a corner of the nearest building he gazed towards the camp entrance. A beaten-up Land Rover had pulled onto the base and stopped just inside the gates. Two men got out and looked around. One of them was carrying a crowbar. He tapped it impatiently across the flat of his hand. Their voices were low, but the breeze carried their words across the flat expanse of the parade ground.

"Did you hook the chain up properly last time we were here?"

Henderson remembered leaving it lying across the lane and swore at his stupidity.

The man who'd spoken was the one holding the crowbar. He was tall and muscular and carried the arrogant body language of someone used to giving orders. His companion was a good head shorter. He scratched at his scalp as if memory wasn't his strong point.

"I thought I did, Luke, but I might be wrong."

The big man cursed. "I can't trust you to do anything, can I? You're fucking useless, Dessie, do you know that?"

Dessie nodded in reluctant agreement. "Sorry, Luke," he said.

His companion seemed as if he wanted to take the argument further and then stopped.

"This is the last time we search that place," he said. "It's getting too risky. I'm starting to think Morgan wasn't telling us the truth."

"Well we can't question him again Luke," Dessie said, and laughed. "Not unless it's through a medium."

The big man scowled. "Shut the fuck up Dessie and get back in the car." He pointed to a Nissan hut standing at the end of a row of buildings on the far side of the compound. "Let's try again," he said, "and this time we'll smash the place apart if we have to."

From his vantage point Henderson watched them drive across the parade ground. The day had grown darker. Headlight beams chased shadows along the flank of a building. Rain had begun to fall. He was scared.

Luke and Dessie had killed Morgan, he was sure of it, murdered the old man for information they weren't even certain was true. *What were they searching for?* It had to be money, something to do with the payroll that years ago had been looted from the back of a hijacked security van.

The car pulled up and the doors opened. Two shadows stepped out and then disappeared from view behind the hut. Moments later sounds of destruction carried over the camp. He looked back at his own vehicle and wondered if it was worth trying to drive away while the pair of them were occupied. Would he have time to make it through the gates? As he hesitated a sudden gust of wind blew two words across the parade ground.

"It's here!"

***

It was dark. The heater was on full blast. He'd watched the windows fog and listened as rain beat against the car roof. Luke and Dessie had left the base twenty minutes earlier, once they'd found what they were looking for they hadn't hung around. As they'd climbed into the Land Rover, Henderson had peered through the slanting rain and saw Luke carrying what appeared to be a pair of plastic holdalls. The two men had been laughing.

When he was sure they were gone he'd driven across to the Nissan hut. The door had been forced. He'd taken a torch from the car and stepped inside. It looked as if the place had been used as a storeroom and never emptied. He remembered Luke's threat: *'we'll smash the place apart if we have to.'* That's what they'd done. Rotting furniture had been thrown across the floor.

Cupboard doors hung lopsidedly from broken hinges. The iron frame of an old bunk bed had been pushed over. Beneath ripped up floorboards he found a hollow large enough to conceal two bags. *Buried treasure,* Henderson had thought, and wondered how long it had been sitting there.

It was still raining as he drove away from the camp. His thoughts kept returning to Barry Morgan and what part the old man had played in something that had led to his death. Then there was the puzzle of the burglaries; break-ins where hardly anything of value had been stolen. There was a connection somewhere but he couldn't make it. All he was sure of was the fact Luke and his accomplice were murderers, and even that he couldn't prove.

He pulled onto a road he didn't recognise and hoped he was heading in the right direction.

***

Once he'd showered and had dinner he went into the bar. The return journey had taken a lot longer than the one to the base. The back lanes had been dark and full of wrong turns. He'd been glad to see the illuminated sign of the Haymow.

The pub was quiet. He checked his watch, there were still a couple of hours until closing time and as he settled onto a stool the barman poured him a pint.

"How's your day been?" the old man asked, and placed the glass on the bar.

Henderson gazed into the amber liquid, tiny bubbles rose to the surface; it was like watching a magic show you never tired of. "It could've been better," he said, and nodded towards his drink. "Are you having one yourself?"

The barman grinned and pulled himself a half. "Cheers," he said, and raised his glass.

Henderson returned the salute. "How long have you been landlord here?" he asked.

The old man rubbed his chin and thought. "Well, I was born in Cotters Grey," he said, "and I took over the running of the Haymow when Eddie Stephens decided he'd had enough of pulling pints and went to live in Spain."

Henderson took a swallow of his beer and listened.

"That was thirty years ago," the landlord said, "and if anybody had told me then how quickly the years would disappear I wouldn't have believed them." As he wiped a cloth over the counter Henderson asked him a question that had been playing on his mind.

"Did you know Barry Morgan?"

The barman shook his head at the mention of the name. "Of course I did the poor old soul. Look at the way he ended up, living alone in that pigsty he called a home." He rested his elbows on the bar and lowered his voice. "He was never the same after what happened to him all those years ago."

Henderson paused in the act of lifting his glass and frowned. The landlord saw his expression and carried on. "Morgan wasn't always a recluse" he said. "In his younger days he was a different man entirely, and not all good, I can tell you. I don't mean to speak ill of the dead but he was a cocky little bugger, had a mean streak a mile wide. Thought he was the bees-knees he did." The landlord gave a grim smile. "Of course," he continued, "he changed after the robbery, that knocked the stuffing out of him."

"Robbery? What robbery?" Henderson thought of a newspaper cutting folded behind a mirror.

The old man seemed to relish recounting the past. "Barry Morgan used to drive for a security company," he said. "That was in the days before wages were paid directly into the bank. He was delivering a double payroll when he got ambushed by a gang of thieves. They cleaned out the van and beat up Morgan into the bargain. The police found him trussed up in the back of own truck." The landlord shrugged his shoulders, as if getting assaulted was only to be expected in that line of work. He finished his beer. "Same again?" he asked.

Henderson hadn't realised he'd emptied his glass; the landlord's words had stunned him. *Barry Morgan was the driver.* As vague pieces of a puzzle began to fit into place the two men he'd seen loading holdalls into a battered Land Rover walked into the pub.

The barman recognised them. He placed a fresh pint in front of Henderson and lifted a finger to his lips in a discreet sign that the subject was closed.

"Two pints please, Arthur." The big man called Luke placed a ten pound note on the bar and stared at Henderson. "You must be the reporter I've heard about," he said.

Henderson forced a smile; he remembered hearing Dessie's joke that they'd need a medium to get in touch with Barry Morgan. "News certainly gets around," he said.

Luke continued gazing at him, sizing him up the way a street-fighter might weigh up an opponent. "Discovered anything interesting?" he asked.

Henderson matched his stare. "What, in Cotters Grey?" he said, and grinned.

There was a pause and then Luke grunted, as if he got the joke but didn't find it funny. He broke eye contact and handed Dessie his drink. "Fella here reckons nothing happens in Cotters Grey."

It was Dessie's turn to eyeball Henderson. "Is that so?" he said, and laughed, a sly sound that matched the look in his eyes.

"Come on." Luke picked up his pint. "Let's go in the other bar, it's time I beat you at a game of snooker."

Dessie followed obediently and as they walked away Luke turned around. "Be seeing you," he said to Henderson.

It was a farewell that might have been a threat.

"What did I do to upset him?" He'd watched the two men leave. Again it was only him and the landlord at the bar; a scattering of customers were seated around the pub.

"You wouldn't have to do a lot to upset Luke Baines," the old man said, "and you're already half way there."

"Why's that?" Henderson asked.

The barman lowered his voice. "You're a reporter," he said. "The chip Baines carries around on his shoulder was put there by people like you. At least that's the way he looks at it."

"What do you mean?" Henderson had no idea what the old man was on about. The landlord continued.

"You know I was telling you about Barry Morgan?" he said. "Well Luke Baines' father was one of the gang who held up that truck."

Henderson was shocked. The old man leaned in closer. "And he was the only one of them to be caught!"

Before the reporter could interrupt, the barman came out with another revelation.

"To make matters worse a couple of months after the robbery a body was found on the disused military base. Although it was never identified the police believed it to be someone connected with the theft. The press tried to pin that on him as well but they couldn't make it stick.

"Of course, old man Baines kept his mouth shut, honour among thieves and all that bollocks, and so the papers crucified him. Luke blamed them for the long sentence handed down to his father." He looked at Henderson. "Mickey Baines died in prison. He had a heart attack. It's something his son's never forgotten or forgiven." The old man uttered a humourless laugh. "Luke's never going to be your bosom buddy."

Henderson was trying to make order of everything the old man had said. He could picture a circle slowly closing; tightening itself around two dead men and a father and son.

"Where does he live?" he asked.

The barman raised an eyebrow. "In a caravan on the other side of Mole Hill, but I wouldn't go prying around there if I were you," he said. "It's a rough old site, the only welcome you're likely to get is a dog set on you and a shotgun pushed in your face."

Henderson laughed. "Is that legal?" he said.

"Luke wouldn't care," the landlord replied. "He's been in and out of prison himself, I doubt if another stretch would worry him. Seriously, I'd stay away from there; he'd like nothing more than to give a journalist a roughing up."

Henderson had a feeling Luke Baines wouldn't be living on Mole Hill much longer. He could afford to move now, he'd come into money and it had been enough to kill for. He finished his pint and ordered a scotch.

"What about his mate?" he asked, as the landlord placed a glass in front of him.

"Dessie Mitchell, that idiot? He's got a little two-up two-down on the Woolpack Road that used to belong to his parents. I think they had a bit of money. Since they died all Dessie's done is fritter it away. There can't be a lot left." He went to serve a customer and spoke over his shoulder. "But Dessie and Luke are as thick as thieves," he said. "He'd do anything Baines told him to."

The old man pulled a pint and then rang for last orders. Henderson checked his watch and decided to have a large one for the road; why break a habit?

Before he went to bed that night he made out a list, he needed to get clear in his head what he knew so far.

1. Barry Morgan had been the driver of a security van that had been ambushed.

2. Luke Baines' father, Mickey, had been the only member of the gang to be caught.

3. Shortly after the robbery an unidentified male had been either killed on Cotters

Grey military base or his body had been taken there and abandoned.

4. Morgan had kept hidden a newspaper cutting relating to the robbery. The letters CGMB had been scrawled on the back.

5. Cotters Grey had suffered a spate of burglaries where nothing of value had been stolen.

6. Barry Morgan had been murdered; presumably by Luke and Dessie after they'd forced him to tell them where the money from the robbery was hidden.

7. How did Morgan know about it?

He read through what he'd written and tried to make sense of it. He couldn't shake the feeling Barry Morgan had known something about the robbery and lost his life because of it. Henderson remembered hearing Luke tell Dessie he suspected the old man might have been lying about the location of the money.

Everything else, the unidentified body and the random burglaries, were a mystery, but one he felt sure sooner or later he might solve. He was still a journalist and he still had a nose for a story, an instinct drink and apathy might have deadened but not killed.

He lay down on the bed. Tomorrow he'd decided he was going to pay Luke Baines a visit. It was probably the wrong thing to do but it felt right.

***

All the morning had to offer was a memory of winter and a sky full of rain. Henderson pulled his jacket around him and made his way across the pub car park. He recalled his surprise at discovering Luke Baines was a local lad whose father had been involved in a robbery that years later was still sending out echoes. As he drove away from the Haymow he wondered how a thief's son was going to take another invasion of his privacy.

Mole Hill Estate was as Arthur the landlord had said, a rough, fenced-in sight that looked more like a gypsy encampment than a residential park. An assortment of run-down caravans and mobile homes stood in ragged rows; car parts and disused kitchen appliances decorated neglected squares of garden. The scene reminded Henderson of the wasteland that had surrounded Barry Morgan's cottage.

He pulled up on the perimeter road and wondered which of the shanty dwellings was Luke's. It looked like a place outside the law. As he stepped from the car a breeze blew clouds over the hill and chilled the day.

An old woman was pegging grey washing onto a lop-sided rotary line. The cigarette dangling from her lips looked like a permanent fixture. Her skin colour matched the laundry. When Henderson asked her which of the homes was Luke's she coughed an answer and pointed in the direction of a tumbledown caravan.

"He's probably still asleep, the lazy fucker," she said, and hung another sheet that would never be white again on the line.

Henderson had rehearsed his excuse for visiting Baines. He planned to tell him about the article he was working on and then drop into the conversation he'd heard Luke's father had been involved in a long ago robbery; could he shed any light on that? He knew his question would provoke Baines and hoped anger might lead to the big man letting slip something that couldn't be taken back. He climbed a pair of uneven steps and knocked on the caravan door.

A dog threw itself against the inside wall and let out a staccato burst of barks.

"SHUT UP!" Luke's voice sounded half-full of sleep. Henderson heard the dog whimper and fall silent. Baines pulled open the door; it looked as if he'd been sleeping in his clothes. He squinted and covered his look of surprise with a scowl.

"What do you want?" Behind him the dog let out a low growl.

Henderson lied. "Sorry to disturb you," he said, "but someone told me you might be able to help with the article I'm writing." He saw the look of disbelief form on Luke's face and carried on. "It's about the spread of rural crime." Again he lied. "I'm researching old robberies and discovered your father was involved in one."

He knew he'd forced what he'd wanted to ease into the conversation. Luke stepped down from the caravan and thrust his face into Henderson's.

"Who told you that?"

The reporter didn't flinch. "The same person who told me Barry Morgan was involved in that robbery."

If Baines was surprised he hid it well. Henderson realised the conversation was spiralling in the wrong direction and there was nothing he could do to change its course. Luke had balled his fists.

"Why don't you fuck off while you still have the chance?" the big man said.

Henderson couldn't help himself, his tongue formed words he was powerless to prevent.

"I went out to Barry Morgan's cottage," he said. "I found paperwork there that suggested he knew money from the robbery had been buried on the abandoned military base."

This time Luke couldn't disguise his shock. There was a moment's silence filled with unspoken knowledge; they both knew this confrontation had nothing to do with a newspaper article. The dog's steady growl had deepened.

"Did you, now?" Baines had taken a step back; he was staring at Henderson with the same weighted expression he'd used in the Haymow. "So what did you do about it?"

Henderson knew Luke was attempting to gauge how much he knew; trying to work out whether the reporter was dealing in suspicion or fact.

"I visited the camp," he said. "Someone had wrecked a Nissan hut. It looked as if they'd been searching for something." He paused and returned Luke's stare. "How's Dessie?"

Baines grinned and laughed to himself. "You think you're very smart, don't you?" He reached backwards and dragged the dog out by its collar. The Doberman bared its teeth and snarled, its claws skittering on the floor in its eagerness to get at the stranger. "I guess he feels the same way about you as I do," Luke said. "If you're not off my property in twenty seconds I'll set him on you, after all, I'm only protecting what's mine." The dog whined impatiently.

Henderson shrugged his shoulders and tried to ignore the fear creeping its way into his stomach. "I'll see you around then," he said. It was his turn to veil a farewell with a threat. Before he reached his car Baines called out to him.

"Don't come back!" he shouted. "Bad things can happen in a place like this! Ask Barry Morgan." His laughter followed him into the caravan as he pulled the dog inside and slammed shut the door.

Henderson drove away and watched the image of Mole Hill Estate grow smaller in his rear view mirror. He wondered what he'd set in motion.

Back inside the caravan Luke Baines pulled out his mobile and dialled a number.

***

This time Henderson found the deserted base without getting lost. He steered the car between open gates and pulled up in front of the looted Nissan hut. He knew he'd riled Baines and he was sure the big man wasn't about to let it go. Luke had a quick temper as well as a large amount of money burning a hole in his pocket. Sooner or later he was going to give himself away, especially now he was aware he had a reporter snapping at his heels.

It had been dark on his last visit, now Henderson wanted to carry out a thorough sweep of the building. Baines and Dessie Mitchell had been impatient in their search for the hidden money; perhaps they'd left tell-tale clues behind, something that might prove they killed Barry Morgan. He pushed open the broken door and stepped into the past.

An hour later he'd found nothing. If the ripped-up floorboards and rotten furniture held secrets he'd been unable to discover them. He brushed dust and cobwebs from his jacket and stepped outside. That was when he saw the battered Land Rover drive onto the base.

Luke swung the vehicle halfway across the front of Henderson's car and climbed out. As Dessie opened the passenger door he pulled a pick-axe handle from the foot-well. The two men stared at him.

"I don't like you," Baines said.

Henderson folded his arms. "It's mutual."

Luke sneered. "What are you doing here?"

"My job," Henderson said.

"Is that so?" Baines nodded at Dessie and before Henderson could react Mitchell swung the club into the small of his back. Henderson collapsed. As he fought for breath Luke pulled him to his feet. Dessie was smiling, eagerly waiting to land another blow.

"I thought you were a reporter," Baines said. "Not a detective."

"Think what you like," Henderson gasped. "But what I do know is that you're a murderer." He saw an expression of worry pass over Mitchell's face.

The grin left Luke's lips. "Have you got proof of that?"

He hadn't and Baines knew it. He pulled himself free; the pain in his back had settled to a dull ache, it didn't feel as if anything was broken.

"Tell me what you do know," Luke said, "and then I'll fill you in on any details you might have missed." He smirked. "Who knows, perhaps we could write an article about it."

Henderson was regretting his visit to Mole Hill, he'd let his instinct for a story get in the way of common sense. It made him realise how out of touch he'd become, how years of living off second-hand scraps had blunted his intuition.

"Well?" Baines impatient demand prompted Dessie to raise the pick-axe handle. Luke blocked his swing. "Not yet," he said. "Let's see what our Sherlock's got to say for himself."

Henderson didn't have a choice; he told them what he knew. Baines listened, his face blank, again it was only Mitchell who was unable to disguise his concern. He nervously wiped his mouth with the back of his hand.

"What does guilt taste like?" Henderson said to him.

Dessie's eyes widened. "It wasn't me who…"

"Shut your mouth, Dessie!" Baines cut him off and then held out his hand. "Give me your mobile," he said to the reporter.

That was when Henderson realised things were about to pass a point of no return. Luke and Dessie had murdered an old man, they wouldn't be afraid to kill an interfering journalist; at least Luke wouldn't. Now the truth had been uncovered Mitchell seemed to be regretting his involvement. Henderson reluctantly reached into his pocket and passed over the phone. When Baines tossed the handset to the ground and stamped on it Dessie laughed.

"Now I'll tell you something," Luke said. "Morgan was in on the robbery, how do you think the gang knew which route he was scheduled to take and how much he was carrying?" He saw the look of surprise on Henderson's face and grinned.

"Everything was arranged until he got greedy and started demanding a bigger share. He said if it wasn't for him there'd be no robbery. After that he was living on borrowed time."

"How do you know all this?" Henderson had a good idea where Luke had got his information but he wanted to hear it first-hand.

Baines stared at him. "My old man told me," he said. "We had plenty of time to talk after he went inside. Your lot made sure he was sent down for a long term."

Henderson shook his head. "I had nothing to do with that Luke, and you know it. Besides, he'd committed a crime, what did he expect, to be let off with a warning and a slap on the wrist?" He saw Baines' eyes narrow, for a moment he thought Dessie was going to club him again.

"I'll make you pay for that later," Luke said. "Now shut-up." He continued with his story.

"The gang agreed to Morgan's demands but behind his back things had changed, he was out and he didn't even know it. When they ambushed the van they tied him up as planned but then they beat the crap out of him.

Before they did they let him know where he stood and threatened to kill him if he squealed."

Luke leant against the truck and pushed his hands into his pockets. "And how could he?" he said. "He'd supplied the gang with inside information, if they went down then so would he. It should have all been hunky-dory but when Morgan was released from hospital he was spitting mad and decided to try and get his own back. That was when it all went wrong.

"He got word to my old man that he wasn't worried about their threats, and unless he got his share of the proceeds he swore he'd go to the police and say the thieves forced him to help them. That caused a few ripples. They agreed it was time to shut Barry Morgan up for good. My dad arranged to meet him here and hand over the money. He brought with him another gang member, Ray Stubbs, a tough old gypsy lad who had no qualms about killing someone. They also carried Morgan's share of the cash with them as bait."

"What happened?" Henderson realised things had been more complicated than he'd first suspected.

"What happened?" Luke said. "I'll tell you; it was that bastard's turn to hold an ambush. My old man never told me all the details because he didn't know them himself. When they got to the base there was no sign of Morgan. Stubbs did a recce while he held onto the money. That was the last thing he remembered. Someone coshed him over the head. When he woke up the police were pulling onto the base and there was no sign of Stubbs or the cash. End of story."

"So the body they found later was Stubbs's." Henderson said. "How come they couldn't identify him?"

"Do me a favour," Luke said. "He was a gypsy. He'd never paid tax, never paid rent, and for all I know Stubbs might not have been his real name." He nodded towards the fence. "He was an outsider, there's a lot like him out there. The police weren't happy though, they were left with a body and a heap of blame they tried to pin on my old man. Bastards."

"What about Morgan?" Henderson asked.

Baines shrugged his shoulders. "He denied everything. Told whoever would listen that he'd bottled out of the meeting and swore that someone was trying to set him up, which was convenient seeing as the police had received an anonymous call informing them my old man was at Cotters Grey."

"Did the rest of the gang buy it?"

"They didn't have a lot of choice," Luke said, "not after what had happened here. They didn't want to make any more waves. What they did do was let Morgan know that if they ever heard of him spending large amounts of cash they'd come back and he'd die screaming."

"So that was why he became a recluse." Henderson wondered how much money a life spent living alone was worth. "How did you find out where it was hidden?"

Baines laughed. "When Dessie and myself decided to carry out a bit of burglary. I thought we'd do over Morgan's place first, it's out in the sticks and I figured I owed him one after what had happened to my old man." He laughed again.

"When we broke in we almost scared the old bastard to death. What we didn't know was that he was practically senile; he thought we were part of the gang come back to sort him out. Then he started blubbing and told us where he'd stashed the money. '*I haven't touched a penny of it, lads, I swear it,*' he cried."

Luke's eyes had grown cold. "He signed his own death warrant with that confession. I remembered where and how my dad had died and knew then it was Morgan's fault. I hit him with a crowbar and he never got up."

"What about the other burglaries?"

"They were just decoys," Baines said. "We wanted to make it look as if someone was attempting random break-ins. That way it'd seem as if the old man had been killed in one of them and there'd be no talk about the past." He looked at Henderson. "It worked out fine until you came along."

They stood silently staring at each other.

"So what happens now?" the reporter asked. The prickle of fear he'd experienced at Mole Hill had returned.

Luke didn't answer. He walked to the rear of the Land Rover. "I've got rope here," he said. "Once you're trussed up we'll sort that out." He made it sound as if the journalist were a medical problem that a bandage could solve. He opened the back door and climbed inside. Henderson saw Dessie glance in Luke's direction and took a chance. He kicked out and swung his foot between the other man's legs. Mitchell screamed and crumpled to the floor clutching at his groin.

"What's going on?"

Henderson barely heard Luke's shouted question. He jumped into his car, pressed the door lock and twisted the ignition key. As the engine caught Baines was suddenly outside, yanking at a handle that wouldn't give. Metal ground against metal as the vehicle scraped along the side of the Land Rover. Henderson swerved onto the compound and Luke lost his grip. For a moment the reporter thought he'd slipped beneath the wheels. He glanced into the mirror and saw Baines scramble to his feet. Mitchell was still on the ground. He pressed his foot to the accelerator and headed for the gates.

When he reached the end of the entrance lane he hesitated and then turned away from the village. He hoped that when Luke and Dessie came after him, as he was sure they would, they'd presume he'd head for the Haymow and follow that direction. They knew the area better than he did, his only hope was to try and fool them.

The road squeezed its way between high hedges and open fields. Henderson followed it like a man possessed. As he sped through tree-lined woodland the branches above him grew into each other and shaded the day with twilight. When there was no sign of him being followed he felt a triumphant rush of adrenalin; all he had to do now was find somewhere he could use a phone and call the police.

He pulled up at a fork in the road and was dismayed to discover he knew where he was. It was the lane that led to Barry Morgan's cottage. Henderson remembered his previous visit and how there wasn't another dwelling for miles. *Had there been a telephone in the house?* He couldn't remember and tried to think. Then he recalled the moment he'd peered down the stairs and imagined a body lying in the hallway. If he wasn't mistaken he was almost certain he'd seen a table standing by the front door and on it had been an old-fashioned telephone. He changed gear and turned into the lane.

Once again he missed the overgrown entrance and pulled up on the grass verge. Knowing it was only a short walk he climbed from the car and made his way back to Barry Morgan's driveway. Little did he realise that leaving the vehicle parked there would save his life.

The wrecked car still stood on blocks; the front door to the cottage remained locked. He made his way to the rear of the house and pushed open the back door. A thought ran through his mind: *he'd left it open on his last visit.* Unless the breeze had blown it shut someone else had been here. Henderson pulled it closed behind him and made his way quietly into the hallway.

The phone was on the table. He saw it at the same moment he noticed the wires dangling loosely above the floor. As he bent down to examine them the sound of a car engine broke the silence. It pulled up outside and he heard doors opening. Through a gap in a boarded-up window Henderson watched Luke and Dessie climb from the battered Land Rover.

The two men disappeared behind the side of the house. Henderson hurried up the stairs and frantically searched for a hiding place. The main bedroom still looked as if it had been ransacked. He heard the sound of the back door scraping open. There was a gap between Barry Morgan's unmade bed and the wall. He squeezed into it and listened.

Two sets of boots clattered across bare boards.

"Where do you reckon he went, Luke?" Mitchell sounded scared. Henderson heard what might have been a panel being crow-barred from a downstairs wall.

"I don't fucking know, Dessie." Luke's voice was tight with anger. "If I did I'd kill the bastard."

There were two thumps: *holdalls full of money being dropped to the floor.*

Henderson suddenly realised Baines and Mitchell didn't know he was there. He guessed they must have driven in from the opposite direction and not seen his car. He also realised Baines had stashed the money from the base back at Morgan's. Mitchell proved him right.

"I still don't understand why you brought it here, Luke," he said.

"Of course you don't, Dessie, because you're fucking stupid." There was a pause. "Did you think I was going to leave it in that shit-hole of a caravan? Christ I wouldn't trust any of the cunts who live on that site." He laughed. "They're worse than me."

"I'd have kept it at my place." Dessie sounded almost offended, as if he thought Luke felt the same way about him as he did his neighbours.

"I bet you would."

Mitchell seemed oblivious to the venom in the words. "What are we going to do?" he asked.

"We?"

Henderson heard the malicious amusement in Luke's reply.

"Dessie, I'm sick of you and I'm sick of Cotters Grey. I'm getting out while I still can. That nosey fucking journalist is going to have every copper in creation swarming around here."

In the silence that followed, Henderson could imagine Dessie trying to work out where he figured in Luke's plans. The reporter could have told him he probably didn't.

"What about the money?" Mitchell asked.

"Pick it up," Baines said. "We'll share it out back at your place."

Henderson knew that wasn't going to happen.

There was another pause and then he heard a dull thump followed by a grunt and the sound of a body collapsing to the floor. A second thump sounded louder than the first. He could picture Dessie bending for the bags and Luke striking him once across the back of the head with the crowbar, and then doing it again to make certain he never woke up.

Henderson listened to footsteps cross the downstairs rooms. A short while later a car door was opened and then slammed shut. An engine fired into life and as the sound faded away he left his hiding place and crept back down the stairs.

Mitchell was lying on the floor. The back of his skull had been caved in. Blood and tissue had seeped onto the floorboards. Henderson crouched beside the body. "I'm sorry, Dessie," he said, and searched the dead man's clothing for a phone. He was out of luck; either Mitchell didn't own one or Luke had taken it. He hurried from the house and made his way down the driveway.

As he went to step out into the road he ducked back into the shrubbery and peered through the branches. The Land Rover was facing him, parked in the middle of the lane. Baines was staring into his car. Henderson swore; Luke had left Morgan's in the opposite direction from which he'd arrived. He'd obviously seen the car and turned around. The big man looked up and seemed to gaze straight at him. Then he went back to his vehicle and took the crowbar from the front seat. Baines began walking towards Henderson.

The reporter backed slowly into the bushes. He crouched as far into the undergrowth as he could and held his breath. Luke turned into the driveway and stopped. He cocked his head to one side, listening. Henderson was sure he'd be discovered. Baines stood there a moment longer. He tapped the crowbar against his palm and then carried on towards the house. When he was out of sight Henderson sprinted along the road.

His car was hemmed in by the Land Rover. He had no choice but to take to take the other vehicle. He pulled open the door and sighed with relief. In his hurry to cause more damage Luke had left the keys in the ignition. Two holdalls were stacked on the passenger seat. The journalist climbed in. As he started the engine Luke came running from the driveway screaming obscenities. He had the crowbar raised.

Henderson took his foot from the clutch and pressed the accelerator. Baines made no attempt to get out of the way. His face was twisted in rage. He drew back his arm and launched the crowbar at the windscreen. As it bounced off the car a split appeared across the glass. Henderson changed gear and put his foot down. Luke ran straight into the front of the vehicle. Henderson felt the impact as Baines disappeared beneath the bonnet. He could hear the body beat against the underside of the car and thought it the worst sound he'd ever heard. When it finally ended he glanced into the rear-view mirror. What was left of Luke Baines lay stretched across the middle of the lane.

Henderson tried to blink the image from his mind. He drove slowly back to Cotters Grey. His fingers shook each time he took them from the steering wheel. When it began to rain the rapid beat of the wipers kept time with his heart.

***

"There you go, Richard, it's on the house." The landlord placed a pint on the bar.

It was late. Henderson was seated in the lounge. The police had finished questioning him. His answers had cleared up an unsolved mystery as well as revealing who'd been responsible for Barry Morgan's death. Henderson's car was still parked outside the cottage and would be for some time; the murder scene had been sealed off. He wondered how much money the police had discovered in the holdalls. The barman's voice interrupted his thoughts.

"You did what you promised," he said.

Henderson looked at him. "What was that?"

"You put Cotters Grey on the map."

The reporter smiled. When he'd phoned the story through to his editor, Philip Morley had concealed his excitement beneath a brief showering of praise. They both knew it would sell a lot of papers.

As Henderson drank his beer his mind went back to another time. Barry Morgan wasn't the only old man who'd sheltered a secret. Reinhardt Braun had been another, and those secrets had cost both men their lives.

This wasn't a once in a lifetime story, he knew that, but it was knowledge he could live with. He'd followed instincts he thought were dead and buried and the result had made him feel like the man he used to be.

His glass was empty but it didn't seem that way. For once he didn't have one for the road.

THE SNOWBIRD

Last night's snowfall had bowed the trees and dragged every sound from the world. The stream was dead, the lane was blocked and Oakwood Cottage stood between the two like an outpost on the edge of some unexplored frontier.

High overhead the creature that flapped its way across a frozen sky looked as old as time. It circled sail-like through the air, a giant silhouette spiralling slowly downwards until it came to land in front of the house. When it beat its wings the sound was like canvas flapping in a breeze.

As it strutted towards the cottage the bird left behind it a trail of broken snow. Once there it rested the hook of its beak against a window and gazed through its reflection into the room. A faint scent of flesh and warm blood stirred the hunger in its belly. It stared a moment longer then turned and walked slowly into the woods.

***

The fire was lit, the oil heating turned on; soon the cottage would be summer warm. Ellie Hooper cocked her head and listened. Apart from the crackle of logs in the hearth there was silence. It was a beautiful sound.

Her daughter's bedroom door hung half-open; beyond it shafts of snowy daylight spilled through the window and fell on her little girl's face. Megan lay in her cot dreamlessly sleeping with a thumb between her lips. Of all the things Martin had left her she was easily the most precious.

Nine months had passed since the morning he left for work and never came home. As soon as she'd opened the front door and seen the police-woman on the doorstep she'd known. *"There's been an accident."* How many times had the officer had to say that to some unsuspecting wife or husband? Even as grief closed in on her Ellie remembered thinking it could never be something you got used to. Just before she fainted she recalled feeling sorry for the young constable.

The weeks that followed carried unbearable milestones, passages of time when she realised she would never hear his voice or see his face again. And the only thing that had kept her mind from going someplace she might never get it back was the child she carried; their child. Four months later Megan was born. By then Ellie had sold the home she'd shared with Martin; walking around its empty rooms had been like living in a ghost house. She'd cherished the memories but couldn't live with them, so she'd moved as far away as possible.

"You're running away," her family had said, and they were right, she was, and if it had been possible to run further she would have. But now Oakwood Cottage was home and it was a place where she thought she might make peace with her past.

From Megan's window she could see frozen willows lining the river-bank and tried to imagine how they'd look in the spring. Then she frowned and moved closer to the glass. There were tracks in the snow. Her heart missed a beat. Who would be out in the woods in this weather and why would they have come to the house?

In the hallway she pulled on a pair of boots and opened the front door. The air was so cold it pinched her skin. She dragged the door to, stepped outside and sank into nine inches of snow. Half-way across the front of the cottage she stopped, hardly believing what she saw.

The tracks weren't a man's, they were a bird's; three toes in the shape of an impossibly large v. From print to print was a distance of at least five feet; what kind of bird had that length of stride? The trail led into the woods. She hesitated and then followed it to the edge of the undergrowth.

Her eyes scanned the frost-bitten trees as she tried to make out shapes in the darkness beyond the tangled branches. The woods were winter silent and full of secrets. She glanced back at the cottage and realised she'd come further than she meant to. As she turned around something shot out of the trees above her head. It flew past, clipping her shoulders and knocking her to the ground. Snow filled her eyes and mouth, blinding and choking her as she struggled to her feet. Then she saw it, a bird from a bad dream. It lifted its wings once and she heard the slap of feathers on air. How could something that big get off the ground? And yet it was graceful, almost floating above the snow before it landed in front of the cottage.

Then it pushed open the door with a clawed foot.

Megan! She suddenly knew what the bird wanted.

"NO!" Her scream filled the empty landscape, losing itself in the drifts and hollows. For a moment the bird's hard eyes looked back at her. Then it entered the house.

Ellie ran and fell, picked herself up and ran and fell again. She'd almost reached the cottage when the bird backed out of the door. It was panicking, its feet scrabbling against the wood in its hurry to get away. Ellie fell again and grabbed for it. Feathers came away in her hand. The bird kicked out, narrowly missing her face, and then it was airborne, rising into the snowy sky, becoming smaller as it left the world behind. It held something in its beak and suddenly she couldn't look any more.

She picked herself up and leant against the wall. Now her mind could go where it wanted and she welcomed that oblivion; there'd be no more running away. The frozen world looked inviting.

At first she didn't hear the cry. The small demanding sounds of a baby interrupted of sleep. When she did she thought she was hearing things. But then the crying became louder. Her daughter wanted breakfast. She stumbled into the hallway and saw tracks of melting snow on the rug. Megan's door was wide open, claw marks were scratched into the frame. She wondered who else was crying and then realised it was her.

She walked into the room. Megan lay in her bed, bewildered and probably cold. Her quilt was missing. The cover that had looked like a small child caught in the beak of a giant bird was gone. She lifted her daughter from the bed and stared into eyes that looked exactly like her husband's. Outside it began snowing again.

Lightning Source UK Ltd.
Milton Keynes UK
UKOW05f0948020115

243823UK00001B/4/P